It hadn't been more than thirty minutes or so since I'd climbed out of the food truck. How did Terry get in there after me? And what was he doing here? Had he followed me back to give me more grief over parking in "his spot" on Dauphin Street?

"What's up out here, young 'un?" Ollie came out of the diner, still holding the sword.

"I don't know. This is Terry."

He nodded. "From the infamous tacky taco truck?"

"Yes. I don't know what he's doing here. And I think he may be drunk or something."

Ollie bent down and put his hand on Terry's neck. "I don't know, either, but he ain't goin' no place else."

"What do you mean? I can call him a taxi or something."

"No, Zoe. You don't get it. The man's *dead*. A taxi won't do him any good now."

Berkley Prime Crime titles by J. J. Cook

Sweet Pepper Fire Brigade Mysteries

THAT OLD FLAME OF MINE
PLAYING WITH FIRE

Biscuit Bowl Food Truck Mysteries

DEATH ON EAT STREET

Specials

HERO'S JOURNEY

DEATH ON
Eat Street

J. J. COOK

BERKLEY PRIME CRIME, NEW YORK

THE BERKLEY PUBLISHING GROUP
Published by the Penguin Group
Penguin Group (USA) LLC
375 Hudson Street, New York, New York 10014

USA • Canada • UK • Ireland • Australia • New Zealand • India • South Africa • China

penguin.com

A Penguin Random House Company

DEATH ON EAT STREET

A Berkley Prime Crime Book / published by arrangement with the authors

Berkley Prime Crime Books are published by The Berkley Publishing Group.
BERKLEY® PRIME CRIME and the PRIME CRIME logo
are trademarks of Penguin Group (USA) LLC.

For information, address: The Berkley Publishing Group,
a division of Penguin Group (USA) LLC,
375 Hudson Street, New York, New York 10014.

ISBN: 978-0-425-26345-7

PUBLISHING HISTORY
Berkley Prime Crime mass-market edition / April 2014

PRINTED IN THE UNITED STATES OF AMERICA

10 9 8 7 6 5 4 3 2 1

Cover illustration by Griesbach/Martucci.
Cover design by Jason Gill.
Interior text design by Laura K. Corless.

ACKNOWLEDGMENTS

We would like to thank our fantastic editor, Faith Black, and our amazing agent, Gail Fortune, for helping us with this book. We couldn't have done it without them!

ONE

It had been the worst day of my life.

I parked my Biscuit Bowl food truck beside the diner and closed my eyes as I rested my head on the steering wheel. Outside, the fiberglass biscuit on top of the food truck stopped twirling.

How could so much go wrong in one day?

I'd worked hard to make my dream come true. Why was it all crashing in on me?

My phone rang. It was Tommy Lee, my boyfriend.

That made me feel even worse.

Tommy Lee Elgin is a real go-getter. He's handsome, makes a lot of money as an investment broker, and is on his way to the top. He's out there busting his butt, making a name for himself every day—as he frequently reminds me.

What am I doing?

I had recently quit my job at the Azalea National Bank where I was a loan officer—not even a *senior* loan officer.

I'd always wanted to own a restaurant. I loved cooking

for other people. I finally got up the nerve to do it after being passed over for promotion—*again*. I cashed in my vacation time and my 401(k). I struck out on my own, filled with entre-preneurial spirit gathered from ten different seminars.

"Zoe, don't hang up." Tommy Lee's voice was as clear and commanding as his picture on my cell phone. "We have to hash this out. You made a mistake. That's all. We can take care of this."

Looking at his confident smile, the dimple in his square chin, and his expensive suit, I almost caved. *What am I doing out here anyway? Why did I think I could do this?*

"There's nothing to hash out." I tried to find the passion and drive that had brought me here. "I've made a commit-ment to my dream. Why can't all of you see that?"

My commitment included taking all of my cash and investing it in a diner. It was a little run-down. I admit it.

Eventually, I knew all of Mobile, Alabama—maybe even Birmingham—would be standing in line, waiting to eat my food. I was going to be the Paula Deen of my hometown.

There had only been enough money to bring the kitchen area in the diner up to code. I had to do something to get my food out to people. From there, I could invest my profits into upgrading the diner into a real restaurant.

Did that sound crazy? I didn't think so.

"I refuse to believe that your dream is to make food for other people," Tommy Lee said. "That's what cooks and housekeepers are for, sweetie. This is a knee-jerk reaction to being passed over for promotion again. You know your mother and I think this is a bad idea. If you want to cook for someone, you can cook for us all you want."

I wasn't sure if I was more offended by his condescending attitude or the fact that he was in league with my mother about this. Both issues made me feel a little queasy.

Quitting the bank had been a big decision for me. I'd worked there for the last five years. When I'd realized that

I was facing my thirtieth birthday next spring, I couldn't let time keep slipping away from me.

The bank had continued to promote men like Tommy Lee—smooth, sophisticated—some of whom I'd trained. Passing me over had been the last straw. It was time for me to go.

"I don't want to work for the bank," I said quite clearly. "My biscuit bowl is going to be a hit. I know it will. Once that happens, it's all gravy. I know you don't understand. I don't understand why *you'd* want to be an investment broker, either. Can't we agree to disagree on this?"

"Zoe. *Sweetie*. Trust me, will you? You'll thank me someday. You don't want to get stuck spending the rest of your life in that sleazy diner or that old trailer you call a food truck. Let me help you. You don't have to go back to the bank. We can refresh your résumé and—"

"That's not what I want, Tommy Lee." I wiped away the frustrated tears and firmed up my voice. "Why can't you see that? I think if you loved me, you'd see that."

"You're making a mistake."

"It's mine to make."

"I can't help you if you won't let me help you."

"Then don't." I ended the call, and Tommy Lee's handsome, smiling face went away.

My head hit the steering wheel again, and I closed my eyes.

"Bad day?"

I sat up quickly and wiped the tears from my face. It was Ollie from the homeless shelter two doors down. I took the extra food that I couldn't sell down there each night. If I could convince the office workers on Dauphin Street to gobble my biscuit bowls down the way the shelter residents did, I'd be rich.

"It wasn't too good again. I made forty-eight dollars and fifty cents, not counting expenses. And I got into an argument with Terry from Terry's Tacky Tacos. He said I was parked in his space."

He nodded. "That's up from yesterday's twenty-four dollars and twelve cents."

That's why I liked Ollie so much. Even though I'd only known him a short time, he had this positive way of looking at things.

"That's right." I got out of the old silver Airstream motor home that Uncle Saul was letting me use. I'd only had to cut open a window and gut the whole inside to make a kitchen and to serve customers. That took the rest of my money.

"So there's leftover food, huh?"

Okay.

Maybe Ollie *was* only there because I fed him regularly. Maybe he wasn't exactly my friend. At least he was there for me, even if it was only because he'd be eating a lot of soup without me.

"I could use some help taking the food over. I don't dare take it inside. I think I heard a rat in the diner this morning."

"What did you expect in this neighborhood?" Ollie shrugged his broad shoulders, covered in a used green army jacket. He gestured to the derelict shopping center to make his point.

"I paid to have the rats exterminated." I really dislike rats.

"If you had a *real* cat, he'd take care if it for you." Ollie opened the cab door of the food truck. My chubby, tabby Persian hissed at him. "See what I mean?"

It was true. I had to leave my cat, Crème Brûlée, in the food truck all day. He didn't like rats, either. He couldn't be bothered to try and catch them, though. That might get his big white paws dirty. Instead he stayed in his basket, hissing as I served the few customers I had.

I checked out the food that was left in the compact kitchen area in the back of the motor home. Some of it would still be good tomorrow. The biscuits, which were my most important food, couldn't be saved. They had to be made fresh daily or they wouldn't be any good.

"If you could take these"—I handed two trays of biscuits to Ollie—"I think the rest will keep."

"You made beef stew again, huh?" Ollie sniffed the container I had used to fill some of the biscuit bowls.

"You said I should change it up."

"I keep telling you, young 'un. Chicken and dumplings and beef stew is fine when you ain't got no money. Those people over in downtown don't want beef stew. They want something exotic—some gator gumbo or crawdad stew. The spicier, the better."

We usually had this discussion at the end of the day. I was having a hard time with my savory fillings for the fried biscuits with the hollow in the middle that I called biscuit bowls. I'd tried plenty of other things, too. None of my favorites had gone over very well.

"The fruit pie fillings were good today." I tried to sound hopeful. "People liked the custard-filled biscuit bowls, too."

"You can put anything in these biscuit bowls of yours." Ollie, who'd once been a marine, took out a little custard from a container. He filled a biscuit before he chowed down on it. "You've got these biscuits down."

"Thanks." I closed the back door to the food truck. I didn't want Crème Brûlée to get out. He'd probably get lost.

"Sweet is easy, Zoe." Ollie started walking with the trays of biscuits. "Savory is hard. You gotta think about the smell. Maybe make some gumbo. You need that aroma to appeal to your customer's olfactory. His nose, you know?"

Ollie might have seemed like an unusual advisor, but he knew a lot about food. He'd been my six-foot-six confidant, complete with skull tattoo on the back of his bald head, since I'd opened the diner door for the first time two months ago.

He'd been a big help moving things in and out of the diner and the food truck, too. He'd also talked others from the homeless shelter into helping. He had this way of making everyone jump when he told them what to do. The labor for food concept was awesome, especially on my budget.

"Gumbo, huh?" I went ahead of him and opened the door to the homeless shelter. It was housed in an old storefront.

"Don't underestimate people's love of unusual foods. Not that I'm saying gator and crawdads are all that weird. At least not to me. But those people you're tryin' to impress aren't like me. I've eaten every kind of snake, lizard, and possum that crawls, slithers, and jumps on this green earth."

Most of that didn't sound too appetizing. I held the shelter door open for Ollie. Several other homeless men started coming toward us right away. Ollie gave them his mean look and they backed off. He didn't like them coming up on the food too fast.

"You have to think beyond bland, Zoe. Think *wild*."

I laughed. "I don't know if people in downtown Mobile can handle your idea of wild, Ollie."

"You got nothin' to lose by trying." Ollie put the trays of biscuits and leftover fillings on a table. "Okay, men. Thank Miss Zoe, and eat hearty."

There was always a note of command in his voice when he talked to the other men. He was more personable with me, but he was good at telling people what to do. Ollie liked bossing people around. I wondered if he'd been an officer in the Marines.

It was a favorite pastime of mine, wondering what had happened to bring Ollie down to this level. He was smart, and wickedly funny. Why had he chosen to live this way?

I opened a container of cherry pie filling and filled two biscuit bowls with it. There wasn't much. The men might as well enjoy it.

"You spoil them, Zoe." Marty Zimmerman closed the back door and smiled at me. He ran the homeless shelter. "You spoil me, too. We're all glad you decided to move into the diner. How did it go today?"

"It wasn't too bad."

I didn't want to go through the whole sob story again with him. Marty was a very nice man with a round stomach that had a hard time fitting into his jeans. His Dauphin Island Festival T-shirt was also about a size too small for him.

I supposed beggars couldn't be choosers. The homeless shelter was run on donations and a little local charity money, according to Ollie. They were barely able to pay the power bill each month.

Marty tasted the beef stew in a biscuit bowl. "Mmm." He closed his eyes. "This is great stuff. The people who haven't tried your biscuit bowls don't know what they're missing!"

"Thanks." I appreciated any compliment.

I watched Ollie draw a gleaming sword out of its scabbard while the other men were eating. "What's that for?"

He grinned, even white teeth strong against his dark skin. "Rat hunting."

I didn't know what to say. I smiled at Marty, took two cherry pie–filled biscuit bowls, and wished them all a good night.

The biscuit bowls were for Delia. She was a cocktail waitress who always seemed to be waiting for a bus at the corner of the old shopping center. I knew she worked at one of those sleazy dives downtown. She said the pay was good and it was the only thing she knew how to do.

Even so, I thought she looked a little lost and alone on the corner with her too-short skirt and red sequined top. I felt the need to feed her. It was about all I could do for her.

I walked the food up to her, and smiled. "Going out?"

"Of course. I saw you come in tonight," Delia said. "I could smell those biscuit bowls a mile off. Sales not so good again today?"

"I'm afraid not." I said it cheerfully. "But their loss is your gain."

"And Ollie's, too, huh?" She nodded toward the ex-marine

who was approaching the door to the diner with all the stealth of a hunter in the wild.

"Yep. Everyone eats on me tonight." I handed her the biscuit bowls. "How are things going?"

"Tips were slow at lunch so I'm going in for the late shift. Have to pay the rent. It'll pick up." She sniffed the cherry biscuit bowls before she took a bite of one of them. "What's wrong with those people downtown anyway? These are the best biscuits, and the cutest idea I ever saw. My granny, rest her soul, would be jealous of your biscuits. And that's saying a mouthful, Zoe."

"There's a lot of competition," I explained. "Terry's Tacky Taco truck and Mama's Marvelous Mojitos all had long lines today. The Dog House was busy, too. I think it has something to do with his food truck. It's so cute. There's a dog face at the front and a tail sticking out back."

"Well, they don't know what they're missing."

"Thanks. Ollie says I need a better savory filling. He says it should be something that has a strong aroma, something unusual."

"He might be right about the savory." Delia closed her eyes as she chewed. "But nothing is gonna beat the sweet. Just don't let him tell you how to make biscuits. You got that down, honey."

I didn't know all of Delia's story, either. I knew she grew up poor and had five sisters. I knew she shared an apartment with some other women who worked at the bar. She had to live close by. I wasn't sure where. That was about it. Delia was smart and beautiful. She was tall and thin, and wore her clothes like a model. It seemed as though she could've done anything she wanted.

I was especially envious of her long legs, since I'd always been on the short side. I was a little plumper than I wanted to be, too. It was hard to make food and not eat it.

"I got something for you, too." Delia did a quick glance around us in the badly lit parking lot. "I thought maybe you'd like them. They aren't much. I just wanted to give you something for cutting down on my food bill!"

I looked at the big, green paper beads she'd given me and stuffed them into my pocket. "Thanks."

A dark green Lincoln sedan pulled in close. Delia popped the last of her biscuit into her mouth and cleaned the crumbs from her bright red lips.

"That's my ride tonight. Gotta go, Zoe. Take care. Thanks for supper."

I watched as she wrapped the other biscuit bowl in a napkin and then stowed it away in her red handbag. Her matching red cowboy boots disappeared as she got in the car, and the Lincoln pulled back into traffic.

I worried about Delia. I'd seen the place she was working once or twice. Tommy Lee had told me the bar catered to the rich crowd in Mobile. I think he'd been in there. It looked worse than my diner.

I'd tried several times to give her my cell number in case she needed any help. She wouldn't take it. She'd been working since she was a teenager, and had taken care of herself and her family. She probably handled her life better than I handled mine anyway.

I walked back through the mostly dark parking lot. Ollie had turned on the lights in the diner. I'd given him a key a few weeks back in case of emergency. I couldn't think of anyone more trustworthy than him, even if he was homeless.

I knew he was working on the rat problem. I didn't want to think about how he was doing it. I decided to clean up the food truck and be ready for another early morning tomorrow.

Crème Brûlée was snoring in his bed on the passenger seat in the front of the food truck. He didn't wake up as I worked. He had taken to ignoring me lately.

I knew he was angry that we'd moved from my apartment. I couldn't afford to stay there and keep the diner.

Besides, there was a shower and bathroom at the diner. It had once been a truck stop. I'd made a small bedroom out of the office. It was fine.

I cleaned and prepped as much as I could in the evenings, but I'd been up baking since four A.M. It was time to go to bed. I closed and locked the back of the food truck then went around to the front.

Crème Brûlée hissed when I picked him up. "You need to go on a diet," I told him. "The only reason you complain when I lift you is because you're too big for me to pick up with one arm. No more treats for you. Maybe then you'll be inspired to catch a few rats."

He yawned and looked at me like I'd lost my mind. Maybe he was right.

I reached over to get my wallet and keys from the driver's side. A man was sitting there, in front of the steering wheel. Probably one of the homeless men from the shelter.

I pushed at him. "Hey you! You have to get out so I can lock up."

He didn't move.

A little annoyed, I grumbled to myself as I went around and opened the driver's side door.

The man slid halfway out of the cab. I could see in the dim light that it was Terry, from Terry's Tacky Tacos—the man I'd argued with that day. What was *he* doing here?

Could this day get any worse?

TWO

I shouldn't have asked that question. Crème Brûlée meowed and tried to jump out of my arms.

We both knew that would be a disaster. I couldn't remember when the last time was that he'd jumped anywhere.

"Just be still and let me think." I rubbed his ears and stroked his silky fur. He wasn't much good at anything else, but he kept himself well-groomed—I had the hair balls to prove it.

It hadn't been more than thirty minutes or so since I'd climbed out of the food truck. How did Terry get in there after me? And what was he doing here? Had he followed me back to give me more grief over parking in "his spot" on Dauphin Street?

"What's up out here, young 'un?" Ollie came out of the diner, still holding the sword.

"I don't know. This is Terry."

He nodded. "From the infamous tacky taco truck?"

"Yes. I don't know what he's doing here. I think he may be drunk or something."

Ollie bent down and put his hand on Terry's neck. "I don't know, either, but he ain't goin' no place else."

"What do you mean? I can call him a taxi or something."

"No, Zoe. You don't get it. The man's *dead*. A taxi won't do him any good now."

Dead? That made even less sense to me. Maybe I was too tired to think straight.

Why was Terry—alive or dead—in my food truck?

"We gotta hide him somewhere." Ollie glanced around. "We gotta get rid of him before someone sees him here."

"We can't do that. We should call the police. That's what you do when you find a dead body."

"Oh? 'Cause you've got so much experience finding dead people?" He chuckled. "You better believe me, Zoe. You think you got trouble *now*, tell the police there's a dead man in your food truck. You'll be in for a heap more trouble."

I knew he was wrong. If something had happened to Terry, regardless of how he got into the Biscuit Bowl, the police needed to be informed. If there was one thing I knew besides cooking, it was the law.

My mother was one of the most prominent attorneys in Mobile. There was even some talk of her getting a judgeship. She'd fed me the law with my pureed carrots and pears when I was a baby. She'd hoped I was going to follow in her footsteps someday.

I was kind of a disappointment in that area.

I took out my cell phone. "I'm sorry, Ollie. I have to call. If you're worried about being here, you should go to back to the shelter. I can handle this."

"I ain't worried about me, Zoe. It's *you* I'm concerned for. What do you think the police will make of you having a dead man in your vehicle?"

I thought about it. "What *can* they make of it? I didn't

do anything. Someone must have put him here. Or he climbed in and died. I'll be fine. Don't worry."

Famous last words.

The police arrived about ten minutes later. The first car came in with sirens blaring, skidding to a stop on the broken pavement in the parking lot. Two more cars, filled with Mobile's finest, joined them a few minutes later. They were followed by an ambulance, and another team of investigators in an unmarked car.

Ollie stayed with me, much to his credit, at least until the police officers started asking questions. He mumbled an apology at that point, and disappeared into the night.

"Do you have a driver's license or any other form of ID?" Officer Frank Schmidt asked me once we were seated in his police car.

"Of course." I handed him my license. I knew what was on it—Zoe Elizabeth Chase, five-foot-two (though really I'm five-foot-two and three-quarters), black hair (short and curly), and blue eyes (on the violet side). Twenty-nine years old. "My address isn't accurate because I recently moved. I'll have it changed as soon as I can."

"Sure." Officer Schmidt handed the license back to me. "Is this your vehicle?"

"Yes. I sold my new Prius and used the money to upgrade it. Uncle Saul is letting me borrow it. I'm trying to make enough money to open my restaurant to the public."

He glanced up. "You mean the diner? Is that considered a *restaurant*?"

His tone bruised my already tender feelings. "It will be when I'm finished with it."

Crème Brûlée yawned and repositioned himself in my arms. My right hand was going numb holding him. I didn't think I should ask to go inside and put him down in the middle of my interview.

"Whatever you say." Officer Schmidt kept typing into

the computer. "What about the man in the vehicle? Do you recognize him?"

"You mean Terry."

"Okay, Terry. What's his last name?"

"I don't know. I've only spoken to him a few times. He has a food truck, too. He sells tacos and other Mexican food. Terry's Tacky Tacos. He's pretty popular."

"What happened to him?"

"I don't know. I was getting ready to go lock up the food truck, and saw him in there. I opened the door and he kind of slid out. He wasn't there when I parked the Biscuit Bowl about an hour ago. I don't know how he got in there."

Officer Schmidt studied me for what seemed like a long time. "He suddenly appeared—*dead*—in your vehicle?"

"That's about it. I wish I could be more helpful." I smiled at him for emphasis, wishing I had a biscuit bowl to give him. Everything went better with food.

"Stay here, Miss Chase. We may need to talk to you again."

That hadn't gone the way I'd planned.

I waved to Ollie. He was standing outside the homeless shelter with Marty. All the other men were out there, too. With the flashing lights from the emergency vehicles, the parking lot was lighted well enough to see everything. It was quite a show. More excitement than most of us got—or wanted.

I yawned, exhausted, wondering how long it would take to deal with Terry. I felt bad for him being dead and all. But I had to get up really early if I wanted to be done cooking in time to get downtown and set up for lunch tomorrow. It didn't take long for the best spaces to get filled up with food carts and trucks. Once that happened, it was over for the day.

My phone rang. It was Tommy Lee again. I was going to ignore it, but I felt a little vulnerable, maybe even nervous about the whole matter.

"Hi, Tommy Lee." I gave in to my need to talk to

someone familiar. I knew he'd be through the roof when I told him what had happened. I hoped it was worth it.

"Zoe, you and I need to talk."

"I don't think that's a good idea right now." I explained about the police investigating Terry's death. "Maybe tomorrow?"

"Don't be crazy. I'll be right over. You keep your pretty little mouth shut. Let me do the talking when I get there."

The phone went dead in my hand. Having Tommy Lee there wasn't exactly what I'd had in mind. I glanced at the time. It was almost midnight. Would this day never be over?

Officer Gil Gayner got into the car as I was watching the paramedics finally move Terry's body out of the food truck.

"I'd like to ask you a few more questions, Miss Chase. Exactly how well did you know the victim?"

"You mean Terry? Not well at all—as I told the other officer. We'd only met a few times. He accused me of parking in his space when we were setting up to sell lunch today. That's about as close to a conversation as we ever got. He wasn't much of a talker, at least not with me."

What I didn't say was that he'd made a pass at me the first time I'd met him. I'd been filling biscuit bowls, and he'd walked into the food truck, uninvited. Before I could ask him to leave, he put his arms around me from behind and bit my neck. He smelled like old tacos and cheap aftershave.

I'd managed to push him out of the food truck and locked the door behind him. I'd been a little nervous afterward about picking up the tiny café tables and chairs I'd set up on the sidewalk. They were the cutest patio furniture I could find, and at a good price, too.

But Terry was gone in his taco truck way before I went out.

"Why do you think Terry got into *your* food truck?" Officer Gayner asked.

"I don't know. The last time I saw him, he was downtown in his taco truck."

"You're sure he didn't come back with you? Maybe he was gonna spend the night or something?"

"Absolutely certain! I wouldn't have brought him here with me."

"You didn't think about finding a place to get rid of him around here? In this neighborhood, most people wouldn't have noticed for a few days."

I was horrified that he'd even ask me that question. "I'm not sure what you mean, but I didn't *bring* Terry here. He left in his taco truck today before I left. I don't know why he's here. Someone had to put him in the Biscuit Bowl, I guess. Unless he climbed in there and died after I got back."

Officer Gayner's face looked skeptical in the light from his computer. "All right. Wait here, Miss Chase. Someone else might want to talk to you."

I couldn't imagine who else that would be. I was starting to get a little cranky. It was almost one A.M. and I was still sitting there, waiting.

More police, this time without uniforms, and some other people in lab coats were in and out of the food truck. They had suitcases full of some kind of gear. I didn't know what they were searching for, but I was beginning to suspect that Ollie had been right about not calling them.

Crème Brûlée began to get restless. I knew what that meant. He had to *go*. Not a pleasant thought when I was holding him inside a police car.

I waved frantically to Ollie. He finally noticed and surreptitiously began to make his way toward the car.

He opened the door in front. "I told you, you shouldn't have called them."

"It's going to be fine. I can't get out right now, and my cat has to go. You know?"

"Go?"

"Use the litter box. I don't want to hold him when that happens. Can you take him inside?"

"Me?"

"I don't have anyone else. The police want me to stay here."

"You mean the police like you for Terry the taco man's murder."

"Terry was murdered?"

"From what I can make out, he was shot."

"Somebody shot him in *my* food truck? How is that even possible?"

"I don't think that's what happened. The important thing is that he was *in* your food truck. Things like that make police ask questions. We should've dumped his body."

Panic grabbed me by the throat at that point. This hadn't seemed like such a big deal to begin with. "What should I do?"

"Don't say anything," Ollie advised. "I got a friend who's a lawyer. He sometimes works for Legal Aid. I already gave him a call. Just remember—anything you say will be used to put you in prison."

He didn't take Crème Brûlée with him, either, after terrifying me. He sent Marty instead.

Good thing, too. My poor kitty was very uncomfortable.

"I'm praying for you, Zoe." Marty awkwardly lifted Crème Brûlée. "Be careful."

I thanked him, and Crème Brûlée bit him. It was only a love bite. Marty moved his hand quickly away from his mouth and smiled, promising to take care of him.

I could understand Ollie and Marty with their grim warnings. They were, after all, used to being around people who could be on the shady side of the law. My involvement with what had happened to Terry was purely coincidental. Nothing to worry about, from my perspective.

Tommy Lee's attitude had been the same as Ollie's and Marty's, I reminded myself. He knew I wasn't guilty of anything. I had absolutely nothing to hide. So, why was he worried about me saying too much?

By this time, my heart was pounding. Surely no one could think *I* killed Terry. That would be crazy!

I saw Tommy Lee's red Jaguar, with the heated leather upholstery, pull up, and heaved a sigh of relief. I watched him get out of the car and tried to get his attention by waving at him. He didn't look my way.

He spoke with the police, and pointed at the car I was in. They wouldn't let him through the barricade. My eyes welled with tears when I realized they weren't going to let him talk to me.

Someone else got out of Tommy Lee's car, on the passenger side. It was Betty, from the bank where I'd worked. She'd handled my 401(k) withdrawal. It was confusing, like everything else at the moment. *Why is she here? Why is she in Tommy Lee's car?*

As I watched, Tommy Lee went over and put his arm around her shoulder. It looked as though he was comforting her. That made me a little suspicious. Betty and I didn't know each other that well. She certainly wouldn't be all *that* upset about what had happened to me.

I understood finally when I saw her put her arms around him and snuggle her head against his chest. Tommy Lee bent his head and kissed her right there in front of me.

Tommy Lee and Betty?

I didn't even know her last name. *My* Tommy Lee and Betty from the bank were *lovers*.

Before I had a chance to absorb this information, the front door to the police car opened again. Another man—plain-clothed—sat down in the seat. He was facing me. More questions with the same answers.

His dark suit was threadbare, though I could see it had once been expensive. It was way out of style. I'm not a fashionista, but I could tell that much in the dim light from the dash. Maybe he was undercover. I couldn't clearly make out his face in the shadows.

"I'm Miguel Alexander. Ollie gave me a call. I'm a lawyer. What have you told the police, Miss Chase?"

I don't know why. It was as though, when he said my name, it was too much. I broke down, sobbing, and told him everything—from my forty-eight-dollar day to finding Terry in my food truck. I even told him about Crème Brûlée being afraid of rats, and seeing Tommy Lee kissing Betty what's-her-name.

I saw a white handkerchief waving in front of my face as I peeked through my hands. Miguel Alexander apparently dealt with weeping women on a regular basis.

I finally had a rational thought, embarrassed by my outburst. "Thank you for coming, Mr. Alexander, but I don't need an attorney."

"I think you might, Miss Chase. You've built up quite a case against yourself. I'm sure the police are grateful for your help."

"That's crazy." *Impossible!* I took a deep breath. "What makes you say that?"

"Let's not talk about it anymore, okay? I know you're upset, and you aren't helping yourself by sharing everything you know."

We both saw two officers approaching the police car.

"Don't say anything else until you ask me first," Miguel said. "All right?"

I agreed. I didn't know what else to do. Tommy Lee was standing in the parking lot with his new girlfriend. My food truck was probably going to be impounded by the police. The whole situation was out of my control. Miguel Alexander at least offered a ray of hope in what seemed like my darkest hour.

"Officers," I heard him say to the approaching police as he got out of the car, "Miss Chase has invoked her right to an attorney and will not be answering any further questions."

"Alexander," Officer Schmidt said in a disdainful manner. "What rock did you crawl out from under?"

"I'll ignore that remark," Miguel responded. "My client and I are going to confer *privately* in the police car."

"Whatever," Officer Gayner said. "I hope you're better at Legal Aid than you were at being an ADA. This girl looks good for murder one."

THREE

His words squeezed the breath from my lungs. I couldn't have heard right. Just because they found Taco Terry dead in my food truck, they thought *I* killed him?

Miguel got into the car again. "Can you tell me again what happened? Leave out the part about the biscuits and the cat and your boyfriend. Just talk about what led up to you finding the man in the truck. I'm going to record what you say."

I looked at the little tape recorder he held between us. Miguel was supposed to defend people who couldn't afford a lawyer. I probably didn't have that problem. My personal wealth was limited, but my mother and father would be able to afford help. No matter how angry they were about the food truck, they wouldn't leave me hanging.

"I should tell you that my family has money," I confided to him. "It was nice of Ollie to call you, but I'll be fine. I don't want to waste your time. My mother is Anabelle Chase."

He whistled softly in the darkness. "I see."

Everyone knew my mother.

"If I'm really accused of killing Terry, she'll find someone for me. Thank you so much for coming out. I felt really isolated in here."

"That's okay. Where is your mother now?"

"I'm not sure. I didn't want to bother her. She and I are having a few *issues* right now. Well, we have issues most of the time. She'll be here for me. Just not right now."

"What are you doing here with this old food truck and a dead body? It doesn't seem like a place Anabelle Chase's daughter would hang out."

I really liked Miguel's voice. It was soothing. It seemed like he'd have a good singing voice. I wished he could stay and talk to me all night. I felt better with him there. Either he was easy to talk to or I was desperate to talk to someone— I wasn't sure which.

It was a little hard to tell exactly what he looked like, besides being thin. His face was angular and he had high cheekbones.

He seemed like a nice man. Maybe I'd offer to make him dinner sometime for his trouble. It looked like I was single again. Why not?

I told him about my biscuit bowls, Uncle Saul, and Ollie's thoughts on savory fillings. I explained about quitting my job, and using all my money to get started on my dream.

He sat back in the seat and turned off the tape recorder. "You're a brave woman, Miss Chase."

My heart did a little flip-flop. "Call me Zoe, please. Everyone does. I don't know about being brave. I'm scared to death most of the time. I hate rats. I let Terry say some terrible things to me today, and didn't even tell the police that he tried to assault me in my food truck."

I yawned. "Sorry. I'm exhausted. I've been up since four A.M., and I don't plan to sleep tonight. I probably won't bother making biscuits. They won't let me have my food truck anyway, right?"

"No. You won't get that back for a while. I'm sorry. Maybe your mother's lawyer can help that problem along."

As if on cue, the door beside me was jerked open. The cool night air rushed in.

"Get out of there, Zoe," my mother's stern voice said.

"The police said I had to wait here for them to talk to me," I replied. "I'm in enough trouble, Mom."

"It's quite all right, Miss Chase." A man, whose face I didn't recognize, stared in the opening at me. "We'll be leaving now."

"It looks like your rescue team is here, Zoe," Miguel said. "Go with them. Do what your lawyer says. You'll be making biscuits again in no time. It was nice meeting you."

"This is Dirk Gordon," my mother explained to me. "He's going to deal with this mess you've made."

I got out of the car and stretched a little. I'd been waiting there for almost two hours.

"I didn't make this particular mess, Mom. It was made for me."

"We can talk later." She frowned across the top of the police car as Miguel got out on the other side. "Well, look who it is. How is the view from the other side, Mr. Alexander?"

"Just fine, Mrs. Chase. As a matter of fact, I like it better."

"What are you doing here, Mom?" I wondered how she knew about the situation.

"Tommy Lee called me, thank God, since you didn't. Let's get out of here. You can tell Dirk your story. I hope you aren't having some kind of psychotic break, though that would explain your recent actions."

Dirk Gordon fingered his blond mustache, which almost glowed green in the bad parking lot lighting. "She has no previous record of violence," he explained to my mother. "A judge would believe a psychotic break. We could sell that explanation. Lucky for us the dead man has a rap sheet. No one will want to prosecute her for killing him."

I finally snapped, or reached the limit of how much I could endure for one day. I glared at my mother in her expensive black suit and lost it.

"I'm not going anywhere with you, Mom. As for my lawyer, I want Miguel Alexander to represent me." I looked at him where he waited on the other side of the car. "We'll pay you, of course. I don't expect the people of Mobile to get me out of this."

"You'll do as I say, Zoe Chase," my mother roared back. "Or so help me—"

"Daddy will pay," I smugly reminded her. "Don't worry about it."

I walked around to where Miguel waited. "Can you do that? Can you defend me even if I have money?"

I could see his face more clearly now. He had dark eyes with slight frown lines between them and a generous mouth. His dark hair looked a little unruly.

"I could." He looked across the car at my enraged mother's face. "Are you sure that's what you want? I know Gordon's work. He's a good attorney."

"I want *you* to be there. I trust you. I'm not psychotic, and I didn't kill anyone. Okay?" I couldn't tell if he'd go for it or not.

He finally smiled. "Okay."

"Oh, for goodness' sake," my mother said. "Why does everything have to be so dramatic with you, Zoe?"

I didn't have an answer for that. I didn't really think she was asking for one. This was our relationship.

Tommy Lee made it through the police line at that point—minus Betty. Though I was a little grateful to him for calling my mother, I couldn't forget what I'd seen.

"Honey!" He approached me with his arms open.

"Get lost," I said. "Save it for Betty."

His face was stricken. It was hard to tell if it was guilt or surprise.

"Is this about Betty?" He laughed. "I ran into her on my way here. Naturally, she was upset when she heard about what happened to you. I gave her a ride. I know you don't think it's anything more."

I got right up in his handsome face and said, "I have rats to kill and a litter box to clean. You might not want to mess with me right now."

He didn't say anything else until I'd walked past him, headed for the diner.

"Okay. I'll call you later," he said. "We'll talk."

"Not if Ollie brings his sword over first," I muttered as I made my way through police officers and crime scene people who were staring at me.

Miguel followed me. "I could give you a lift home."

I opened the door to the diner and flipped on the light. The overhead florescent began buzzing loudly, as it always did. "This *is* home. Would you like some coffee?"

The health department had given me an 89 percent rating once I'd cleaned up the front of the diner, replaced the broken tiles that had been on the floor, and pretty much put in a new bathroom. It still didn't look like anything that could be open to the public, but it was good enough for me to get started.

"You know, it's not really legal for you to live here," he said.

"I know." I put on a pot of coffee. "I'm not telling anyone else that. I hope you'll keep it to yourself."

He sat on one of the refurbished stools at the counter. "I won't say anything. The police might, if they find out."

"I gave up my apartment. I could use my father's address. He wouldn't mind."

"Your parents are divorced?"

"For years. Would you like a biscuit?"

"No, thanks." He swung around on the barstool. "I still

don't understand why you're here. Your family is rich. Why not have them buy you a nice restaurant?"

"No one understands, especially not Tommy Lee."

"The boyfriend in the parking lot?"

"Well, ex-boyfriend. Could you believe that lame story? The only time I even spoke to Betty was when she closed my 401(k). He must really think I'm dense."

Miguel smiled. "I'm sure he doesn't. You caught him with his pants down. He had to think of something to say. That's what men do."

I examined him a little more closely now that we were in bright, albeit annoying, light. He was about six feet tall, a good-looking man—not by Tommy Lee's standards, but he also didn't have the personality of a used-car salesman. Miguel seemed very serious, and a little intense.

Not usually my type. I reminded myself that he was only my lawyer, not a potential boyfriend.

I was right about his clothes being old. His tie and shoes were, too. Everything about him seemed as though it had once been first quality, but hadn't been new in a long time. But his dark brown eyes (I was right) were kind, and a little troubled. Instead of a smooth, well-practiced line of conversation, his words felt carefully thought out.

"What about *you*?" I asked as I got out cream and sugar. I had to keep everything in the refrigerator to keep the rats out of it. "You were with the DA's office? What happened?"

"I'd rather not talk about it. I'm here to handle your case."

"I told you about my whole life tonight. I think you could tell me why you left the DA's office."

"You're kind of snoopy, aren't you?"

"Maybe. It's hard to help people if you don't know their stories."

"I'm not looking for help. You wanted to hire *me*, remember?"

"That's true." I studied the coffee cups for inspiration. I really wanted to know more about him. It was only professional, of course. He was representing me. I should know about his past, right?

"Consider it an interview." I was inspired. "How can I hire you if I don't know more about you?"

Miguel got to his feet. "I might not be the right man for the job, Zoe. Dirk Gordon would be happy to tell you all about his past, I'm sure."

Ollie walked in, glancing back at the scene still going on in the parking lot. "Wow! You're in it now, young 'un. Good thing I called Miguel. He knows how the DA thinks, seeing as how he was almost in that office."

"I don't think it's going to work out," Miguel told him.

Ollie took a seat. "Of course it will. Zoe needs you. You probably need her, too. I smelled that coffee brewing all the way down at the shelter. Let's all have a cup. Did Miguel tell you about the big scandal that made him leave the DA's office?"

I smiled and put out a third coffee cup. "Not yet. I think he was about to."

Miguel sat back down. "I hope you have plenty of coffee."

FOUR

"I wouldn't call it a big scandal," Miguel said as I poured coffee into their cups.

Ollie laughed. "You were gonna be the next DA. Someone set you up to take the fall for 'irregularities.'"

"What irregularities?" I asked.

"Miguel was accused of falsifying evidence in a big murder trial. Remember the one about the girl getting killed on the tourist ferry? That's the one."

"Thanks for reminding me," Miguel added.

"What? They dropped the whole thing—*after* the election. It was all a ruse to keep you from beating the old DA." Ollie slurped his coffee.

"Is that really what happened?" I asked Miguel.

"I'm afraid so. Maybe not as dramatic as Ollie tells it. I left the DA's office after that. I'm happy working for myself now."

"Sure you are. Like a shark is happy in a big tank at

SeaWorld." Ollie slapped Miguel on the back, knocking him forward.

Lucky he wasn't drinking his coffee, I thought. "At least you were innocent."

"It didn't *feel* like it at the time." Miguel held his cup while I poured more coffee into it. "I'm warning you that there could be some tough days ahead when you might question if you really are innocent."

"Thanks. I'm glad you can represent me."

He raised his dark brows. "That means the interview is over?"

"It was just a *ruse* to find out all that stuff." I borrowed the line from Ollie.

"You know, it's not too late to change your mind," he said. "I have plenty of work to keep me busy. You might be better off with Dirk Gordon."

"Hell, no!" Ollie declared. "She's not better off without you. You got me out of a dozen scrapes I probably didn't deserve to get out of. You can get her out of this one, Miguel. She's a good girl who works hard."

Looking past them through the windows, I saw a woman in a suit approaching the front door to the diner. She was accompanied by a uniformed officer. All the good energy that had welled up in me after sharing jokes and stories with Miguel and Ollie fled like the darkness before sunrise.

I remembered how tired I was and how overwhelmingly unfair all of this was. The weight of it crashed down on me.

"What's wrong?" Miguel asked.

"I think the police might be coming to arrest me." I nodded at the windows behind them.

"Don't worry," he said. "Be calm. You didn't kill anyone."

I heard him, but my heart still beat a terrified tattoo in my chest.

"Zoe Chase?" the woman in the pretty brown suit asked as soon as she opened the front door.

"That's me." I waved at her.

"What did I tell you about saying anything without my permission?" Miguel got to his feet and approached them. "Detective Latoure. I assume you have news for my client."

Detective Patti Latoure nodded, shaking his hand. "Miguel Alexander! I haven't seen you in a while. You're representing this woman?"

"It's been a few months. Your news?"

"It looks like Terry Bannister was shot with a .22-caliber pistol close up. The medical examiner is working on time of death and whatnot. Does your client want to make a statement tonight?"

"My client and I are conferring at the moment. We'll be glad to come down to police headquarters first thing in the morning. This has been a traumatic event for my client. I assume you know that she's Anabelle Chase's daughter. She's not a flight risk."

The detective studied Miguel with sharp blue eyes that seemed to see everything. Her hair was pale blond, scraped back from her tired face. "Her mother told me the same thing. Let me assure you, Miguel, as I did Mrs. Chase—Zoe isn't a suspect. We'll be expecting the two of you in the morning. I want to hear all the details then, all right?"

"Absolutely," Miguel promised. "Everything that's fit to tell."

Detective Latoure agreed in a voice dulled by too many rules and not enough patience. She and the officer went back out to the crime scene, which was finally beginning to clear.

I collapsed on the countertop when they were gone, taking in big gulps of air. I think I'd been holding my breath the whole time.

It was almost three A.M., according to the big, biscuit-shaped clock on the wall. I'd managed to find it at a local thrift store. It didn't keep time very well, but it was cute and went with my theme.

"You okay, Zoe?" Ollie asked.

"I'm fine." I didn't raise my head. "I need some sleep, and my food truck."

"That's not going to happen today." Miguel was apologetic but certain. "Get some rest. We'll get together in a few hours before we go to the station. We need to go over your statement again."

"Okay." I raised my head. "I suppose I can stay home tomorrow. How long do you think it will take to get the Biscuit Bowl back?"

Ollie laughed as the tow truck pulled my food truck out of the parking lot. "You have a terrible funny bone, girl. You'll be lucky to get that back in time for Mardi Gras, next year."

"It won't be that bad," Miguel said. "But it will be a while before the crime scene people are done with it."

"Thanks. How much do I owe you? There must be a retainer or something?" I asked him.

"We'll talk about that tomorrow, too. Try not to worry. We'll get this straightened out." He looked around the shabby diner. "You really *live* here?"

"No." Was that a test? "You said to say that I live with my father."

"*Really.* Do you live here?"

"Yes. I have a cozy spot in the office. Crème Brûlée and I are fine here."

"Crème . . . what?"

Ollie laughed as he walked to the door. "It's her cat, man. You know how single chicks dig cats. Good night, Zoe. Good luck tomorrow."

"Thanks, Ollie."

"And don't worry about rats bothering you. I took a few of them out with my sword. They're not coming back for a while. Rats are smart animals. They know when they're outclassed."

When Ollie was gone, Miguel left me his business card.

"I guess I'll be going, too. Try to get some sleep. I'll be here to pick you up at seven. Call me if you need anything."

I wanted to say thank you. It would've been polite. I was too far gone for politeness. I nodded and he left. I locked the diner door behind him, and turned off the buzzing overhead light.

Crème Brûlée was already asleep on my makeshift bed, hogging up the whole thing as usual. I moved him over a little to make room for myself. He hissed and rolled anyway. I fell down on the bed without even taking off my shoes.

"This *has* to be better tomorrow," I told him. "It was really just a bad day. Tomorrow will be better. Let's get some sleep."

His purring was the last thing I heard as I snuggled next to him and put my arm around his furry body.

- - - - - - -

Someone was pounding on the front door and calling my name. I checked my alarm clock—seven thirty. I'd forgotten to set my alarm.

After disentangling Crème Brûlée from my arm, I got up and ran out of the office. Of course, he hissed at me. He rolled over and went back to sleep. How dare I disturb his slumber?

It was Miguel. He pointed to his watch before I opened the front door.

"We're supposed to be at the police station by nine. We need time to talk before we go."

I yawned. "I just woke up. I need a shower and a change of clothes."

He looked at my rumpled jeans and T-shirt from yesterday. "You look fine. Let's go."

He had to be joking. I searched his very sincere face. He wasn't joking.

"I'm not going in the clothes I slept in. Help yourself to some coffee while I get dressed. It will only take a few minutes." I blew a curl that had fallen into my face and swiveled to leave him.

"We still have to talk about everything that happened yesterday," he maintained. "We have to get your statement right."

Yeah, yeah. "We'll have time while we're driving. Have some coffee, please."

He said a few other things before I grabbed my clothes and went into the shower. I didn't hear what they were, and I ignored him.

How could he think I looked fine to go anywhere? Had I looked that bad yesterday?

I turned on the shower. Immediately, I knew what the problem was. We'd mostly seen each other in the dark last night. There was only that brief time in the diner with the painful overhead lighting. He'd forgotten what I looked like, or was too intensely occupied with his defense strategy to pay attention. That had to be it.

The hot water gushed out of the showerhead. Crème Brûlée had crept into the bathroom, leaving the door wide open to the kitchen area. He was meowing for his breakfast, poor kitty. He was used to eating much earlier. He had to be starving.

In answer, my stomach growled. I hadn't eaten dinner last night. I was used to being up and grabbing a snack at four A.M. I was hungry, too.

I turned off the water and moved aside the goldfish-covered shower curtain. Miguel was trying to lift Crème Brûlée. He looked up at me—naked as the day I was born—and smiled.

"The cat sounded hungry," he explained. "I didn't think about you being in there—you know—like *that*."

Words had clearly failed him. Time seemed to pause for an instant and then started back up again.

I grabbed an orange towel and quickly wrapped it around the most important parts. All of me had to be red with embarrassment. I looked okay naked, but I wasn't prepared for an audience.

"Well, turn away or something! I told you I was going to take a shower!"

"Sorry!" He turned away, a little red-faced himself. "I made coffee. Hurry up. It's not good to be late for your first interview in a murder investigation."

I closed the bathroom door behind him, and looked at my face in the misty mirror. I was breathing hard and my heart was pounding. Miguel had to be one of those seriously laid-back kind of people. If that had been Tommy Lee, he would've reacted much differently. Of course, Tommy Lee wouldn't have offered to feed my cat, either. And Crème Brûlée wouldn't have let him hold him.

I dried off quickly, and did what I could with my hair. Curly hair does what it wants to do. It's like an entity all its own that happens to live on my head. I get my curly hair from my father, who wears his in a crew cut so you can't tell it's curly at all.

I chose to wear something dressier, one of the suits I normally wore to the bank. It was peach colored, a good hue on me. By the time I'd put on my makeup and matching shoes, my face wasn't so red. My heart had stopped beating so quickly, too.

Ollie was making breakfast on the old grill while Miguel set out coffee cups.

"That smells good." I sniffed and smiled. I already knew Ollie was good at cooking the basics—pancakes, eggs, and toast. "I'm hungry."

"You're going to have to roll up eggs in a pancake so you can eat on the way." Miguel poured coffee into paper cups. "Where are the lids for these things?"

"Under the counter." I sat down as Ollie heaped food on a plate for me.

"She has to eat," my large friend maintained. "Who

knows how long the police will interrogate her. She has to be prepared."

"She's not a suspect right now," Miguel said. "Only a person of interest. The police are also talking to Terry's taco truck partner. The two had a fight yesterday over some missing cash. The police will probably like him better for the murder than they do Zoe."

"Why are we going at all then?" I sipped some coffee. "Maybe we should skip it and let the police get on with questioning Terry's partner."

Miguel did exactly what he'd said and wrapped my plate-sized pancake around my eggs. "It's not nice to stand up a police investigation. Believe me, Detective Latoure wouldn't like it. We have to get you cleared of this completely if you want your food truck back."

Ollie was already eating his pancakes and eggs. "Do what he says, young 'un. Miguel knows what he's talking about."

At least I think that's what he said. It was hard to tell around the food already in his mouth.

"Okay." The pancake-wrapped egg made me feel a little queasy. I wasn't as hungry as I'd thought. "Maybe we could put this in the fridge for later."

"Good. Let's go." Miguel started for the door.

"No. She needs to eat," Ollie argued. "I've been through this. I know what it's like."

"It'll be fine," I assured him. "I'll eat later."

"At least take it with you." Ollie wrapped it all up in some aluminum foil. "Just slip it into your pocket. It will stay warm that way."

That sounded even less appetizing. I took the pancake anyway. I was pretty sure I wouldn't eat it, but I didn't want to offend Ollie.

"Will you look after Crème Brûlée for me? Miguel fed him. He might get lonely."

"I'm not much good at looking after animals, especially
spoiled fat cats." Ollie glared at Crème Brûlée, who immediately hissed at him and ran back to the office.

"Thank you." Miguel grabbed my arm and we headed
out the front door.

The morning was bright and sunny, already warming
up—full of sounds from the city. I could glimpse the blue
water of Mobile Bay from the parking lot. There were fishing boats, tourist charters, and ferries from the city to Dauphin Island. Every tourist should have a chance to see the
city this way.

"Here." Miguel handed me the foil-wrapped breakfast
and then started his car.

"Thanks. And thank you for coming to get me this morning. I'm sorry I was so messed up. Yesterday was awful. I'm
hoping today will be better."

"Most people going to a police interview aren't that opti-
mistic. I guess that's why you can handle your food truck
not making much money. Optimism."

"Uncle Saul was in the food business for thirty years
before he retired. He says you have to be patient, like a
spider. When the right insect flies into your web, you grab it."

"I wouldn't have thought of applying that image to the
food business." He pulled into the heavy traffic, headed for
downtown Mobile. "Your uncle must be an interesting
character."

"He's my father's brother," I confided, "but you couldn't
find two men more different if you tried."

I told him about my father's close-cut curly hair. Uncle
Saul wears his gray-streaked, black curly hair like a big bush
on his head. My father wouldn't be caught dead like that.

"And my father is the president of an old, established
bank, while Uncle Saul lives in the swamp in a log cabin he
built himself. They don't get along all that well, either. My
father blames that on my mother, but I think they're too
different to be friends."

"Don't you believe in opposites attracting?"

"I suppose it all depends. It can happen. I don't know how long a relationship like that can last."

"Is that what happened to you and your boyfriend?"

"That's a little personal. I've only known you a few hours, if you don't count the time I was sleeping."

He repeated my words back to me. "I'm your lawyer. I have to ask personal questions sometimes."

I looked at him in his dark suit, white shirt, and blue tie. His clothes today were better than they had been last night. Maybe he'd thrown on whatever he could find to come and help Ollie. Maybe he saved this suit for special occasions.

His black Mercedes was at least ten years old. The brown leather interior was spotless. He maintained what he owned, I considered, but wasn't making as much money as he had in the past. Possibly a reflection of his problems at the DA's office?

I knew those attorneys didn't make much money, either. Intuition told me that somewhere along the way, he'd had money in his life.

I wasn't rude enough to inquire.

"Are we clear on your statement?" Miguel asked as we pulled into the parking lot for the police station.

"Yes. I know what I need to say."

"And not say, right? Don't elaborate on your statement. Look at me before you answer any question they ask you. If I don't tell you to answer, don't answer. Are we clear on that?"

"Clear as rain," I assured him.

We got out of his car and I felt nervous again. I'd been fine while we were talking. Now that I was about to be interviewed, I wasn't quite so fine.

"What's wrong?"

"How do I look?" I didn't move away from the Mercedes.

"What do you mean?"

"I mean, does my hair look okay? I know it can be a little

goofy looking sometimes because it's curly. Is my lipstick straight? I think the peach color works on me, don't you?"

"You look good." He glanced at his watch. "We have two minutes to get upstairs."

I put my hand on his. "Could you *really* look at me? Am I a mess or something?"

Finally, it seemed that I had his full attention. His brown eyes, with a hint of sherry in them, roamed from my feet to the curls on my head. His gaze lingered on a couple of places that made me take a deep breath.

"You look *really* good, Zoe. Much better than you need to for this interview. Your boyfriend is losing a very lovely lady."

That assessment, spoken in his sexy baritone, made me feel better. *Too much better.*

I had to be careful, I realized. I was drawn to Miguel, but it was probably just a rebound thing. After all, my relationship had only broken up last night.

Tommy Lee probably didn't even realize we'd broken up yet at all.

"Thank you." I fingered the lapel of his suit. "You look very good, too."

He took my hand, and we got in the elevator.

I had never been in the downtown police station before, even though I was born and raised in Mobile. I guess that you'd have to have some reason to be here. Apparently I'd never had a reason before.

The police station was very busy with what seemed like hundreds of police officers in uniform, and people in all states of dress and undress—probably criminals.

A thin man in uniform at the front desk called Detective Latoure when Miguel told him we were there to see her.

"You showed up," Detective Latoure greeted us. "I had money on you skipping town."

Was she talking to me? I looked around. Miguel and I

were the only ones within hearing distance, besides the officer at the desk. Why would she think such a thing?

"If you're saying that you thought I'd leave town rather
than come here this morning—"

"Miss Chase has nothing to say about that since she isn't
here to talk about your opinions of her, Patti," Miguel butted
in before I could finish.

It was hard to remember not to talk.

"Maybe we should start easy," Detective Latoure said.
"Did you kill the man you found in your food truck?"

FIVE

"Of course not!"

"Zoe!" Miguel called out.

Detective Latoure laughed. "I'm gonna enjoy this."

Since I wasn't supposed to say anything, I gave Detective Latoure the same look I'd seen my mother use on the gardener and the housekeeper when she wasn't pleased with them.

I couldn't tell if it had the same effect on her that it did on them, but it allowed me to put my nose in the air and walk past her to the interview room as though she were someone beneath my notice.

"Have a seat, Miss Chase." Detective Latoure opened the door to a tiny room with a table and three chairs in it.

There was even a small window that was obviously a two-way mirror, the same as they show in movies and on TV. I wasn't as familiar with detective shows as I was cooking shows, but I knew that someone was on the other side of the mirror.

Detective Latoure sat down across from me and Miguel. She opened a file and started reading out of it.

I glanced at Miguel. He shook his head and lounged back in his uncomfortable chair, apparently waiting for the detective to make the first move. He seemed completely at ease.

I tapped my fingernails on the table. I needed a manicure. It had been weeks since my last one. I'd been so busy setting up my food truck and cleaning the diner, I'd forgotten many of the niceties.

That was probably one reason Tommy Lee and my mother thought I'd lost my mind.

Detective Latoure put down the file and stared at me for a few minutes.

I stopped tapping my nails and tried not to fidget. The chair was *very* uncomfortable. I hoped Ollie wasn't right and that I wouldn't have to spend all day sitting here.

"Miss Chase," she finally began.

"Call me Zoe. Everyone does."

Miguel's dark eyes made it clear that I wasn't supposed to speak yet. I tried lounging back in my chair as he was. I couldn't pull off the look and sat back up.

"Okay. Zoe." Detective Latoure smiled. "You're from a very well-known family here in Mobile. You've had a good education. Auburn, right?"

I looked at Miguel, as I was supposed to. He nodded. "Yes. I went to Auburn."

That had been easy. I could do this whole talking-when-I-was-supposed-to thing.

"You worked as a loan officer at the Azalea National Bank for the last five years. There are nothing but glowing reviews from the people you worked with, and your supervisors there."

Did that need an answer? I peeked at Miguel. He didn't nod. I didn't speak.

"What are you leading up to, Patti?" Miguel asked. "I don't think my client needs a history lesson on her own life."

"I appreciate that, Miguel. My point is that Zoe led a sheltered, uneventful life—until a few weeks ago. Out of the blue, she quit her job, gave up her apartment, decided to open an old diner, and started driving a food truck. Does that sound *normal* to you?"

"*Normal*?" I asked. "Are you saying I'm not normal? And what do you mean uneventful? I'll be thirty next year. I did all of those things to find my dream. I want to make people happy with my food. I don't think that makes me a killer."

Oops.

I could tell I'd said something I wasn't supposed to. Miguel's expression was as dark as a thundercloud above Mobile Bay.

Was I supposed to sit there and let this woman disparage my life?

I sat back again. "Sorry." I was never very good at keeping quiet about anything. I also tend to talk when I'm nervous.

"What's your point?" Miguel's voice was calm. "People frequently leave their jobs. How does that have anything to do with the taco truck owner's death?"

"I'm getting to that," Detective Latoure promised.

"Let's expedite it." Miguel sounded impatient.

"My point is that Zoe is living a very stressful life—*for her*—right now. We know that she and the victim argued yesterday on Dauphin Street in front of a crowd of people at lunch."

"Argued? He tried to *assault* me." I tossed out the words like they were firecrackers. "If he wasn't dead, I'd file charges against him."

"Really?" Detective Latoure took out a tape recorder. "Tell me exactly what happened."

I opened my mouth to speak. Nothing came out because Miguel's hand went over it.

"I need a moment alone with my client," he said abruptly.

I knew what that was all about.

Before Detective Latoure could leave the room, the door burst open, and my father strode into the tiny space.

"Zoe! Baby! Are you all right? Why didn't you call and tell me about all of this? Daddy would've taken care of it."

Daddy was an impressive man. He was tall, broad shouldered, lean, and fit for a sixty-something-year-old. He was tan from his frequent fishing trips. He was always going on cruises and sailing to exotic places since he and my mother had divorced.

He was dressed to the hilt in an expensive gray suit and a red tie. He even wore the matching onyx cuff links and tie tack I'd given him for his last birthday.

He knew how to make an entrance. Funny how much he suddenly reminded me of Tommy Lee.

"Daddy!" I ran and threw my arms around his neck. I was very happy to see him. If anyone could understand and make all of this go away, it was him.

"I'll give you all a few minutes to sort yourselves out." Detective Latoure got to her feet, taking her file with her.

Before she could leave, my father stepped forward and shook her hand. "I'm Ted Chase, president of Bank of Mobile. I'm sure there's been some terrible mistake, ma'am."

Detective Latoure shook his hand and smiled. "I hope for your daughter's sake that's true, Mr. Chase."

I thought I heard Detective Latoure mutter, "And my sake, too," as she walked by me and out of the room. I could've been mistaken about that.

Once the door was closed behind her, my father turned to Miguel. "Ted Chase. You are?"

"Miguel Alexander." They shook hands. "Your daughter's attorney."

"So I heard." My father stared at Miguel. "I think we should consider someone else, Zoe. Your mother has a good friend who is an excellent criminal lawyer."

I glanced apologetically at Miguel. Maybe by this time

he was hoping I'd find another lawyer, too. I still had confidence in him. I hoped he still felt the same about me.

"Daddy, I like Miguel. I want him to represent me."

"I know you do, angel. I think we should consider your mother's experience in all this. She wasn't very happy with your choice."

"I wasn't happy with hers, either. He wanted me to pretend that I was having a meltdown or something. He wanted to blame the murder on me because I quit my job and bought the diner. The police detective sounds just like him. I don't need that kind of negativity."

Daddy glanced away. "Honey, I want to support you through this terrible time. I'm here for you, whatever you need. We'll fight this together. If they find you guilty, we'll make sure you never see the inside of a prison. There are several good hospitals in the state."

I stared at my handsome father, thinking about all the time we'd spent together while I was growing up. We'd done everything from playing tennis to sailing. He was right. He'd always been there for me. *Until now.*

What was wrong with everyone?

"Daddy, there was a dead man in my food truck. I can't sell my biscuit bowls because my vehicle has been impounded. People think I killed this man. Do you have any idea how I feel right now?"

He smiled. "No, pumpkin. How do you feel?"

"Angry!" I yelled. "I'm *really* angry. I want Miguel to be my lawyer—I don't care what Mom says. I don't care what *you* say. Can you handle that?"

"Of course." He smiled at Miguel. "I know you'll do a good job for my daughter."

"Thank you for your confidence. But I can't do anything if your daughter won't listen to me. I told her to keep her comments to herself about what we'd said. She keeps trying to incriminate herself."

"Sorry." I felt really foolish. He was trying to help me. It made me so angry for people to think that I killed Terry, especially since that made me stupid enough to hide his body in my own food truck.

"I can't represent you if you won't listen to me." Miguel's very sincere dark eyes fixed on me. "You have to let me do the talking unless I tell you to speak. If you can't do that, Zoe, I'm leaving."

"Don't leave. I won't say anything else. I promise."

"Okay. Let's bring Detective Latoure back in. This time, stay quiet."

"I will." I pulled the imaginary zipper across my lips.

My father decided to stay in the interview room with us. Detective Latoure came back, this time with no folder in hand.

"We're ready," Miguel told her.

"I'm very happy to tell you that we've made an arrest in this case, Miguel. Your client is free to go. She's no longer on our person of interest list. I'm sorry if we've caused you any distress, Zoe. Have a nice day."

"Was it his partner?" I asked the detective.

"I'm afraid we're not at liberty to discuss that matter."

"You dragged me in here and acted like I murdered Terry. Surely I deserve to know who you've arrested," I argued.

Detective Latoure took a deep breath and glanced at my father. "It will be out in the media later today anyway. I guess it doesn't matter. We've taken a waitress from the area into custody. We think that she was Terry's Bannister's lover at one time. Her name is Delia Vann."

SIX

"Delia?" I couldn't believe it. "You arrested Delia?"

"She fits." Detective Latoure shrugged. "They used to be lovers. Separated on bad terms. She has no alibi, and she was at the shopping center when the medical examiner thinks Bannister was killed."

"What about his partner who was stealing money from him?" I demanded.

"He has an alibi. We feel sure Delia followed through on a threat she made against Bannister for keeping some of her possessions when they broke up. We have a witness who can testify to that."

Miguel nodded. "Bannister's partner, right?"

"Maybe. Let us handle the police work."

"You know this waitress she's talking about?" My father sounded like he couldn't believe it. "Where did you meet her? Your mother was right. This is no life for you, Zoe."

"Never mind that, Daddy." I turned to Miguel. "Will you represent her instead of me?"

Miguel looked surprised. "You really *know* this woman well enough to believe she didn't kill Terry Bannister?"

"Yes. She's a wonderful person. Will you represent her? I know I can trust you to do a good job."

"The down-and-out waitress with a heart of gold." Detective Latoure snorted. "I love that fable."

"Zoe, who's going to pay for Miguel to represent this woman?" My father's words implied that it wasn't going to be him.

"If I have to, I can sell my shares in Bank of Mobile," I bluffed, hoping he wouldn't call me on it. That bank had been in our family for a hundred years. I hadn't even wanted to touch those shares to get my food truck business going.

"You *wouldn't*!" His face turned pale. "The bank is your family legacy, Zoe. You'd lose that for this woman?"

"If I have to. I'd rather borrow the money from you to pay Miguel. I'll pay you back when I get the business up and running."

"What do you know about Delia Vann?" Detective Latoure appeared intrigued.

"I know she's had unfortunate circumstances," I said. "And I know she's a good person. That's all I need to know." I hoped they wouldn't ask me what those circumstances were, since I didn't know her complete history. Maybe I'd only known her a short while, but I had a sense about people. I always knew who was good and who was bad. I was usually right at the bank when they hired someone new.

It was a knack I'd inherited from Uncle Saul. The rest of the family scoffed. I knew it was true.

It also occurred to me that Delia may have been talking to me at the bus stop when the real killer was putting Terry's body in the van. I told Miguel and Detective Latoure about my theory. Detective Latoure said she'd look into it.

"I'll talk to her," Miguel agreed. "No promises until then—money or not. I only represent people I think are innocent."

"So you thought all along that I was innocent?" I took a step toward him but stopped short of hugging him. I didn't want him to get the wrong idea. "Thank you so much, for me, and for Delia."

Miguel picked up his briefcase. "It's been a pleasure."

As he left, I turned to Detective Latoure. "When can I have my food truck back? Today is lost, but I can be ready for tomorrow."

"I'll check with forensics. I think they already know Bannister wasn't killed in the food truck. The ME thinks he was stuffed inside because it was convenient."

I know it sounds terrible, but the first thought that came to my mind was that it was going to take a boatload of disinfectant before I got behind the wheel again. I could still see Terry's body, and smell the old tacos on him. *Eww!*

"I'll give you a call," Detective Latoure promised.

"I'll wait here. I have nothing better to do until I get my food truck back."

"Miss Chase. Zoe—"

"I'll take you out for lunch," my father offered.

Was it that late already? I looked at my watch. It was nearly noon.

"Lunch then," I agreed. "I'll be back right after lunch, if I haven't heard from you by then, Detective."

I walked out of the little interview room, glad that my part in Taco Terry's murder was over.

I thought I heard Detective Latoure say to my father, "Your girl is very determined, Mr. Chase."

"She's a lot like her mother," my father replied. "Who do you bank with, Detective?"

I saw Miguel across the crowded squad room. He was already talking to Delia. As I watched, a police officer escorted them to another tiny interview room.

Miguel was a good person, too. Instinct had told me that about him right away—just like with Ollie.

There was some sadness behind his dark eyes and calm

demeanor that I thought was more than just losing his bid to be the next DA. I wasn't sure if I'd ever know what it was that I sensed. I hoped he'd stay in my life, but it seemed doubtful. Still, a girl could dream.

I liked Miguel. I hoped he liked me, too.

We left police headquarters on Government Street and headed to Daddy's favorite restaurant, Wintzell's. He loved to eat shrimp and cheese grits there. I opted for the seafood au gratin. It was awe inspiring. We also splurged for some of their amazing Key lime pie.

Wintzell's doesn't look like much on the outside, but the interior had original wood walls and everything was there from when it opened in 1938, including old Oliver Wintzell's sayings on the wall. Some of them I had memorized after seeing them so often, such as: *"Every girl waits for the right man to come along, but in the meantime, she gets married."*

Is that what I'd almost done with Tommy Lee?

Daddy had been telling me about his last fishing trip to the Florida Keys when my mother showed up. She was wearing her tight gray suit. That meant she was there for business. My heart sank as I knew I was about to sit through another tirade.

As often happens when the two of them are in the same place at the same time, sparks flew. You know how some people are sad that their parents get divorced? I was glad. It made my life more bearable. I was just out of high school when they'd decided to split. I was as happy for me as I was for them.

I was pleasantly surprised when they didn't want to discuss my future without Tommy Lee. He was their personal favorite—I knew it would come eventually.

Instead, even though I'd been cleared of my part in Taco Terry's death, they still argued about my choice of lawyer. Sometimes they didn't know when to quit.

"I checked Miguel Alexander out, by the way." My

mother stopped arguing with my father and turned to me—
never a good thing. "I knew he was a loser who couldn't
make it in the DA's office. Then I found out his wife and
infant daughter were killed, with *him* at the wheel. He went
off the deep end, as some do. Is that the kind of person you
want defending your life, Zoe?"

"I didn't know." That's what I'd sensed about him, the
terrible sadness. The poor man. What hell had he gone
through?

"How was I supposed to know?" Daddy demanded. "Zoe
wanted him for her lawyer. I didn't know the particulars."

"Zoe doesn't get to have everything she wants, Ted. How
many times have I told you that?" She was sitting next to
me in the booth when she reached over and grabbed my
wineglass, draining the dregs from it. "You've always
spoiled her. It's easy for someone like Miguel to come along
and take advantage of her."

"Mother!" I couldn't believe she'd say that about someone
who'd experienced such a terrible tragedy. "If anything, that
would make him a better attorney, as far as I'm concerned.
He deserves our compassion."

"Oh, grow up, Miss Goody Two-shoes." She called for
the waiter to bring more wine.

As if it couldn't get any worse, I heard Tommy Lee say,
"Well, look who's here! What a surprise! I just happened to
come by today for lunch. Imagine finding you all here. I had
no idea."

Tommy Lee is the worst liar in the world.

Then I realized why he was there. I'd been set up.

From the looks on my parents' faces, I had to say they
were both in on it. There were times they could get away
from arguing long enough to make my life miserable. This
was one of them.

Both of my parents loved Tommy Lee. I was beginning
to understand why my father praised him to high heaven all
the time—the two men were peas from the same pod.

My mother's motives weren't so clear, except that she believed he was from a good, old Mobile family, like ours. They both agreed that Tommy Lee and I belonged together.

Daddy played the game. "Why bless my soul, it's Tommy Lee. What a surprise."

Did I mention that my father is *also* a bad liar?

He slid over on his side of the booth and let Tommy Lee sit down. I was trapped against the wall with my mother on the outside. I had to hand it to them. It was a master plan, even for them.

"I think we should talk about this little tiff you and Tommy Lee are having." My mother finished a full glass of wine and told the waiter to bring the bottle.

"*Tiff*?" I glared at both of them as I tried to keep my voice from going off the scale. "Tommy Lee brought another woman, his *new girlfriend*, to watch the police harass me last night."

"Betty is *not* my new girlfriend," Tommy Lee denied. "And I called your mother for you. Don't I get some credit for that?"

"People make mistakes." Daddy cleared his throat and began his gospel on couples staying together through the bad times. "We have to forgive and forget, Zoe. How will we ever be happy if we can't make up with our loved ones?"

"You sounded pretty happy about not being with Mom anymore a few minutes ago," I reminded him. Was it possible to crawl out by going under the table without anyone noticing?

"That's different, honey. Your mother and I are divorced."

"Let's just consider that Tommy Lee and I are divorced now, too."

"Let's just consider that you need to get over this slight, Miss Zoe," my mother said. "Your father and I feel the same way. You've uprooted yourself from your home and your career at the bank. You've taken up with people you normally wouldn't even meet. You need some stability in your life."

Tommy Lee sat there with a pathetic look on his hand-some face, eyes staring into mine. He was, of course, excellently groomed in his navy blue sport coat and pale blue button-down shirt.

I knew what he was thinking. He thought we wouldn't break up with my parents on his side.

Wrong.

"I didn't do anything wrong. Hear me out," Tommy Lee implored. "You know you mean everything to me."

"I saw you with Betty last night. How do you even know her?"

"Through business contacts. We're on LinkedIn together. Believe me, there's nothing personal between us."

"I saw you *kiss* her!"

Daddy appeared uncomfortable about that fact. My mother gave him a murderous glance that *dared* him to speak.

"She was only seeking comfort from me during the crisis, as a woman sometimes will," he explained with a nervous smile. "She was saddened by your dilemma. Thank God you've been spared!"

It was all I could do not to lose the wonderful lunch I'd recently eaten. "You'd better come up with a better story, Tommy Lee." I didn't give him an inch to wiggle around. "This one isn't cutting it."

"What about something else?" Daddy nudged Tommy Lee with his elbow. "Wasn't there something you wanted to show Zoe?"

"Oh, right." Tommy Lee took out a small ring box. "I want to end all your disbelief, honey. I'm asking you to marry me."

He looked so sure of himself sitting with the bulwark that was my parents for support. He opened the box and slid it across the table toward me.

It was a beautiful engagement ring. Big square diamond in the middle, lots of smaller diamonds around it. Nothing particularly imaginative about it, but it was really big and definitely expensive.

I closed the box and slid it back toward him. "No, thanks. Try Betty."

"Oh, for God's sake." My mother drained another glass of wine.

"Throw the boy a bone, pumpkin," my father said.

"Excuse me. I have to go to the ladies' room." That was one sure way out.

"Do you really have to go or is this just an excuse?" My mother's blue eyes narrowed to razor slits as she searched my face for the answer.

"I really have to go, Mom. All this excitement has been too much for me."

She threw down her linen napkin (actually *my* napkin) on the table, got up with a labored sigh, and let me out of the booth.

"I'm coming with you."

"I'm old enough to do this by myself, thanks."

"You'll leave before we're finished with this conversation." She looked accusingly into my eyes. "That's not going to happen."

I didn't blink, but I did cross my heart. "I'm only going to the ladies' room, Mother. I'll be right back."

She sank back down. "I'll give you five minutes."

It was more than enough time. I was out of Wintzell's in two minutes, and hailing a taxi in three. Lunch was over. I wanted my food truck back. I asked the driver to go to police headquarters.

No amount of pressure was going to make me get back together with Tommy Lee. It wasn't only seeing him with Betty last night. It was also the past few months. He'd berated me about my decisions. He'd scoffed at my diner, and my food truck. He'd even refused to eat a biscuit bowl. We were over.

It was hard enough making decisions about my future

without the people closest to me giving me grief every five minutes. I couldn't get rid of my parents. I knew they'd come around eventually—they always did.

I knew Mother and Daddy were unhappy about the decision I'd made. They couldn't be all that surprised.

I kind of had a history of suddenly standing up for myself. Like that time at Auburn when I refused to write another sexist paper for my sexist civics professor.

Waiting for things to turn around was fine. I thought of myself as a patient person. Once the football was dropped, I kicked it. It was the same in this case.

I couldn't help it. I'd tried to live the life everyone wanted for me. It hadn't worked. Now I was going to find what *did* work. Maybe it wouldn't be food, although that was hard to believe. The only thing I liked better than making good food was eating it.

First I needed my food truck back. Next, I planned to gear up for Dauphin Street again tomorrow.

I paid the taxi driver when we reached police headquarters. He wished me well and said he was glad it wasn't him going in there. I tried to assure him that I had already been cleared of a murder charge. He didn't seem impressed by that, either.

Detective Latoure told me it would be at least an hour longer until my food truck was released. "We're doing the best we can, Zoe. Be fair. We found a dead man inside it. It has to be processed."

"That's fine. I'll wait." I sat down in one of the hard wood chairs at the front of the office. They definitely needed some comfortable furniture.

"Suit yourself." She shrugged. "I'll give them another call."

"Thank you."

I was watching the police drag in people they'd arrested. It was a terrible waste of time since I could have been cooking for tomorrow. I felt like my presence was necessary, though. Detective Latoure couldn't ignore me if she saw me every time she looked up from her desk. Proximity is important.

I saw Miguel about to leave the office, and thoughts of baking flew from my mind like four and twenty blackbirds baked in a pie.

SEVEN

"Miguel!" I called to him over the constant flow of people.

"Zoe?" He looked surprised to see me there. "Have you been here waiting the whole time?"

"No. I just got back from lunch. Did you decide if you can defend Delia?"

Miguel stopped. "Let's step outside for a moment so we can talk."

I walked out with him. The day seemed suddenly brighter. Where had that blue sky been hiding when I'd been out before?

Knowing his tragedy made me respect him even more. I wished I could say something about the untimely death of his family. I would've liked to give him my condolences, no matter how much after the fact.

Of course, saying something would mean I'd been gossiping about him. I didn't want him to think that was going on.

As we hit the sidewalk outside the building, I noticed two food trucks parked there. There were long lines at Suzette's

Crepes, and at Charlie's Tuna Shack. I hadn't realized I could park my food truck here. I made a quick mental note to check out the regulations. Business seemed to be brisk. The area could handle another vendor.

"You mind if I get something?" Miguel nodded at the food trucks. "I skipped breakfast this morning, too. Would you like anything?"

"No. That's fine. I'll get a table."

I hated it, of course. I was jealous of every minute Suzette was selling crepes and Charlie was selling tuna. I begrudged them every dollar they brought in. It was so hard getting my food truck up and going. I hoped later to look back at this and realize it had all been worth it.

Even though I put on a brave face for my parents, sometimes I was terrified. If I failed, I'd be back working at a bank, or someplace similar, again. And then I'd be afraid to dream.

I tried not to think about it that way. Once Mobile discovered my biscuit bowls, I was going to be a sensation—and so was my food.

There was an open bench—no table, but better than nothing. Miguel came back a few minutes later with a big hunk of roasted tuna on his plate, and some sweet tea. He sat down and balanced his plate and drink on his worn briefcase.

"I'm going to take Delia's case," he told me. "I believe her when she says she's not guilty. I understand Patti's point of view. She doesn't really have any viable suspects. Delia's been intimate with Terry Bannister. They broke up, and there was a fight. That gives her motive. Ex-lovers make the best murder suspects."

"If that's all she has, it should be easy to beat the charge, right?"

"I don't know. She was also at the scene. We know Terry wasn't killed in your food truck, but the ME thinks he was killed behind the shopping center. That gives her opportunity. We'll know more when the report is finished."

"What about me talking with her right before I found him?"

"That gives us something to work with on Delia's behalf."

"I'll be glad to testify for her, if that would help."

Miguel smiled at me in a strange, kind of quizzical manner as he chewed his tuna.

"You don't even really know her, Zoe. Why would you go out on a limb like this for her? She was completely surprised when I told her you'd offered to pay for her defense. She didn't even know your name. I had to explain that you were the woman with the food truck."

"I don't really see it as going out on a limb. Testifying that she's a good person isn't going to hurt me. And I was talking to her at around the time someone had to put Terry in the truck. Besides, I don't have to know someone well to know about them. Take you, for example."

He swallowed his tuna quickly. "Okay. Take me, for example. Am I a good person?"

I used his question as an excuse to deeply study his face. The sun showed a few childhood scars at his chin and forehead. He had deep smile lines fanning out from his dreamy eyes. In their dark depths was the soul of an artist.

"Yes. You are a very good person." I smiled at him and felt my heart flutter a little. He was so different than Tommy Lee. Not that I should be comparing them, since I wasn't thinking about dating Miguel. Still . . .

He laughed outright at that statement. "And you can tell this by looking into my eyes?"

"No. I have an extra sense about this. I got it from Uncle Saul. He loves food, too. We can tell things about a person by looking at them. Delia is a good person, too."

"Any witches or voodoo priestesses in your family tree?"

"Not that I know of. I suppose it's possible. I'll have to ask Uncle Saul. My parents would never discuss something like that, even if they knew about it."

He finished eating and drank the rest of his sweet tea. "I guess that's good enough for me."

"So . . . are you?"

"Am I a good person?" He threw his plate and cup into the trash. "I believe people show themselves with their deeds. In which case, *you* are a good person, Zoe Chase. I guess we'll have to know each other a little better for you to know if your assessment of me is correct."

I was more than willing to go along with that plan. The sun had warmed the day considerably, and I removed my peach-colored jacket. The white silk top beneath it was pretty and feminine. I thought it showed off my skin . . . and other attributes . . . very nicely. I hoped Miguel would notice.

"That's fine." I tried to keep my tone cool and light. "What do we need to do first for Delia?"

"She'll have a bond hearing this afternoon. I don't think she'll make bail."

"How much do you think it will be?"

"I'm not sure. Nothing, if a property owner agrees to put up collateral. As long as she doesn't skip town, the property goes back to the owner after the trial."

"Okay. I can take care of that. What about looking for the real killer so we can clear Delia's name?"

"That's Patti's job. Do you need a lift somewhere?"

"I'm going to wait for them to finish whatever they're doing with my food truck. Thanks. You know the police aren't going to look for anyone else, right? Delia's a good suspect."

"I serve the court, Zoe. I don't believe the police quit looking because they think they have the killer. Patti will follow through. She's a good cop."

"I suppose you know best. I thought finding the killer would be top of the list, that's all."

"Giving Delia a good defense is top of the list for me. I'll interview as many people who knew Terry as I can find. People might be willing to testify on Delia's behalf. I'll let you know if anything out of the ordinary comes up. Patti will take care of it, if it does."

That was much different than I'd expected. I thought we'd be investigating, too. Maybe Miguel had too many expectations of the Mobile Police Department. I was sure they'd do their best, but they were understaffed and underfunded, like all police departments. They'd probably welcome a little help.

My cell phone rang—it was Detective Latoure. My food truck was being released. All I had to do was go to the impound lot and sign for it.

"I might need to take you up on that offer of a ride," I told Miguel. "Do you know where the impound lot is?"

He knew where it was. We got in his car and drove there. Along the way, we talked about general subjects. He liked Mardi Gras. I liked Mardi Gras. He had his tonsils. I had mine removed when I was six.

"What made you decide to become a lawyer?" I asked as we followed slowly through some heavy traffic.

"I was the first person in my family to graduate from college. I wanted to impress people. That's why I joined a big law firm for a while. It was good money. When I realized that wasn't what I was looking for, I joined the DA's office. I wanted to make my mark on the world and put away bad guys."

I wanted so badly to ask about the accident that had killed his wife and baby. I looked out the window at the road construction that had slowed our progress. It would be cruel to bring up his loss.

"Aren't you going to ask me what happened?" He spared me a sidelong glance. "It's okay. Everyone does."

"I know you ran for district attorney," I answered as kindly as I could. "You didn't win, and left."

Maybe everyone asked about his tragedy, but I couldn't.

"That's putting it short and sweet. Thanks."

"And you became the champion of the underdogs, like Ollie and me."

"I wouldn't call the only daughter of Ted and Anabelle Chase an underdog. Why didn't you become a lawyer? I feel sure your mother urged you to."

"Well, for my family, I'm an underdog and underachiever, I guess. We always lived in this big house over on Julia Way. I wanted to live in the swamp with my uncle. He has a rustic log cabin that he built himself."

"You graduated from Auburn with a degree in business."

"Yes, thank God. I barely made it, though. They created the phrase 'skin of your teeth' for me." I glanced at his profile as he drove. "You've been checking up on me."

"I admit it. I wanted to know all about you because I thought I was going to represent you. My father built houses. He always taught me to study the foundation before building. It makes sense with clients, too."

"Then you know why I'm not a lawyer. I could barely stand being at the bank for the last five years. All those unhappy people. I went home every night and watched the food channels. I wanted to make people happy with my cooking."

"I take it that wasn't something your parents had in mind?"

"No. They'd rather see me married and having babies than anything else—since I'm not a lawyer. The bank was only a stopgap until that could happen. Not now. I'm dedicated to my calling."

"Feeding people?"

"Yes. I like looking at their happy faces as they eat my food. It's what I was meant to do."

We'd reached the impound lot. The guard at the gate knew Miguel and asked for my ID. He pointed out where the food truck was parked.

I told Miguel he could drop me right where we were. I

didn't want to take up any more of his time. He insisted on driving me to the spot.

"I hope you have your keys," he said.

"Oh yes. Not a problem." I fished them out of my bag.

I hadn't thought to bring a towel or anything to clean the seat in the Biscuit Bowl. Maybe the police crime people had done it. I opened the driver's door. It wasn't bloody, but *eww*.

"Something wrong?" Miguel asked when I hesitated.

"No. Everything's fine. I have some spray cleaner and paper towels in the back. I'm going to clean up a little. There was a dead man in here recently."

Miguel waited. He'd wanted to help, but I insisted I could do it alone. Even when the seat had been cleaned, I was reluctant to get behind the wheel. I couldn't get the image of Taco Terry out of my mind. I didn't know what I was going to do. My life was invested in the truck. I had to get back on the road with it.

"Still thinking about the dead man?"

Miguel's voice behind me made me jump.

"Yes. I'm afraid so." I felt a little foolish. "Once I get back in there, I'm sure everything will be fine. It's just convincing myself that he isn't there anymore."

"I have an idea. Give me the keys."

I handed them to him, the little ceramic biscuit dangling at the end. "What are you doing?"

"I'm making a new memory for you. Get in. We'll drive around the impound lot. That way, I'll be the last person you remember sitting here."

It was so sweet that I almost started crying. I *knew* he was a good man. Who else would even think of suggesting such a thing?

I got in on the passenger side. Miguel started the food truck. The police had backed it into the spot so it was easy to pull out. I did similar parking wherever possible.

"Thanks so much for doing this." I smiled at him, hoping

my eyes weren't glistening with tears. If he'd remarked on it, I would've told him I had allergies.

"No problem. It's not easy getting over your first dead body."

"You've seen a lot of them?"

"I've seen my share."

"Not because you're a lawyer. My mother would never leave the house again if she'd ever seen a dead body that wasn't at a funeral."

He laughed. "It comes with the territory when you're an assistant DA. It never gets any better. You have to develop a tough skin for it, like cops do."

He didn't look very tough. I wondered what he thought of me.

I admit that I took advantage of him and had him drive the food truck around the impound lot a few times before I took over. When I finally got behind the wheel again, Miguel was right; all I could see was him driving me around, trying to help me feel better.

"I think I have it. Thanks again." On impulse (it was either this or hugging him) I said, "I want to cook for you. Dinner would be nice. I have to work tomorrow. What about tonight?"

It was about as forward as I had ever been with a man I didn't know well. Since Tommy Lee had been my only boy-friend since college, I wasn't even sure I was saying it right. I winced, waiting for his response. It was too late to develop that tough skin Miguel had talked about in case he said no.

"I'd love to. At the diner?"

"Absolutely. Seven P.M. Don't dress up. I can't guarantee that the counter stools won't ruin good clothes."

"Great. See you then."

I drove the food truck back to the diner with a light heart and a smile on my face that wouldn't quit. I even turned on the spinning biscuit on top of the Biscuit Bowl and enjoyed the funny looks I got from people as I passed.

I had every right to be happy. I'd been accused of murder, and that charge had been withdrawn. I'd broken up with my boyfriend, and maybe found someone new to be interested in. And I'd eluded my parents' designs for me once again.

Yes, I could be blissful.

Ollie was waiting at the diner when I got back. He was excited when I told him I wasn't on the suspect list anymore. We walked down to the homeless shelter and gave Marty the news. He invited me to stay for cake—a donation from a bakery on the other side of town—to celebrate.

I couldn't. There was so much to do before tomorrow morning if I was going to take out the food truck again and make dinner for Miguel that night. It already felt like it had been a week since I'd had the fight with Terry.

I put on my rubber gloves and old jeans. Crème Brûlée watched me like he thought I was demented. I gave him a few cat treats and put him back in the office.

Since Ollie had hunted for rats there, I hadn't see any sign of them. I knew we both appreciated Ollie's efforts. It might mean Crème Brûlée could feel comfortable at the diner and not have to accompany me when I went out to sell biscuit bowls tomorrow morning.

The back of the food truck was a mess. It looked like a hurricane had gone through. My food and cooking utensils were flung everywhere. It took me an hour just to get everything back where it belonged.

I didn't know about other food truck owners, but for me, everything needed to be in its place. There wasn't much space to keep the biscuits warm and the savory fillings hot. I also had a small refrigerator to keep the dessert fillings cold. There were specific spoons for each filling.

I hadn't really experienced a large crowd of people, but I was organized and ready for them when they came.

At least I hoped they'd come.

Once the back of the food truck was scrubbed clean and ready for the next day, I moved into the driver's area. I got out the disinfectant again and scrubbed both seats, the floor, and the dashboard. The doors came next, and then I cleaned the windows inside and out.

I thought about Terry as I cleaned. I couldn't help it. Even though he'd been an ass with me, I still felt bad about the way he'd died.

A chilly breeze swept through the truck and I shivered. There were worse things than losing a day with my biscuit truck.

EIGHT

"Give you a hand with something?" Ollie asked.

I jumped, startled from my thoughts of Terry being murdered.

"I'm almost finished. Well, at least I'm almost finished cleaning up. I have to get the food ready for tomorrow. Then Miguel is coming to dinner."

Ollie waggled his black eyebrows. "That the way it is?"

"Not the way you're thinking. I invited him to dinner because he was very nice to me today. It was a difficult time. I was glad to have him there. Thanks for calling him after we found Terry. Why don't you come for dinner, too?"

He looked at his clothes. He was wearing the same T-shirt, hoodie, and jeans that he wore every day. "Don't know that I'm dressed for dinner."

"Don't be silly. You look fine. Come inside and let's talk about savory fillings. I'll make some coffee."

We spent the next few hours working on biscuit bowl

fillings. Ollie took over my kitchen, throwing bits of this and that into a spicy gumbo.

It almost drove me crazy. He had no recipe, no idea what he was going to put in next. He kept finding new ingredients and adding them to the pot. He'd stop, put a spoonful on a plate each time, and slurp it up to taste it.

I watched him as I checked my laptop to make sure it was okay for me to park the Biscuit Bowl outside police head-quarters in the morning. My permit was good for that area.

"How can you cook like that?" I tidied up behind him. "I'd go insane if I had to work that way."

"What way?" He rolled his latest sample around in his mouth with a pleased expression on his face.

"How do you know what to put in without a recipe? What if it's too much, or not enough? What if the spices don't blend well?"

"Chill, Zoe. Give this a taste and see what you think."

Before I could protest, he'd stuck the big stirring spoon in my mouth.

It took me a minute to get over that assault. By the time I had, I realized a new flavor was circulating through my mouth, tantalizing my palate.

"Oh my God!" I cried out in ecstasy. "It's amazing! How did you do that? You have to show me."

"Sure." He spread out his ingredients again. "You take a pinch of pepper, and throw in some salt."

"No. I mean I need the recipe."

He pointed to his head. "It's all in here. No need to write it down. I got it from my mama who got it from her mama who got it from her mama. It's never been written down."

"That doesn't mean we *can't* write it down." I grabbed a pencil and paper. "Okay I'm ready."

He stood there mute and defiant. I put down the pencil.

"Can't be committed to paper," he said. "It would ruin everything."

That was the craziest idea I'd ever heard. I could see by his face that he was serious. I wouldn't be able to coerce him into letting me write down the ingredients.

Not right then, anyway. I'd keep working on him.

"Let's make another pot." I redirected our conversation. "I can't wait to take it out tomorrow. People are going to love this, Ollie."

I made the sweet fillings as he worked on the savory gumbo. I kept glancing over to take note of what he was using. It was hard to tell. I think he was purposely trying to keep me from seeing what he put into it. I didn't understand why he'd be so secretive about it, especially since he was willing to share it.

Uncle Saul had plenty of secret recipes. He rarely shared them with anyone. He wrote them down and hid them. Someday after he passed, I expected to unearth an entire cookbook.

When we were done, I put the savory filling into a metal pan and put it in the refrigerator. It would stay warm in the food truck tomorrow over a vat of hot water, after being heated up in the morning. The sweet fillings were in a bowl that would stay in the refrigerator until I needed them.

The biscuits would have to wait. I wouldn't dare make them and heat them up tomorrow. Everyone would know.

I glanced at the biscuit clock above the door. I had a little over an hour to shower, change clothes, and get dinner ready. I had a special dish in mind that I hoped Ollie and Miguel would love. It was one of Uncle Saul's recipes that he'd been willing to share.

Crème Brûlée got up from his nap, a little on the cranky side. He walked over and bit my ankle then licked it a few times. Normally that meant he was hungry. I was staring at his full food bowl. I knew that wasn't the case.

He hadn't touched his food. I picked him up carefully and held him in my arms, rubbing his warm, furry tummy. "Aren't you feeling well?" I asked him.

That's all I needed—a big vet bill. I hoped it wasn't something serious.

He purred loudly and closed his eyes. I realized that he was probably attention deprived. Crème Brûlée could be quite the diva when he chose.

"I love you." I kissed his nose. He returned the favor by biting mine and then licking it. "You know you always come first. But mama has to make some money. We gave up our apartment. If we lose the diner, we'll have to move back home with my mother. You don't want that, do you?"

He hissed, and even gave a tiny snarl. That was the height of emotion for him. I knew he understood what I was talking about. He never liked going to my mother's house.

I put him down, and he started eating. I stroked his fur and praised his efforts. He was going to be fine. He *had* to be fine.

After showering and putting on clean jeans and a pink T-shirt, I started cooking the pepper and onion strips for dinner. I defied anyone to walk into the diner and not immediately be starving. Not much smelled better than sizzling peppers and onions.

Sure enough, it wasn't long until Ollie came back to the diner. He'd actually changed his T-shirt, though he still wore the same old hoodie.

He took a sniff and grinned. "That's got my mouth watering. Smart girl! Hook Miguel with the food. That always works."

"It's not that way," I assured him again. "I'm just saying thank you."

He laughed and sat down at the counter. "And those tight jeans are saying please?"

I blamed my suddenly heated face on the cooking food. Ollie could be a handful sometimes. People in my life mostly weren't so plainspoken. He reminded me of Uncle Saul, who also called things the way he saw them. That was one reason my parents had nothing to do with him.

I was glad to see Miguel's Mercedes pull up in front of the diner. I hoped my hair wasn't too frizzy from double shampoos today. I couldn't help it, anyway. I suppose my hair couldn't, either. Naturally curly hair doesn't like being abused.

I was surprised to see Delia come in first. She'd obviously come with Miguel.

"I didn't expect to see you here," I said to her.

Immediately, she took a step back. "I told Miguel we shouldn't surprise you this way. You were expecting him. I'll wait in the car."

This was truly Delia—all the smart mouth and quick banter gone, she didn't even look like her in her plain, knee-length black skirt and gray top. It was so sad to see her this way. I flew around the counter and wrapped my arms around her. "Don't be crazy. There's plenty to eat. I'm happy to have you here. Come and sit down."

I made the introductions. Delia had met Ollie briefly before. Miguel and Ollie shook hands. They all sat down at the counter while I finished the meal.

"So what happened?" I asked after I'd thrown the fresh-cut tomatoes on the grill with the peppers and onions. The rice was already perfect, each grain standing apart from the others, not too much liquid.

"The judge set bail at a reasonable amount," Miguel said. "I called your father and he stood good for it. We have three weeks before the preliminary hearing."

"I don't know what to say," Delia began. "I don't know why you wanted to help me, Zoe, but I appreciate what you've done."

Ollie snickered. "Zoe is like Marty—she wants to help everyone, *and* feed the world."

I wasn't sure what to make of that. I was glad I was cooking and I had to face the grill, away from them. Ollie had made me sound like some do-gooder. I never meant to come off that way. I wanted to help Delia and make food for people. That didn't make me a saint!

"The DA doesn't have a very strong case," Miguel said. "I'm not saying it's going to be a walk in the park, but I think we can get Delia out of this."

The surprise ingredient in my peppers, onions, and tomatoes with rice was a hint of orange zest. I also garnished each plate with a few fresh orange slices and some radishes. The effect was colorful and tasty.

There were biscuits, of course. They weren't deep-fried, like the biscuit bowls. These were plain, buttermilk biscuits. I was glad to see everyone reach for one as I put the plate out.

"Zoe Chase makes the best biscuits in Mobile," Ollie declared. "Maybe in the South."

"They are *very* good," Miguel agreed after taking a bite of one.

Delia nibbled on one. "I can't eat this whole big one by myself."

"Of course you can," I assured her. "You need your strength for the days ahead. Where are you staying?"

"I had a little place I shared with two other girls." She shrugged. "They don't want me there anymore. They're worried about the police looking into their backgrounds. I lost my job at the bar today, too."

"Maybe I can find something different for you," I suggested.

I wasn't sure exactly where I was going with this. I barely had enough money to feed me and Crème Brûlée until the food truck started making more.

"What were you thinking I could do?" Delia asked. "I'm not really good at much."

"I really need help with the food truck," I explained. "I can't pay you a lot, but you can eat your fill. And you could stay here. What do you think?"

Delia appeared to be a little overwhelmed by the offer.

"I don't cook, Zoe. I can wash dishes. I can learn to do almost anything."

"Okay. We'll try it tomorrow. I leave here at six A.M. I have to get to a spot where I can park the food truck well before lunch. Otherwise all the good places are gone. Can you do that?"

"Yes. Thanks." Delia smiled at me. "I'll try not to let you down."

"How long do you think the trial will take, Miguel?"

"It's hard to say. We'll do the best we can. Sometimes it can take a year to process the crime scene information. The DA won't go to trial until that information is complete."

Delia's beautiful face looked daunted.

I smiled and tried to cheer her up. "Don't worry. We'll work it out."

Dessert was one of my favorites—deep-fried ice cream. I rolled the scoops of vanilla ice cream in a mixture of coconut, honey, and almonds and then put them into the hot deep fryer for a moment. It didn't take long to create a hard, sweet crust on the outside while preserving the cold ice cream center.

I served it with a dollop of real whipped cream. When I heard three people making satisfied sounds of pleasure and not talking, I was thrilled.

This was what I was looking for, what I couldn't get at the bank. This was the part no one in my family understood, except Uncle Saul.

After everyone had finished eating and was enjoying my own special blend of coffee (with a little chicory), I asked Miguel if he'd seen all the evidence against Delia.

"It's mostly circumstantial, but people have been convicted on less," he said. "A new suspect could wipe it away, as it did in your case."

"What about an alibi?" I said. "I'm her alibi, remember? We were talking at the corner at about the same time someone was putting Terry in my truck. If it wasn't so dark in the parking lot, we would've seen it happening."

"I'd be glad to give her an alibi too," Ollie said. "Tell me what I need to say. I've done worse."

"And everyone knows it," Miguel answered. "Delia needs an alibi from a *credible* witness."

Ollie laughed at him, the dark skin on his face wrinkling. "You know too much, old man. I might need to take you out for a moonlight cruise of the bay."

"What about the man who picked up Delia that night in the dark green Lincoln?" I didn't want the subject of Ollie getting rid of Miguel to go any further. "He came from behind the shopping center. He might have seen something."

Delia immediately shied away from that idea. "We don't want to mess with him. He's bad news. Besides, he wouldn't have been hanging around waiting that long for me. He's too important."

"All the more reason to ask him what he saw," I suggested.

"Again, we'd need a credible account of someone witnessing the killer moving Terry's body to the truck. Or seeing someone kill Terry. That would work, too."

"That would be before he picked me up," Delia added with a sigh. "I didn't tell the cops about him because he's an important man. He wouldn't like me involving him in this."

"Are you afraid of him?" I asked her.

"No." She smiled slyly. "I have a few aspirations for his affection. I'd rather him not be bothered. I don't want to make him hate me."

My little dinner party began to break up after that. Miguel took Delia back to her apartment. She needed to pick up a few things. Ollie helped me clean up and then went back to the homeless shelter.

Delia and Miguel returned about thirty minutes later with boxes and a few worn suitcases.

"Are you sure this is going to be okay?" Delia asked again.

"I don't have much to offer. But I could use the help, and you're welcome to stay. We'll have to find you a bed."

"I can sleep on the floor." She grinned, and thanked Miguel for his help. "I don't know what I would've done without the pair of you today."

Ollie brought a cot down from the homeless shelter for her. We made room for it in a pantry so she'd have a little privacy.

Miguel left, after wishing us luck tomorrow with the Biscuit Bowl. It was weird hearing Delia humming in the bathroom as she got ready for bed. I was used to living alone.

Everything was set for the morning. I put on a T-shirt and shorts before I snuggled in with Crème Brûlée for the night.

I was excited about taking the food truck out again tomorrow. I thought that was a good sign. Despite everything that had happened, the idea of getting up at four A.M. and making biscuit bowls was enough to make it hard for me to sleep.

Tomorrow, I might get a great spot and the crowds would find me. It only took one day, and big lines of customers, to have a television truck come out and change everything.

"By the end of the week, Crème Brûlée, we could be famous. We could be turning people away from the Biscuit Bowl. After that, they'd find out about the diner. We'd have to upgrade real quick to accommodate more than five people eating here at the same time."

As if he understood, Crème Brûlée bit my hand—a love bite—and licked it.

"That's right," I whispered fiercely to him. "Take that, all you people who didn't believe in me."

I said good night, and was almost asleep, when there was a loud banging on the front door.

I'd never had any problem staying there, despite the shabby neighborhood. Still, after Terry's death, I approached carefully, not turning on the inside light until I saw who was there.

"Who is it?" Delia was right behind me.

"I don't know. It's probably nothing."

As I spoke, I saw a man in a ski mask. He pulled out a gun and pointed it right at me.

NINE

"Duck!" I yelled, pulling Delia down with me. "Gun!"

She was on the floor before me. We lay there, covering our heads with our arms for a few minutes. I finally peeked out, and the man was gone.

I called Miguel, and the police.

Delia and I took turns breathing into a paper bag so we could calm down. I'd thought I was acting like a big baby, but she'd been scared, too. She seemed tough to me, so I didn't feel so bad.

Police officers showed up first. We gave them what we could of a description—about six feet tall, medium build. He was wearing faded jeans and a white button-down shirt.

They took a look around, but couldn't find anyone. Since there was no damage done to the diner, or us, I thanked them and they left again.

Fifteen minutes later, Miguel was there looking cute and half-asleep in cutoff jeans and a Pearl Jam T-shirt. He asked us questions about what had happened. There wasn't much to tell.

"He was wearing a ski mask," I said. "I didn't recognize him."

"We couldn't see his face, but he was about the same size as Terry's partner, Don Abbott." Delia knitted her hands together.

"It seemed like he was trying to scare us," I told him. "Why show us the gun and then just walk away?"

"This location, and Terry's death, have been all over the news," Miguel said. "There might be a few people checking out the area."

That made sense to me. I didn't like it any better, but it made sense. If the man had really wanted to hurt us, he could have shot us and been gone long before the police had arrived.

"I'll talk to the police on your behalf right now, and ask for a few more patrols until things quiet down," Miguel offered. "I think they might be willing to do that."

I wanted to go. I really wanted to go. But if I went with him, it could take hours. I'd miss the opportunity to take my food truck out again in the morning. It was already almost midnight. I couldn't do both things, especially after having been up most of the night before.

"Thanks, Miguel," I told him. "I wish I could come, too, but I have to work tomorrow."

"I'll let you know what happens," Miguel promised me. "Make sure you're careful until we know what's going on. Do you have a gun?"

"A gun?" I giggled a little at that. It wasn't really funny. I was nervous and I sometimes giggle when that happens. I sobered at once. "No. I have an attack cat, and a few frying pans. I'll be careful."

After he left, I turned the lights out and we went back to bed.

"I sounded stupid out there, Crème Brûlée. I would've been better off biting him and licking the spot after, like you do. You're lucky you don't have to worry about the right words."

It took me a long time to get back to sleep. I jumped up at every noise I heard. Delia was up and down a lot, too.

The last time I looked at the clock, it was a little after two A.M. Morning was coming too fast. I hoped my enthusiasm would get me through another long day with no sleep.

I guess I finally fell asleep again. The alarm was suddenly going off. For a moment, I wasn't sure why it was making that awful racket. It was four A.M. Time to get up and bake biscuits.

I mixed my biscuit dough together, and set the first tray in the oven. I took that opportunity to shower and get dressed. By that time, I put in another tray of biscuits.

Delia wasn't sure what to do to help. I wasn't sure, either, since I hadn't had anyone helping me before. I had her look outside in the dark parking lot. We seemed to be alone.

There were no new messages or texts from Miguel. I wished he would've said if the police were taking the event seriously. It was hard to focus on the day ahead and get everything right.

Ready to load the food truck, I picked up a tray of cool biscuits and headed out the door with them—straight into Ollie.

At first, I was afraid it was the masked man with the gun again. The idea of having a gun at that time sounded pretty good, though I wasn't sure I could actually shoot anyone.

I realized the person I'd run into had caught, and was holding, my tray of biscuits, which would otherwise have fallen to the ground.

"Ollie." I didn't know whether to be angry that he'd scared me or happy that he'd kept me from dropping the tray. One thing was for sure—he was the immovable object. I don't think he even budged when I ran into him.

"I want to help you," he said.

"Stocking the food truck?"

"Yes. And going with you. You need a good strong hand, Zoe. I've got two good arms and legs. Nobody is gonna mess with you, like that taco man did, with me there. I guarantee nobody will think about sneaking up on you and Delia."

It made sense, I supposed, in an Ollie kind of way. I told him I'd pay him what I could. He said he didn't care.

"No sword, though." I made my restrictions up front.

"No sword," he agreed. "I won't need one with all the kitchen equipment anyway."

I knew it was possible I could be sorry, but after yesterday, having somebody with me seemed like a good idea.

"Okay. Let's get going. If we're going to beat Suzette's Crepes to a spot in front of police headquarters, we have to get there early."

Ollie was a big help loading up, too. He could take two trays of biscuits at once.

Delia brought the water out to get the heating pan started, and put the fillings into the refrigerator. The last thing in was Crème Brûlée and his bed. He hissed at me and then went back to sleep when he was safely in the front of the food truck. I had to make room for him between the seats for me and Delia.

Ollie rode in back.

"Thanks for doing this," I said to him again. I was still alive with excitement and energy about the coming day.

"Ain't nothin' to it," he drawled. "Besides, you think I want you to get all the credit for my savory filling? I don't think so."

That was fine with me. We rode through the dark, nearly deserted streets of Mobile. Morning traffic was getting started in the downtown area when I pulled the food truck into the same parking space where Suzette was selling her crepes yesterday.

I hoped for the same success the crepes seemed to enjoy.

Delia made some coffee and then poured a cup for each of us.

"This is all there is to it?" she asked.

"Pretty much, unless we get busy. I hope we get some morning business, too. Some people like to get their lunch early and heat it up later."

Ollie made a face much like Crème Brûlée did when I offered him something to eat that he didn't want.

"Heat up a biscuit? What's wrong with those people?"

I shrugged. "It saves them another trip down later. They can eat at their desk. I did that a lot of times at the bank. I brought my own lunch. You get the idea."

"I don't understand why a person can't take some time to eat without working. It's not healthy."

"They're eating fried biscuits." Delia laughed. "I don't think they're worried about being healthy."

I warmed up to my subject with such an appreciative audience. "I'm hoping to sell some breakfast biscuits, too. I think people might even enjoy a biscuit bowl for breakfast. I didn't bring eggs this morning, but I was thinking that scrambled eggs might be good. Maybe with some sausage, bacon, or peppers.

Ollie rubbed my head, a bad habit that I thought he might have picked up because he was so tall. I'd seen him do it to Marty and some of the others at the homeless shelter.

"You're always thinking, aren't you?" he asked with a grin. "Don't you want to stop for a while and just enjoy?"

"I don't think that would be good for business," I said pertly. "Would you like to help me set out the chairs and tables, and lift the sides? I have to add your gumbo to the menu list, too."

Ollie was ready to help in any way. He didn't want to think about much, but he was right about using his strong arms and legs. We had the food truck set up in no time.

Delia wrote *Ollie's Spicy Gumbo* on the menu board in a pretty script. My menus were easy to change. Uncle Saul had added two big chalkboards to the swing-open doors on the side of the food truck.

Delia used different colors of chalk to highlight my specials. She even drew some pictures of biscuits and fruit. I'd found that it was always helpful to bring a few café-style chairs and petite tables with me. My chairs and tables gave my potential customers a place to sit and enjoy their food, if they were so inclined. I thought I might invest in colorful umbrellas for my tables later, after I made some money.

My special was a plain biscuit and a cup of coffee for ninety-nine cents. Uncle Saul had told me to use my specials wisely. "Get them to try something cheap and reel them in for something more expensive later," he'd advised.

I hadn't had much of a chance to try this food law of economics yet. I was ready for it. I just had to put it into practice.

After everything was set up, I started cooking a few biscuit bowls. I made some plain biscuits that I could use for my special. My biscuit bowl biscuits had to be made in cupcake pans. The biscuit batter cooked up solid and round with a depression in the middle where the fillings went.

I'd experimented with deep-frying the biscuits at the diner before I went out. That had left them greasy and cold, not even good heated up.

They had to be deep-fried at the spot where I was working. That meant a small deep fryer that could do a few biscuits at a time. They came out crispy and brown. The biscuit bowls held up well to the sweet and savory fillings I'd tried. Soup was too liquid, but things like chili, stew, and, hopefully, Ollie's gumbo worked. There was no problem at all with the sweet fillings.

"What are you all cooking in there?" Our first customer of the day walked up to the food truck. "It smells wonderful. I don't care what it is—I want some. And some coffee with it, please."

Ollie grinned at me. "Of course, sir. Step right up. Would

you like the biscuit plain or a biscuit bowl with some cinnamon apple filling inside?"

I was totally blown away. Ollie looked so big and fierce, like a warrior from a fantasy movie. Who knew there was a great customer service rep hidden under that tattooed skull?

That man wasn't our last customer, either. About twenty more followed him before nine A.M. After that, things got slow for a while. Everyone was at work. I couldn't expect another rush before eleven.

Still, I was ecstatic. I'd made more money in that one morning than I had the other whole days I'd taken the food truck out. It was possible, if the rest of the day went as well, that I might even make enough money to pay Ollie and Delia.

Feeling very pleased with myself, I went out to make sure my tables and chairs were clean. The sun was shining warmly down on the spinning biscuit on top of the food truck. Birds were singing in the live oaks, Spanish moss swaying in the breeze from the bay. Life was good.

A man, who looked like a college student, approached. He was wearing a backpack and a red ball cap on his stringy, long hair. He walked right up to the side window. I thought I'd stand back and see Ollie in action from this angle.

"Can I help you, sir?" Ollie asked as the young man drew near.

"Yeah." The seemingly harmless man drew a gun out of his backpack. "I'll take whatever you've got in the cash drawer, Pops, and whatever Terry gave you before he died."

Imagine that! Right in front of police headquarters!

What did he mean—whatever Terry gave him?

I looked around for a uniformed officer but didn't see one. I tried to think of something I could do to keep our hard-earned cash from disappearing down the street in this man's backpack.

Ollie's eyes narrowed on the man. His face transformed. I hoped never to see him look at me that way.

The man took a step back. The gun shook in his hand.

"I mean it." His voice, which had been insolent and demanding, quivered. "I want that money, and th-that stuff."

Ollie folded his arms across his broad, muscled chest. "You'll have to come through me to get it, son. Do you think you're up to the challenge?"

The thief stood there for another moment. I couldn't tell if he was trying to decide if he could get through Ollie or what. In case he decided to go ahead with his plans, I picked up one of the café chairs and held it, ready to hit him.

Lucky for me, I'll never know what I might have done to try and stop him. The man threw down his gun and ran away, his backpack sliding down one of his arms.

I dropped the chair in relief and sat down on it. In all my planning and calculating, I'd never thought of anything like that happening.

"Are you okay?" Ollie seemed more concerned for me than for him.

"I'm fine. Are *you* okay?"

"It was just some punk. He wasn't even big enough to keep. He had to run home to his mama. Maybe she'll take a switch to him and teach him better."

"I guess you were right. I'm glad you were here."

"Why? You would've hit him with the chair, right? We had him covered, either way."

"Do you think you could show me how to make that face that scared him off?"

Ollie studied me. "No. You don't have what it takes, Zoe. Just stick to making your food. Let someone else take care of the other stuff."

It was good advice. I had a feeling you had to be tall, mean-looking, and big as a mountain to scare someone away with only a glance and a few words. The thief probably would have laughed at me if I'd tried it.

Maybe I needed to start building some muscle. Of course then I'd have to shave my head and have it tattooed. I was pretty sure it was the whole look.

Delia came out of the front of the truck where she'd been reading a magazine and looked around. "Is everything all right?"

That meant we got to tell the story again.

While we were telling her all about it, I thought back to what the young man had said.

"He thought we had something of Terry's," I told Delia. "He wanted the money and something he thought we had."

"Don't pay any attention to that," Ollie advised. "He was probably just saying that because he saw it on TV."

Delia seemed doubtful, and even a little nervous after that. I asked her what she thought, but she shrugged and walked away.

"What should we do about the gun?" I asked Ollie.

"What kind is it?"

"I'm not really sure." I stepped closer to it on the pavement and inspected it without touching it. "I don't really know much about guns. I think it's real, if that helps."

Ollie went back inside the food truck. "It's too small to be any good—like that boy. Just throw it over there in the bushes. That's what everyone does before they go inside."

"You're kidding, right?"

He shrugged, and started stirring the warming gumbo.

That idea didn't sit well with me. I called over the next police officer I saw going into the building and pointed out the gun. He thanked me and picked it up.

Maybe I should have told him about the boy who'd left it there. After the incident the night before at the diner, I thought not. Nothing really happened.

Things were dead slow for about an hour. I put the harness on Crème Brûlée and let him relieve himself on a little patch of grass across the street. I hoped it wouldn't be long before he began staying at the diner by himself while I was working.

A few customers came by and bought biscuit specials after that. I was getting anxious about lunch. I hoped I had enough food. I hoped I had enough customers to eat all the food. My stomach was jumping around like a fish out of water.

It was ten thirty when the Suzette's Crepes food truck pulled up beside us. A man almost as big as Ollie jumped out of the truck and quickly headed our way.

"I think this could be trouble," I told my companion.

TEN

"He doesn't look like trouble to me," Ollie said. "He looks hungry. Probably starving to death eating crepes. What kind of food is that for a man to live on anyway?"

Sure enough, the man came and pounded on the back door. I couldn't let Ollie take all the tough situations. "Can I help you?"

"You can get your biscuits out of my spot," he roared back. "I was here yesterday. You can't come in and take someone's place."

"I didn't see your name on it." Ollie loomed up behind me. "Go find your own spot. Get up earlier. We were here first."

Suzette, or whatever his name was, didn't like that idea. He kicked the tire on my food truck as he walked by. "You really want a battle?" he asked as he came to the open customer window. "I'll give you a battle."

"Maybe we should move," I whispered to Ollie. "I really don't want a battle."

"What's he gonna do—throw his little crepes at us?"

Suzette (I didn't know what else to call him) kicked a tire again and flipped us off. Then he went back to his crepe truck. I let out a sigh of relief.

We waited as the lunch crowd began to trickle out of the surrounding buildings. I saw people heading for us with delight. When they suddenly veered away, I wondered what was wrong.

"I'm going outside to see what's happening," I said after this had happened several times.

"Let me," Ollie said. "I don't like people messing with our business."

I waited for a few seconds after he'd left the food truck. I finally followed him, imagining all kinds of things that could be going on.

What I didn't imagine was that "Suzette" was standing in front of our food truck giving away free samples of *his* food and directing people to his crepe truck.

I heard Ollie growl when I came up behind him. That couldn't be a good sign.

"Get me some biscuits, Zoe," he said. "Two can play at this game. I'll bet I can play it better."

I scurried to do what he asked. I stood beside him with a big, welcoming smile on my face, giving out little menus as he gave out biscuits. Delia watched from the window as she put apples into biscuit bowls.

"Suzette" looked our way a few times as people began to come toward our food truck. I had to give up handing out menus to serve our customers.

I was thrilled when people began ordering both sweet and savory biscuit bowls. A few sat on the café chairs and smiled when they bit into the treats. Some even ordered a savory biscuit bowl and then came back for a sweet one.

There was actually money in the cash register. The crowds I'd remembered from yesterday were lining up at our window. It was almost too much to keep up with. That wasn't a good thing since poor service has been the death of many a restaurant. I called to Ollie so he could give me a hand. It was all Delia could do to keep up with filling the biscuit bowls.

For the next hour, we were so busy, I didn't have time to look up from the rapidly disappearing biscuit bowls. My fears about not having enough food were almost right. We were down to the last pan of biscuits when the crowd vanished as fast as it had appeared.

It was almost two P.M. "That was the lunch rush." I took a deep breath.

Delia let out a sigh of relief. "How were you doing all that by yourself, Zoe?"

"I wasn't. This was my first really busy day!"

Ollie grinned. "I think they liked us."

"I think so." I smiled back, elated. "You and Delia were my lucky charms. Well, your gumbo, too."

"I told you, give them what they want, and you'll be fine."

"That, and being an aggressive marketer, and scaring away potential thieves," Delia said.

I agreed. "Thanks for your help, Ollie."

"Happy to be here for you, Zoe. You should take a breather. I'll straighten up a little."

I liked that idea, though I felt guilty once I was sitting outside on one of the café chairs. I was lucky to have Ollie and Delia. I hoped I'd made enough money to pay them both something by the end of the day.

"I heard you were down here."

I looked up and shaded my eyes with my hand. "Tommy Lee! What do you mean you heard?"

He sat across from me. "I heard it on the radio. I came over to see how you were doing."

I couldn't quite wrap my mind around what he was saying. "You mean the radio station was telling people where to find us?"

"They were telling people you and that other food truck were giving out free samples." He frowned. "Zoe, we need to talk."

I was so excited that they'd called my name on the radio. The possibilities from that were amazing. I could give out free samples every day. Biscuits were cheap and easy to make. Of course, I could try other things. A biscuit bowl could be lightly filled with a pie filling and cut into four pieces. That could work, too.

"Zoe?" Tommy Lee was snapping his fingers in front of my face.

"Oh. Sorry. What were you saying?"

"I asked you to marry me. You didn't answer. I think we should at least get engaged. We don't have to get married right away. Weddings take time to plan anyway. I know you want a big, showy wedding where your mother and father can invite all of their friends. My parents do, too."

"I'm sorry, Tommy Lee." I put my hand on his. "I can't get married, or engaged, right now. I don't think you really want to marry me anyway. You just feel obligated."

"What are you talking about? We've been together for a long time."

"Most of that time wasn't me. It was the girl my parents wanted me to be. You, too, I guess. I'm not that girl anymore. I don't think you want to marry a woman who owns a ratty old diner and drives a food truck."

"Zoe, that's *now*." He smiled very tenderly. I could feel his old pull on my heartstrings. "When we get married, you won't need a career or a business. I make enough money that my wife doesn't have to do anything—except attend charitable functions and support me in my work."

"I think you have the wrong person." I wanted to say he should ask Betty to marry him, but that sounded like sour grapes, and I really didn't feel that way. "I wish you all the best, Tommy Lee. I don't think we're right for each other anymore."

The shock written on his handsome face was terrible. I felt so bad for him, despite everything. I even started to take it back so his feelings wouldn't be hurt.

"Customers coming," Ollie called out.

"Gotta go." I smiled at Tommy Lee. "You'll see this is for the best. I wouldn't be good at what you expect from a wife. Come over to the window and I'll give you a free biscuit bowl."

He sat at the café table for a long time, staring at me. Ollie and I waited on a few customers who'd heard good things about our food from their coworkers in the building.

Finally, when everyone was gone, Tommy Lee came up to the window. He stared at Ollie instead of me.

"Is it *him*?" He pointed to Ollie. "Are you in love with this man?"

I was surprised and embarrassed. "No. I'm not in love with Ollie. He's working with me."

Tommy Lee made an ugly snorting noise. "Is that what you want from a man, Zoe? Somebody who will put on an apron and work in this sweatshop with you?"

Ollie had that mean look on his face that had scared off our early morning thief.

"You're embarrassing both of us," I whispered. "You should go now."

"Yeah? Who's gonna make me go? *Him?*" He really noticed Ollie for the first time. That closer study made him gulp hard and step back from the window.

Ollie lunged at him. It was fake, of course

Tommy Lee almost tripped over a chair as he tried to get away. I felt bad for him again.

I put my hand on Ollie's big arm. "No need to threaten him. He's only upset and disappointed."

He nodded and walked to the front of the food truck to sit down by Crème Brûlée.

"Go home, Tommy Lee. Or go back to the office. This isn't going to work for us. I'm sorry, but getting angry won't change anything."

"That's fine." Tommy Lee spared a glance at the front of

the Biscuit Bowl where Ollie was sitting. "If that's what you really want, Zoe. That's fine."

I don't know if it was Ollie's warning face or my persistent entreaty that our relationship was over. Tommy Lee finally turned and left without a backward glance.

What did I do?

I had to wipe away a few tears even though I knew it was for the best. The change in my life wasn't our only problem. We'd been together for a long time. Suddenly, I was alone.

Delia patted me on the shoulder. "You'll find someone else. There's no point in being with someone when it's wrong."

"You okay back there?" Ollie asked.

I sniffed, thanked Delia, and wiped my eyes. "I'm fine. thanks. I'm sorry you had to hear that."

"I've heard worse. How many biscuit bowls we got left?"

It turned out to be plenty. A few people stopped on their way home, leaving police headquarters. Nothing like the lunch crowd. We still had six biscuit bowls left as we got ready to pull out of our lucrative parking space.

I saw Detective Latoure for the first time that day. I told Ollie I'd be right back and jumped out of the food truck to talk to her. I thought I might be able to butter her up with a strawberry-filled biscuit bowl.

"What's this?" Detective Latoure asked as I hailed her.

"I brought you a biscuit bowl," I told her cheerfully. "On the house. Try it."

She studied the biscuit bowl but didn't seem inclined to accept my offer. Maybe she was afraid to eat my food. It hadn't been that long before that she'd thought I'd killed Taco Terry.

"I'm sorry, Zoe. I'm not a big fan of biscuits. Too many carbs. Sorry."

"That's okay. I'm glad we were near police headquarters today. A man tried to rob us."

Detective Latoure frowned

"There are several other guns and some knives over there in the bushes, too," I told her. "Do you want me to get them out for you? You're wearing that nice suit. Green is a good color on you. I don't want you to get dirty."

Her mouth kind of dropped open. It took a minute or two for her to come around. "I'll have an officer pick these up. You shouldn't handle them. Thank you for letting me know about this."

"You have to try my biscuit bowl."

Naturally she felt obligated at this point to try a bite. She took a big crunch out of the warm, strawberry-filled biscuit bowl, and rolled it around in her mouth a little, finally smiling.

"This is good. I really like it. It doesn't taste like most biscuits, not doughy at all." She grinned, finishing it. "I'll have to swim an extra few laps to get rid of it. I've always had to watch my weight. You know how that is!"

I did indeed, and surprisingly, we had pleasant, girl-talk about everything from drinking vinegar to eating grapefruit to lose weight. Patti was very warm and human when she wasn't so busy being a detective.

She bought two savory biscuits to go for her and her husband's dinner.

Word of mouth was everything. I was happy to oblige. "Thanks, Detective Latoure."

"Patti."

"Thanks, Patti."

"I'm really sorry about your near robbery," she said. "Do you have a description? You never can tell when other people have had the same experience, but not gotten away so lucky."

"Of course." I told her what the man had looked like, and she wrote it down. "I'm happy to help out. Did you hear about that man at my diner last night?"

She was still smiling and licking what was left of the strawberry filling from her finger tips. "I heard. Miguel came by and let us know, not to mention the police report from the responding officers. I had them run an extra patrol through there at night for this week."

"Thanks. It probably didn't have anything to do with the murder, but it was really frightening. There was something else about that attempted robbery today, too. The man asked for something of Terry's. He didn't say what."

"Something of Terry's? You mean the man who was killed?"

"I think so."

Her pager went off. Patti apologized. "We'll have to talk about this later, Zoe. I have to go."

I watched her walk quickly up the stairs, admiring her spring green suit again.

Ollie had vanished while I'd been talking to Patti. "Did you see where he went?" I asked Delia.

"He's out there somewhere."

I went to look for him and found him behind the food truck.

"Is she gone?" he asked.

"Yes. Is something wrong?"

"I don't like cops." He shuddered. "They don't like me, either."

It was funny seeing a big man like Ollie crouched down behind the food truck, worried about *anyone* seeing him. I turned away to keep from smiling. I wondered what had made him so afraid of the police.

"I think we should go," I said. "Let's get everything packed up."

Ollie and Delia helped me pack quickly. Ollie glanced around nervously after that. It took only a few minutes before we were ready to go.

I was pleased to give Delia and Ollie each fifty dollars when we were in the food truck. "Thank you so much for your help."

"You don't need to give me this much." Ollie put thirty

dollars back into my hand. "It's not like I got expenses or anything. This is enough to buy a few smokes without Marty asking me to move out and get my own place."

"Wouldn't you like to get your own place eventually?" I asked him.

"Not really. Been there, done that. It's overrated. I like where I am right now."

"Isn't there someone who might like to have you live with them? Family?" Delia wondered.

I wasn't sure how far we should question him. He didn't owe us any answers. I didn't want him to feel like we were prying and get angry.

"You're not trying to reform me because I helped you out today, right?" Ollie put on his mean face. "I don't want to do or be anything that I'm not right now. Got it?"

"Got it." I rolled my eyes at Delia and started the food truck. "Thanks anyway. You were both a big help today. Everyone loved your gumbo, Ollie."

He made a growling sound. "Yeah, well, don't get used to it. I'm not good with schedules or promises. I happened to be hanging around when you were leaving this morning. You can't depend on me, Zoe."

"I completely understand." I guess I'd found out how far I could push Ollie. This was probably why he lived in the homeless shelter. If he had family or friends, he wasn't interested in being part of their lives.

We drove through the crowded streets of downtown Mobile in silence. I was sorry I'd tried to figure out anything about him. I enjoyed his friendship, whether I could depend on him or not. I hadn't really meant to pry.

In my mind, he was like Delia—a person who needed feeding and some hope. I chastised myself for thinking I could be the person to help them. I certainly had enough problems of my own. I shouldn't have meddled in his life. Maybe not Delia's, either.

We got back to the diner, and I groaned when I saw

Tommy Lee's car in the parking lot. Why couldn't he take no for an answer?

I wasn't sure if Ollie would help me unload the food truck. I didn't plan to ask him. I'd done it before by myself. The other times there had been a lot more food left, too. There wasn't so much this evening. It made me happy enough to want to do a little dance.

I refrained because Tommy Lee was there looking hopeful. Ollie slammed out of the food truck, his brow furrowed. Neither man looked like a good dancing partner to me.

Ollie fooled me. He got right out, and started unloading the food truck. "Still taking leftovers to the shelter?"

"Yes. There's still some gumbo left, and the last of the biscuit bowls."

He suddenly grinned at me. "Not as much as the men at the shelter would like, I can tell you that. Your success is gonna mean they miss out on some good food."

I smiled back at him. Just like that, we were friends again. I vowed never to ask about his personal life again.

"Don't worry," I assured him. "We'll mix them up a special batch on the weekend."

Ollie started walking toward the shelter. Delia took some things inside.

Tommy Lee took that opportunity to get out of his car and come toward me. I heard Crème Brûlée meowing from the food truck. No doubt he needed the litter box.

Before I could reach in and get him out, another man joined us in the parking lot. It was our thief from outside the police building that day. He'd followed us here.

He'd also found another gun.

"I want what you took from Terry," he said. "Do it now, or I'll kill you and your friends."

ELEVEN

I had no idea what he was talking about. I didn't have anything that belonged to Terry.

"I think you have the wrong person." I tried to sound
very calm and reasonable. I kept hoping someone else might
show up. I wasn't sure how to handle the situation. My first
impulse was to run away screaming. That seemed less than
useful.

He waved the gun around, his hands shaking. "Don't play
games with me. Give me what Terry gave you. You know
what I mean."

About that time, Tommy Lee decided to get involved. I
knew him well enough to know he was about to try and
prove himself to me. Tommy Lee wasn't a hero, but he liked
me to think of him that way.

"Excuse me! That's my ex-girlfriend you're threatening.
I'm sure we can come to an equitable understanding."
Tommy Lee whipped out his wallet with a wry smirk on his
handsome face. It was the same look he wore when we were

involved in charitable events. He liked to think being rich made him a little better.

"I don't want your money," the thief with the gun said. "I want what's mine. Terry promised to share."

Tommy Lee's expression never changed. He took out a hundred-dollar bill and waved it in front of the man, a little like a matador flashes a red cape at a bull.

The thief's eyes got interested. "I can take both."

"You leave this lady alone, and you can have this hundred-dollar bill." Tommy Lee smiled at him in a satisfied way.

"I tell you what." The thief snatched Tommy Lee's wallet, and the hundred dollars. "I'll take all of it. You tell your girlfriend to give me what's mine. Otherwise, I shoot you both, and take everything anyway."

"You can't do that," Tommy Lee exploded. "That wasn't part of the deal. Give me my wallet. I'll call the police."

The thief advanced on Tommy Lee. I thought he was going to shoot him. Instead, he hit him in the head with the gun. Tommy Lee went down like a sack of potatoes. He groaned and put his hand to his temple.

I was next in line. The thief started toward me. Suddenly, Ollie rose up behind him like a mountain. Before the thief could reach me, Ollie took one large fist and pounded it on top of the other man's head.

The thief dropped to the pavement next to Tommy Lee.

Ollie picked up the gun. "Where did he get another one?" He put the gun into a nearby trash can. "Did he follow us back here?"

I ran to him and hugged him tight. "Thank you. Thank you. I don't know. I guess he followed us. He kept asking me for something that Terry owed him. I don't know what he was talking about."

Ollie's big, dark face twisted in embarrassment. It made his skull tattoo more noticeable. "No need to get hysterical, Zoe. He's down. He didn't shoot you, did he?"

His big hands went quickly and very professionally across my body. It was my turn to be red-faced.

"No," I squeaked. "I'm fine."

Tommy Lee was still groaning and asking for an ambulance. Ollie picked him up and slung him across his shoulder. "You'll be fine. Sit down in the diner for a while, and Zoe will put a wet towel on your head."

"I may need stitches," Tommy Lee gasped. "I may need a tetanus shot. I need to be at the hospital."

"What should I do about him?" I asked Ollie about the unconscious thief.

"You should get some plastic tie straps and put them on his hands and feet. Then call the police, but wait until I'm back at the shelter."

"How am I going to say I subdued him?"

"You'll think of something," Ollie assured me. "Just don't mention my name."

With those words of wisdom, my guardian angel put Tommy Lee down in the diner, and stalked back to the homeless shelter.

I wasted no time putting the plastic ties around the unconscious thief's hands and feet. Once I knew he was secure, I called the police, and Miguel.

By that time, Crème Brûlée was meowing pitifully. I'd almost forgotten him while everything else was going on.

"Poor baby." I smoothed his ruffled fur. "You'll be fine. We'll go inside and help Tommy Lee. After that, we'll make some coffee and think about all of this."

After I got Crème Brûlée inside, I got a wet cloth and an ice pack for Tommy Lee. Ollie had left him, unceremoniously, on the floor in front of the counter. Tommy Lee sounded almost as bad as my cat. Then I called 911.

"What happened?" Tommy Lee's head flopped from side to side. "Who hit me? I hope my brain is still working. I need a CAT scan."

"The police are on their way," I reassured him. "If you want, I'll call an ambulance."

He definitely wanted an ambulance, but he was starting to sound like himself. "Who was that man, Zoe? Why was he trying to shoot you?"

I couldn't tell him, since I had no idea. Instead, I entertained him with stories about my day at the food truck. He didn't find the stories as amusing as I did. I guess you had to be there.

Miguel arrived around the same time as the police and the ambulance. I saw a television news van pull into the parking lot. Good golly! What would my parents think about me being on the news again?

"What's going on?" Miguel came in as the police were talking on their radios. "Who is that man in the parking lot?"

I told him the whole story, including the part about Ollie knocking the thief unconscious. "Ollie doesn't want to be involved. He wants me to say that I knocked the thief out. Does that sound plausible to you?"

"Right now, anything sounds plausible." He nodded at Tommy Lee. "Did Ollie hit him, too?"

"No." I explained again about Tommy Lee's run-in with the thief. "I don't know what he was looking for. He said Terry gave me something."

Miguel excused himself and went to take a quick picture of the thief on the ground. He came back into the diner, and we looked at the man's face. "Here come the police. Be careful what you say if you don't want to include Ollie in your statement."

"Has Ollie actually done something that could get him into trouble?" I asked quickly. "He was hiding behind the food truck today when Detective Latoure came to buy a biscuit bowl."

Miguel smiled. "Where were you parked?"

When I told him how well I'd done at police headquarters, he was amazed that Ollie had even stayed there with me.

"So he's in trouble with the law?"

"Not currently." Miguel greeted the two uniformed police officers and our conversation ceased.

Officer Schmidt and Officer Gayner were on duty again. I told them my version of what had happened in the parking lot. They looked a little skeptical, but when I showed them the gun in the trash can, they had to believe me.

Marty came over from the shelter. He hadn't seen anything, but Ollie had told him what had happened. He didn't tell the police that Ollie had been involved, either. He kind of offered to be of assistance if he could. He smiled, winked at me, and was gone.

The ambulance drivers got Tommy Lee on a stretcher. Officer Schmidt asked him a few questions before they took him to the hospital. Tommy Lee said he couldn't recall what had happened. That was just as well for my lie.

Another ambulance came for the still unconscious thief. I guess when Ollie put them out, they stayed out.

There was a flurry of activity in the parking lot. Most of the men from the homeless shelter—not Ollie, of course—came out to watch. So did the shoppers who'd been inside the consignment store.

I should've had menus to give out. It never hurt to advertise wherever possible.

The responding officers were getting ready to leave when Patti Latoure showed up. That meant going over my story again with her. This time, I sat in the diner with a big mug of coffee. I was starting to feel the long day and lack of sleep the night before.

"So this man came up to you at the food truck today and tried to rob you," she said. "You thought it was random, but it must not have been. He followed you back here. You said he wanted something you took from Terry Bannister. But you have no idea what that is?"

"That's what she said, Patti." Miguel reiterated my statement.

"Doesn't that seem a little odd to you, Zoe? Obviously this is something important, probably valuable. The man was willing to approach you with a gun *twice*. But he didn't tell you what he was looking for. Is that right?"

"He acted like he thought I knew what it was," I answered. "I don't have any idea what he's talking about."

Patti flicked her ponytail off of her shoulder and studied my face carefully. "Do you know who that man was that you knocked unconscious?"

I glanced at Miguel before I answered. He shrugged. "I only saw him today outside police headquarters for the first time."

"He's Don Abbott, Bannister's partner in his taco truck business. You're sure, in your dealings with Terry Bannister, that you didn't see his partner?"

"Honestly, Patti, I didn't even know Terry had a partner until all of this happened. I'd heard some talk on the street about the two of them fighting over some money. But the only person I ever saw from the food truck was Terry."

I realized that this was the man the police thought could've been a suspect in Terry's murder. He was supposed to have an alibi.

"All right." Patti put away her pen and notebook. "I hope you're telling me the truth, Zoe. I don't know how long we can keep Mr. Abbott in custody. He may be back. Or someone else might be looking for whatever it is that they think you have."

"Terry didn't give me anything except a headache and the feeling that I needed a shower," I told her. "Maybe you need to look into Mr. Abbott's alibi a little more closely. If he was willing to shoot me for whatever he's looking for, he could have shot Terry, too."

"We'll do our job," she assured me. "You make sure you're not in the middle of whatever is going on. Don't hide something that could get you killed. I don't want to have to explain *that* to your parents, Zoe. Good night, Miguel."

"I have a few questions for you, Patti." Miguel walked out of the diner with her.

I was ready for bed. I hoped all of that mess was over, but I couldn't help wondering what Don Abbott had been looking for.

The crime scene people had gone over the food truck with a fine-tooth comb. I had cleaned it as well as I could. There was nothing there that didn't belong.

I couldn't figure out what else Terry could have left behind, but his legacy to me was becoming more dangerous. In two days, I had been accused of murder and threatened with being shot. Both of those events revolved around him, and the limited time we'd spent together in my food truck.

It didn't make any sense, but as Patti had said, something was going on. I hoped I could figure out what it was before anything else bad happened. As Ollie had made clear to me, I couldn't rely on him to save my life all the time.

Miguel came back a few minutes later. I could tell by the frown on his face that he had something on his mind that I wasn't going to like.

"I think you should consider closing shop for a while, Zoe. Go and stay with your mom or dad."

"I can't stop now," I said. "I had my first good day with the food truck. I have to build on that. My customers will forget me if I'm not there every day."

"It could be dangerous staying here. We have no idea why that man was willing to shoot you. Whatever he thinks you took from Terry is important to him; it may be important to someone else, too. Right now, you're in the middle of what's happening."

I only wanted to be in the middle of what was happening with the food truck business in Mobile, Alabama. Maybe I was at least on the verge of being important in that industry—I was on the radio today. How could I give that up and run away?

I couldn't.

"I have to stay. Everything I own is invested here, Miguel. They announced where my food truck was today on the radio. Free advertising. I can't stop now. For all we know, I'm on the fringe of what happened to Terry. It's a series of events that I'm slightly involved in. It may be over now since they arrested Don Abbott."

"I can't make you leave. I wish you would, for your own safety. If you won't go, at least look around carefully from now on when you go outside. Don't let anyone in the diner that you don't know. Try to keep Ollie with you when you go out tomorrow."

"I'll be fine. You don't have to worry. Ollie might be with me. I'm not sure."

"He gave you his 'don't count on me' speech, didn't he?"

"Yes. I understand. I felt the same way before I left my job at the bank. Everyone had these expectations of what my life was supposed to be."

"I know that feeling, too."

"Would you like some coffee?" I took out another cup and put it on the counter.

"Are you sure? You look exhausted."

"I'm sure." *How bad did I look exactly?* I peeked at myself in the shiny steel side of the coffee maker. Not that bad. "It's the least I can do after dragging you out again."

"Okay." He sat down on one of the stools. "I didn't mind coming."

"I hope you have me on retainer or something. I don't want to reduce your billable hours. I know my mom is always worried about that, at least with the lawyers who work for her."

He added sugar to his coffee and smiled. "The retainer thing would be the other way around. You'd have *me* on retainer."

I took out some cookies I was saving for a special occasion. *I'd like to have you on retainer, or any other way.* "Well maybe we should do that. I don't want you to go bankrupt while you take care of my legal needs."

Was he seeing someone? Or was he still traumatized from his wife's tragic death? I hoped it wasn't either case. There was no way to know without hinting around in a sneaky way to find out.

"Thanks for worrying about me. Your father and I have come to a good financial agreement. He's worried about you, too."

"He's always worried about me. He doesn't try to stop me like my mother does. He just worries, while he's fishing or whatever."

"As for billable hours," Miguel said, "I'm lucky to be my own boss. I don't have anyone looking over my shoulder or asking me why I'm doing what I'm doing. It's great."

"Good. I'm glad that's all settled." I bit into a cookie and smiled at him. "What's Ollie's story? I know he was in the military. You said he's been in trouble with the police. Was there something that happened to him?"

"Ollie killed his wife," Miguel said, without hesitation. "But he's a good man."

TWELVE

"Ollie killed his wife?" I squeaked a little in surprise.

I was imagining that he had some disorder left over from being in the military. I hadn't thought about him killing anyone—*especially his wife*.

"It's not what you think," Miguel explained. "Let me tell you ahead of time, he doesn't like to talk about it."

"I won't mention it to him." That thought was furthest from my mind. But if I was going to be alone with him in the food truck, I felt like I deserved to know the truth. "What happened?"

"Ollie's wife was in the military, too. She developed PTSD. No one realized. She came home on leave. Ollie was sitting across the breakfast table from her. She pulled out a gun and started shooting at him."

"Oh my God! Poor Ollie—and his wife."

Miguel shrugged. "He tried to restrain her. The gun went off. The shot killed her. She'd managed to shoot him three times. He barely survived, and he lost it for a while. He was discharged, and then started wreaking havoc on the civilian community. That's when I met him. I got him into rehab and he began to get better."

The terrible ordeal tugged at my heart. I knew Ollie was a good person. It was awful that he'd had to go through so much. No wonder he didn't want anyone to depend on him.

"I don't know how he survived." I ate another cookie, promising myself it was the last.

"You get through one day at a time," Miguel told me.

I knew he spoke from experience. I wanted to ask him about *his* tragedy, too, but I couldn't find the words.

He didn't stay long after that. I didn't get to hint around about any possible girlfriends he might have. I told myself to be patient. He was on retainer. I could call him anytime I wanted.

I locked up the diner after he left. I saw his car pull out of the parking lot and I turned out the lights.

Delia was finally out of the shower. She'd been on the phone laughing and talking most of the evening. I didn't ask her who she was talking to.

When I told her about Don Abbott, she said she hadn't heard anything. I knew she was lying. She probably didn't want to be involved.

I managed to take a shower and put on my pajamas before I fell into bed with Crème Brûlée. It was hard going to sleep. I thought about Ollie and his wife. Then I thought about Terry and his partner, Don. *What could he be looking for?*

Terry certainly hadn't said anything to me about something valuable that he was hiding. I couldn't imagine that he wouldn't have sold whatever it was right away. Goodness knew he needed repairs on his taco truck. I knew that's where I'd put my money if I had something worth enough money to kill someone over.

He must have told his partner about it. Maybe they'd even found, or stolen, it together. Anything was possible.

I snuggled up with Crème Brûlée, who bit my arm softly and then licked it.

Maybe tomorrow there would be more answers. Maybe there would also be more customers buying biscuit bowls. I hoped this was only the start. I hoped I was finally on the road to success.

- - - - - - -

I was up before the alarm went off in the morning. I got dressed, and fed Crème Brûlée. He was tired of the chicken-flavored cat food and stuck his nose up at it. He sat down and looked at me expectantly. I got another bowl and tried tuna-flavored food. He liked that.

I made ten trays of biscuits. Delia put the first two in the oven. While they were baking, we made scrambled eggs with sausage and peppers for the breakfast crowd. There was a new recipe for my savory customers—spicy chili with jalapeños. It smelled good, as Ollie had suggested, and filled a biscuit bowl nicely.

Next came my sweet fillings. Today, I was trying an apple with rum sauce filling, and planned to use the rest of the strawberry from yesterday.

Delia was a big help in her cheerful pink tank top and cutoff jeans. She was good with a knife, too. We made short work of everything. I liked working with her.

From time to time, I glanced outside to see if Ollie was there. It looked like he was staying home for the day. I knew I'd miss him. He was good company, as well as a strong arm with setting up, and getting the food truck ready. He also made me feel safer with everything going on.

I reminded myself that I'd started this venture alone, and hadn't planned to hire anyone until I'd made a profit for a while. I wasn't sad or worried about it then. I wasn't going to be now, either.

When everything was ready, I walked outside and backed

the food truck close to the front door. It was cool and dark. It felt like rain was coming. I could do anything except control the weather.

Of course, people still had to eat. I had awnings for them to stand under. Even if I didn't make as much money as I would on a sunny day, my customers needed to know they could depend on me.

I went back inside the diner. I'd forgotten to print new menus. Handing those out with samples yesterday seemed to be a winning combination. I learned something new about the food business every day.

I started up my little printer—it took some pounding to get it to work. Delia waited for the copies to come out. I grabbed my rain poncho, and Crème Brûlée's bed, and headed for the food truck again.

Before I could get out of the door, a face appeared in the dark glass. I jumped back, startled, and held my cat bed in front of me like a shield.

"Sorry. I didn't mean to startle you."

It was Miguel. I sagged in relief, and started breathing again. "You scared the *life* out of me. What are you doing here so early? Did something else happen?"

"No. I didn't have any meetings today. I thought I'd come by and check out the food truck business in Mobile."

"I have the flyers, Zoe," Delia said. "Hello, Miguel!"

As Delia and I were setting up the food truck, Miguel offered to help. "I can do something, too."

I noticed that he wasn't wearing his usual suit and tie. He looked much better in his jeans and pale blue T-shirt, a dark blue waterproof jacket covering them. I couldn't believe he wanted to spend the day in the food truck.

My little heart was beating double-time at the thought! I kind of realized then that I liked him a lot.

I knew I couldn't afford him. I didn't want my father to pay my lawyer to help me serve biscuit bowls.

"I don't know," I hesitated. "I'm not sure I'll make enough

money to pay both of you. I've had days when I didn't make enough money to buy supplies for the next day."

He shrugged. "I'm just along for the ride. You don't have to pay me. Neither does your father."

That alleviated my problem with him. I was still a little unsure about what had brought him there. It would have been nice to think he wanted to spend time with me. It was probably more like he was worried about me.

While I wasn't crazy about that idea, I wasn't going to pass up an opportunity to get to know him better. I thanked him for his offer and sent him to bring out the rest of the biscuits.

I went back for water to put in the warmer and almost walked into Ollie, who was carrying the pot of chili.

"This is good," he told me. "It needed a little cayenne. I added it. Don't worry."

I didn't mention that he'd told me not to depend on him. I was glad he was there. If he decided to stop helping at some point, I'd have to get over it. In the meantime, it looked as though I had a full crew.

Crème Brûlée was always the last on board. I tried to make sure he'd visited the litter box before we left. Usually, he was good for the day after that. If not, I had his harness and could walk him a little in the grass. I was a little worried about the tuna—his little tummy sometimes had problems with fish. There was nothing I could do about it then.

Ollie rode with me to police headquarters. Miguel and Delia took his car. They were going to park in the public lot that adjoined the building complex and join us there.

Suzette's Crepes beat us to the prime location. I sighed but took the second spot without complaining. People would be willing to walk the few yards that separated us.

"I'll take care of this." Ollie started to get out.

"No. It's fine. Like we told him yesterday, it's the early bird. He got here first. That's okay. We have biscuits, scrambled eggs, and chili. People will find us."

Ollie wasn't happy with that. I finally convinced him that it was for the best. The sky was turning gray as we set up. A light rain was falling. People were running by with newspapers over their heads.

I hoped the rain would be gone by lunchtime. Ollie had set up the tables and chairs between us and Suzette's Crepes. Miguel had put up the awnings, and I'd filled out the menu. We were ready for customers.

While Ollie stirred the chili, and Delia was ready to take orders at the window, Miguel and I sat in the front of the food truck and talked.

"What did the police say about Don Abbott?" I asked him for news.

"He made bail, and they had to let him go. I showed Delia his picture. She said she recognized him as Terry's friend and his partner in the taco truck. That was about it. She said they argued about money sometimes."

I made a face. "What's going to happen next with Delia?"

"Well, nothing has changed in her case. Don Abbott may be violent, but he has a good alibi for where he was when his partner was killed."

"So we're right back where we started."

"Not exactly. What do you think Abbott wanted from you? Have you thought about it at all?"

I admitted that I had thought about almost nothing else. "I don't have any idea what he thinks I have. Believe me, Terry and I didn't spend any quality time together when he was in my food truck. I don't know why someone put him here."

I glanced around, uncomfortably, at the seat I occupied.

"It sounds like it could've been Abbott that put him here. He obviously knew you and Terry had a disagreement. It would be the perfect way to throw off suspicion. But it would help if we had some idea of what Terry had that was so valuable."

"I don't know. I keep thinking about it. It doesn't make

any sense to me. I barely knew Terry. Why would anyone think he'd give me something valuable?"

"I hope we find that out before Delia's trial," Miguel said. "She's got a record, mostly petty violations. But she has one arrest that helps the police—she was picked up with a gun last year. Since she had a relationship with Terry that ended badly, she's the perfect suspect."

I agreed with Miguel. I hoped the police would sort it all out in time. Whatever Terry had, people were willing to kill for it.

Customers started coming up. The rain had slowed to a light drizzle again. The smell of biscuit bowls frying had enticed them to visit us. Delia was smiling and courteous as she asked for their orders and took their money. Ollie was dipping steaming bowls of chili, even though it was still early.

We had a break at about nine thirty. I was glad because all of the scrambled eggs were gone.

Note to self: make more eggs next time.

Ollie and Miguel were outside, drying off the café tables and chairs. Delia was helping me get ready for the lunch crowd. I was expecting it to be huge.

"I don't know how to thank you for giving me this chance, Zoe." Delia fussed with some paper towels, eventually putting them in the trash.

"I'm glad to have you. You might not want to thank me once the big lunch crush starts." I smiled at her.

She looked even prettier without all the glitzy makeup, her hair down on her shoulders. She still needed feeding, though.

She laughed. "Once you've been in as many tough scrapes as I have been, honey, you don't get too messed up over things."

I thought about the questions Miguel and I had posed to each other earlier. "Delia, do you have any idea what Terry's partner could've come looking for at my place?"

"You know, I thought about it after you told me what happened last night. I don't know, Zoe. Abbott is a crazy man. It could be anything."

"Was there something special—something valuable—that Terry had that Don could be looking for?"

"Honey, Terry Bannister never had a blessed thing that was worth spit unless he got rid of it. He'd never hold on to something that way. If he was skulking around your parking lot at the diner the night he was killed, you can believe he was trying to sell whatever he had."

Her tone was ironic, but I couldn't help noticing that her hands were trembling.

"How long had you and Terry been broken up when he was killed?"

She smiled in an especially girlish way. "When weren't we broken up? The longest we were together was a few months. Then he'd start drinking, and that would be it. I'm not gonna let no fool slap me around. I'm my own woman. Just because I make my money waiting tables doesn't mean I'll put up with stuff. You know what I mean?"

I agreed with her. "I'm sorry for all the questions. I know the police have asked you plenty."

She put her hand on my arm. "You're no bother, Zoe. You have such a good heart, it makes all of you glow."

"Thanks. Would you like a biscuit bowl?"

"Except for that. You have to quit feeding me. I'll look like a buffalo in no time. I don't want to end up looking like my mama. All she could wear before she died were these big, flowered dresses that hung down to her ankles like sacks. Shoot me if I ever get that bad."

I laughed at her request. "I'm sorry. It's what I do. And I'm sorry, too, about your troubles with the police. I'd like to help, if I can."

"You're helping plenty. I got myself into this pickle. I'm praying Miguel can get me out. If he doesn't, it's all on me. It's the life I've led. I didn't know any better. Maybe if I have to go away for a long time, I can come out with a degree. I've always wanted to fix people's hair. I think I'd be good at it."

We spent the next few minutes with her giving me tips on different ways I could wear my curly hair. I knew none of them would work. My mother had tried everything when I was in school. My hair always went its own way. Short of shaving it off and wearing a wig, it always would. I'd come to terms with it.

Customers began to come in fitfully as it got closer to lunch. By ten thirty, we had a line from the window. I could still see people passing us to go to Suzette's Crepes. I sent Delia out on the sidewalk to give away menus and entice others to come to us instead.

At eleven, another food truck pulled in beside us. It was the Dog House—with the head in the front and the tail in the rear. They sold all kinds of hot dogs and sausages along with French fries and onion rings. The wonderful aroma almost overshadowed my biscuit bowls.

I didn't know the owner of the Dog House, but I remembered seeing him talking to Terry on Dauphin Street after we'd had our run-in.

I started wondering how well the Dog House man knew Terry. Maybe he could shed some light on what Terry had that may have gotten him killed.

It was a remote possibility. If Delia didn't know, it seemed unlikely the Dog House man would. Still, Delia was running out of options. As Miguel had said, she needed a hand. It was worth asking.

I asked Delia to come inside the food truck. She went back to the window to take orders. Miguel was frying biscuit bowls, and Ollie was filling them. They wouldn't miss me for a few minutes.

"I'm going to say hello to the man in the Dog House," I told them, leaving out the part about asking questions. "I'll be back in a few minutes. You're doing such a great job. Thanks for your help."

Miguel wasn't fooled. He put the next batch of biscuits into the deep fryer and nudged Ollie. "I'm going with her."

I wasn't fooled by *him*, either. I saw right away that he was carrying a small gun. He had it in a holster under his jacket.

"I should go," Ollie said. "You make the food."

"Ollie, we talked about this," Miguel said. "I'm not on parole. You need to stay out of trouble."

I was walking out of the back of the food truck when Miguel came after me, apparently having convinced Ollie that he shouldn't accompany me.

"What's up?" Miguel asked. "Did you think of something?"

I told him about the day Terry and I met. "I saw the Dog House owner talking to him later. I thought he might know something about what Terry was into. I don't know."

"Okay. You should've said that. Don't try to do anything foolish, Zoe."

I didn't think trying to keep Delia from going to jail was foolish. I didn't say so because there wasn't time to argue about it. The man from the Dog House was walking toward us as we went around the back of the food truck.

"There you are," the Dog House man said. "I heard Terry was killed at your place. You don't know what kind of mess you're in."

THIRTEEN

Miguel got in front of me like a Secret Service agent. His hand went to his gun.

I saw the look on the Dog House man's face. I knew this could end in a nasty confrontation if I didn't step in.

"Hello. I'm Zoe Chase, owner of the Biscuit Bowl. I don't think we've actually met, even though I've seen you around." I stuck out my hand and smiled at him.

"Zoe—" Miguel warned in an icy voice.

The Dog House man, however, responded with surprising civility. After a cautious peek at Miguel, he stuck his hand out and shook mine. "I'm Reggie Johnson, owner of the Dog House. Terry told me about you, and all the fun you two had in the back of your food truck."

"First of all, unless you call me hitting Terry for making a pass at me *fun*, we didn't have any fun in my food truck. I was thinking you might know why Terry was killed."

Reggie shook his head. His brown ponytail, which stuck out of the back of his Dog House baseball cap, flopped from side to side. He wasn't an attractive man. Most of his teeth were missing and he had deep acne scars on his face. He and Terry looked a lot alike—and they both smelled like old grease.

"I might have an idea." He looked down his twisted nose at me. "What's it worth to you?"

"Maybe you should tell me what you know and we'll discuss it." He wasn't out-bartering *me*.

"How about you trade sites with me today, and I'll fill you in." Reggie spit in his hand and held it out to me. "Deal?"

Reluctantly, I shook his hand. I tried not to feel bad about giving up my spot at police headquarters. People would find me anyway. Letting his spit-filled hand touch mine was a whole other thing. I kept reminding myself that there was hand sanitizer in the food truck.

"Okay," Miguel said. "What do you know?"

Reggie scratched his head under his ball cap. "That day on Dauphin Street, Terry told me that he had something worth a pile of money. He wouldn't tell me what it was. I asked, believe me. He said he already had a buyer for it. He was selling it that night. It's probably what got him killed."

"Did he say what he was selling?" I asked.

"He didn't give you any indication what the item was or where he'd acquired it?" Miguel questioned.

"Nope. One thing I *do* know—it was in his pocket."

"You mean a particular pocket?" I started thinking about all the pockets it could have been in.

"I mean—it was *in* the pocket of his jeans. He kept fiddling with it while we were talking. I kept egging him on, hoping he'd show me. No dice. Are you ready to switch places?"

It was what I'd agreed to. I had the spit in my hand to prove it. I told him I was ready. Miguel and I went back to the Biscuit Bowl.

"I don't think that was much of a deal, Zoe," Miguel said.

"All we learned is that whatever we're looking for is small. We're no closer to figuring out what it is."

"We're closer," I disagreed. "We know it's small and valuable. We know Terry might've had it on him when he was killed. We know he was trying to sell it. All we have to figure out is what *it* is."

"You're not going to have a very good day with your food truck parked way over there," Miguel observed.

"Don't worry about it. I'll be fine."

What I should've said was, let *me* worry about it. I proceeded to do just that. Miguel was right. Customers were less likely to walk farther on a rainy day like this. I'd baked a ton of biscuits and made a boatload of chili. The homeless shelter would eat well that night.

Still, I knew I'd do it again to help Delia. She deserved a break. It could change her life for the better. Marty, at the homeless shelter, had told me many times that an act of kindness could make a difference in the lives of the men he cared for.

If he could make that kind of difference, so could I.

Besides, it wasn't like I was going to go hungry. There would be plenty of biscuits and chili. I wasn't sure what Crème Brûlée would eat when he ran out of cat food, especially since he could be finicky at times. I was pretty sure I could convince my father to loan me some money for that. He'd enjoy it a lot better than taking care of my cat for a few weeks.

Reggie backed his Dog House out of his parking place and we switched positions. I saw "Suzette" watching us from the street as we changed places. It probably wouldn't matter much to him. Reggie's menu wasn't a conflict with crepes.

No sooner had we changed spots outside police headquarters than the cloudy sky above us decided to throw buckets of rain our way. The heavy rain swamped the sidewalks and the parking areas, flowing like streams under and around the Biscuit Bowl.

"It might not matter that we switched places," I said to Miguel from inside the food truck.

We hadn't even had time to put the tables and chairs back outside.

"What do you do in a case like this?"

I shrugged. "I give it a while, and then I go home. There's not much else to do."

"I'm sorry. I know you were hoping this would be a big day for you."

"Well, at least I didn't lose anything by taking Reggie's offer." I was still cleaning my hands with sanitizer. I wasn't sure anything less than a hot bath would actually take care of the problem. Too bad all I had at the diner was a shower. I'd have to make do.

"And you may be right about what we learned from Reggie," Miguel offered. "Knowing that what Terry was trying to sell was small cuts down the possibilities."

"Thanks. It was the best I could do. Maybe the next person I think about questioning will have more information."

"I'd like to take you out for dinner, to celebrate even a small break in the case," Miguel said. "That's assuming you can clear it with your boyfriend. I wouldn't want to cause any problems for you."

My heart was racing. Was this a *romantic* invitation? Was this the chance to learn more about Miguel's life that I was looking for?

"I wouldn't want to cause any problems for you by accepting, either." I smiled at him. "Would *your* girlfriend mind if we went out for dinner?"

"I don't really date—no girlfriend. Even if I did, she'd have to understand that I occasionally have dinner with clients that happen to be women."

All my hopes were deflated like a big hot air balloon. In other words, this wasn't a *romantic* proposal. He was thinking about business, and figuring out how he could help Delia.

On the other hand, he'd said no girlfriend. I figured the

no-dating part was only there because he hadn't met the right person. Also, a business dinner could lead to something more.

"Sounds good," I accepted. "The way things look right now, anytime would work for me."

"Great. I'll pick you up at seven."

With that settled, we watched the rain, and my business, flow down the streets of Mobile and into the drain. I didn't wait much longer. The sky looked heavy with water, and the weather forecast was calling for much of the same the rest of the day.

Suzette's Crepes left before the Dog House. Delia rode back to the diner with me in the Biscuit Bowl, and Ollie rode with Miguel.

Delia had organized that switch. I wondered why—until we left the parking lot and she slapped my thigh.

"Girl, you got it going on with the handsome lawyer. I don't blame you. Who wouldn't want to play house with him?"

"It's only dinner." I assumed she'd heard our conversation. "Business dinner, at that."

"I think that's up to you, Zoe. I could glam you right up and Miguel's eyes would pop out when he saw you. You're beautiful. I love your hair, and you have great skin. Let me do this for you. He won't think about you as a business deal ever again."

I was tempted. After all, that's what I wanted. Knowing Delia as I did, I wasn't sure if that was the right way to go. I wasn't a *glam* kind of person. Probably more often than I liked to think about, I smelled like old grease, too.

"I appreciate the offer, but I'm going to visit Tommy Lee at the hospital. He's been texting me like crazy all day. He was trying to help me last night when he was hurt. It's the least I can do."

Delia stared at me with knowing eyes. "Now's not the time to get cold feet, if you know what I mean. You want it, you gotta take it. Maybe if you don't want my lawyer, I do. You go visit Tommy Lee and think about it."

I drove back to the diner, thinking about all the strange turns my life had taken since I'd decided to follow my dream. In some ways, I guess I could see why my parents were upset. I'd done some crazy things before, but never anything this drastic. It was as though I'd become another person.

Miguel and Ollie were at the diner, waiting. Ollie had once again opened the door and blocked it for easy access. I didn't mind him being ready to unload the food truck. He was making it a little hard *not* to become dependent on him.

It was still pouring rain as we unloaded everything. The biscuits and the rest of the chili went to the homeless shelter. Marty thanked me many times over. He took me aside as Miguel and Ollie put the food out for the hungry men.

"I'm sorry if this seems like I'm butting in," Marty said. "I'm just worried about you, Zoe. You've had a lot going on the last few days. I hope you're okay."

I thanked him for his concern. "It's been crazy, that's for sure."

"Ollie told me that the man who held the gun on you yesterday was demanding something he thought you'd taken from the other man the police thought you killed." He smiled and shook his head. "Is that right?"

He looked scared. It made me feel bad that I might have, however inadvertently, brought this into his life. "It's true, but it's going to be fine. The police will figure it all out. I might have an idea for them, too." I told him what I'd found out from Reggie that day. "I know it's not a lot, but it takes us one step closer."

"I'm not sure I understand what that means," he admitted. "I hope things get back to normal for you, and the rest of us. If you need any help, don't hesitate to ask. You've been such a blessing to the shelter. We'd all like to repay you."

I thanked him. I didn't really understand any of it, either. How could I expect him to?

I left the shelter, got everything off of the food truck and in its appropriate places. Ollie, Miguel, Delia, and I were soaked.

I tried to give Ollie something for his time. He refused. I didn't offer Miguel money, but I thanked him for being there.

"I'm glad nothing unusual happened," Miguel said. "I'm going home to catch a shower. I'll see you later."

Ollie and I stood at the door to the diner, watching Miguel get in his car and leave.

"You know he likes you, right?" Ollie said. "I don't mean like a client, either."

A little thrill went through me. Maybe Delia was right. Maybe the business dinner wasn't only about business. Men have a way of hiding their intentions sometimes. I hoped this was one of those times.

"I like him, too. Not like my lawyer."

Ollie turned and stared at me. "What about Tommy Lee? I don't want Miguel to get hurt in some kind of scheme to make your boyfriend jealous, Zoe. Best you make a choice and stick to it."

He walked casually out into the streaming rain. I watched him go, wondering if he and Delia were either telepathic or had discussed us while Miguel and I were questioning Reggie.

I counted my money when I was alone. I'd made enough to cover my expenses. That was all. Crème Brûlée meowed at me from his bed on the floor.

"We'll be fine," I assured him. "You're not going to starve."

I think he believed me. He climbed out of his traveling bed and made his way onto my bed where he snuggled down into the sheet and blanket.

It had been a trying day for us both. But there was always tomorrow. All I could do was keep making the best biscuit bowls I could, and hope my dreams came true.

I took a quick shower and changed clothes. I had a flirty little red dress that I sometimes wore to parties. I thought about wearing it now. The problem was that I wasn't sure if I was going to have time to change after going to visit Tommy Lee. It was perfect for a date with a prospective boyfriend. Not so perfect for an obligatory visit to an *ex*-boyfriend. It could certainly give Tommy Lee the wrong idea.

Instead, I wore dark pants and a jacket that I'd usually reserved for the office. My pink top had a frothy neckline that verged on being flirty. I could wear the jacket when I saw Tommy Lee, and take it off when Miguel came to get me. That seemed like the best idea.

I was careful with my makeup, and packed some of it away in my bag. I could freshen up before I left the hospital. My curls were a little frizzy, even after I'd used gel on them. I sighed. They were going to have to do.

When I was through, I took one last look in the mirror and decided I was as good as I was going to be.

I called a taxi and waited inside until the driver showed up. With my only vehicle being the food truck, I had no choice. Gas was too expensive to drive it all over town.

I pulled the hood up on my rain poncho when the taxi arrived and dashed out of the diner, quickly locking the door behind me. I wasn't sure where Delia was. Maybe she'd gone down to see Ollie. They'd make a nice couple.

As we drove through the wet streets of the city, I thought about Delia's offer of helping me look better for Miguel. I still didn't think that kind of mojo was for me. Either Miguel and I had something between us, or not. I'd find out.

The taxi driver, a man named Cole, who happened to know Uncle Saul, agreed to wait for me while I went inside to see how Tommy Lee was doing. I thought I could use that as an excuse, if I needed one, to leave after a few minutes. I wasn't sure what Tommy Lee was going to be like.

The driver and I had a pleasant conversation about gator stew that made me want to pay my uncle a visit. The weekend was in front of me. Why not? Maybe he'd have some savory recipes he'd want to share.

I checked in at the front desk. The gray-haired woman there smiled and gave me Tommy Lee's room number. I made a quick stop at the gift shop and reluctantly purchased a get-well balloon for him.

It was hard not having the resources I'd had before. A ten-dollar balloon made me wince. I had to remind myself that Monday would be the start of a new week for my business. It could be the week everything turned around for me.

I told myself that *every* week.

The door to Tommy Lee's hospital room was open. I knocked anyway, and went in. It was a surprise to see both my parents—and his—standing on opposite sides of his sick bed. All of them glared at me as I put the weighted balloon on the bedside table.

I ignored them. "Hi, Tommy Lee. How are you feeling?"

He didn't look so bad. He had a bandage on his forehead. Otherwise, he looked fine. I felt guilty that he'd been injured trying to save me from Don. He'd meant well.

I didn't feel guilty enough to get back together with him, but enough to get me to the hospital and make me smile at him.

"Hello, Zoe." His voice was a whisper. "I'm glad to see you're still alive. I don't mind that I was almost killed trying to help you."

"How do you *think* he's feeling?" his mother (a great deal like mine) demanded. "You've ruined your life, Zoe, and now you want to kill my son. Have I ever told you the story of when my precious Tommy Lee was born? You know I could never have more children after him. He's all I've got."

To my dismay, Martha Elgin started crying. Herb, her husband, put his arm around her and shook his head at me. I felt terrible.

Daddy was visibly upset. My mother never cried, but she was very stern looking. I thought maybe she was practicing for being a judge. If that was the case, she'd been practicing my whole life.

"I'm very sorry about this, honey," Daddy said. "We've all agreed. You need an intervention. Try not to get upset. This is for your own good."

I started to ask what he was talking about when a dark blanket that smelled like wood shavings came down over my head. I tried to push it off, but the person holding it was much stronger than me. He picked me up and slung me across his shoulder.

"It will all be fine, Zoe," I heard my mother call out. "We love you."

FOURTEEN

I screamed. I kicked my feet and tried to pound on my abductor's back with my fists. I couldn't imagine why no one stopped him. Where were the cops, security guards, and hospital personnel?

I felt the elevator start down. Why was this happening to me? Wasn't it bad enough I'd had to shut down the Biscuit Bowl early and come back with almost a full load of food? Did my parents have to gang up on me, too?

Assuming Daddy had hired someone to kidnap me, I knew my only hope was reasoning with the person once I managed to get out of the blanket. This whole intervention routine was extreme. I had no doubt that it was my mother's idea.

I was bounced unceremoniously into what felt like a car seat. The driver of the car started forward right away. After a few minutes of driving, my abductor pulled the blanket from my head. I didn't even want to think what my poor, abused curls looked like at that point.

My eyes needed a moment to adjust to the light again. It appeared that I was back in the taxi. I started to ask what was going on when I heard a familiar voice beside me.

"You been a bad girl," Uncle Saul said with a chuckle. "I know times are desperate when your daddy calls *me* for help."

I hugged him, glad that my kidnapper wasn't some hired hand. I'd had a friend at Auburn who'd been through an intervention for smoking pot. She'd been held against her will for three days before escaping. She still smoked pot— she just never said anything to her parents again.

"What's going on?" I asked him. "What kind of intervention is this? Why didn't anyone stop you?"

"Your mother and father paid everyone to look the other way, of course. It was a brilliant plan—except for asking me to execute it. I suppose I was as close as they could imagine to the kind of person who'd do such a thing."

Uncle Saul was a tall, strong man, used to chopping firewood and living in the wild. He didn't look much like my father, either.

Where Daddy was smooth and always well-groomed, Uncle Saul had wild curly hair that looked like he'd dyed it in wide streaks of black and gray. His clothes were handmade and could have been something from the Middle Ages. He insisted store-bought clothes had poisons in them that caused premature death. Too bad he'd never really learned to sew.

"The best kind of intervention you're gonna get, Zoe." He grinned and messed up my curls even more than they were. He looked at his hand after he'd had it in my hair. "What is that junk you put in there? You need to wear your hair like mine—natural. Curly hair has magic. It shouldn't be tamed."

Uncle Saul hadn't always been this way. Daddy said he'd snapped one day about twenty years ago at his popular restaurant in downtown Mobile. I could barely remember him before. After that, he'd sold everything and bought some land in the swamp where he'd built his log cabin.

"I know you're not here to give me a curl intervention." I was happy to see him, like always, especially since I'd been thinking about him. He rarely came to town. On the other hand, I wanted to know what was going on.

"No. I'm here to save your life. You don't want to become like *me*, do you?"

There was a glint of humor in his bright blue eyes. I never knew when he was serious.

"My mother was looking for some way to make me quit my business, right?" I guessed. "Daddy came up with a plan to get me out of town and forget about it."

Uncle Saul laughed and slapped his thigh. "You must be getting psychic, child. Your daddy drove out to see me and begged me to take you back with me. He said your mother was thinking about having you committed to some fancy-pants clinic in Switzerland or something. She thinks you've lost your mind."

I laughed at that. "And somehow Daddy convinced her that *you* could help me find it? That's the funniest thing I've ever heard. Maybe *she* needs an intervention."

"That's about what I was thinking." He shrugged. "I wasn't gonna argue with him. I set this up and told him I'd take you back to the swamp with me for a few weeks. Your mother thinks that will be enough time to make you want your old job back, and to make up with your boyfriend."

I'd heard some crazy things in my time. This had to be the craziest.

"I don't want to go to the swamp, Uncle Saul. Even if I have to spend a month there, I'm not giving up on my dream. I love what I'm doing. My mother doesn't get it. I think Daddy would be okay with my decision if she'd quit bugging him about it."

Uncle Saul hugged me again, almost cracking my ribs in his enthusiasm.

"I'm not taking you anywhere, except your place. I brought some food to make a mighty fine dinner for my friend, Cole, here." He patted the driver on his back. "Besides, I want to see what you've done with the food truck. How are your biscuit bowls going over?"

In short, my father's visit had prompted Uncle Saul to come and see me to find out what was going on. I was surprised Daddy or my mother didn't realize what a sneaky man he was.

"Did they pay you to do the intervention?"

"Why yes, ma'am, they did." Uncle Saul grinned. "I've had my eye on a log splitter for a while now. I ordered it before I left home. I have the Internet now, you know."

Talk about things not going the way people planned! The taxi driver, Cole, took us back to the diner. As though the weather was smiling at the joke, too, the sun came out and chased all the rain away.

I helped Uncle Saul and Cole take cloth bags of roots, herbs, and vegetables into the diner. I took them on a grand tour of the diner and the food truck. Uncle Saul commented here and there about what I'd done.

"I like the chalkboard on the sling-up door," he told me. "I used to have a little sign I put on the ground. This is much better. When are you going to make me some biscuit bowls? I think I have some ideas for you on what you can serve inside."

We talked nonstop while Cole sat at the counter drinking coffee. It wasn't long before Ollie and Marty came down to see what was going on. Uncle Saul invited them both to dinner as he chopped vegetables and sautéed some fish and chicken. No wonder those bags had smelled so bad.

Delia had come back. She'd gone out shopping with some friends. She had several large bags of clothes. I didn't ask where she got the money. That would have been rude.

There were introductions all around. Ollie reminded me

a lot of Uncle Saul. He wasn't as outgoing—Uncle Saul had been known for his hospitality at his restaurant before his breakdown. Ollie helped Uncle Saul at the grill while I went to work on my hair.

It was almost seven P.M. I didn't know what Miguel would make of all this. I couldn't leave Uncle Saul, even for the possibility of a romantic dinner out.

I waited by the front door until I saw Miguel's Mercedes pull up. With one last pat on my hair, I went out to greet him and explain the situation.

"I can't go out. I'm sorry. I was looking forward to dinner."

"That's fine." Miguel smiled and didn't look upset at all. "Am I invited to the feast?"

I was a little put out that he didn't seem disappointed that he couldn't be alone with me. Maybe I'd overestimated the romance part of the meal. "That would be great. I'd love to have you meet my uncle."

My personal radar that could spot bad people was nothing compared to Uncle Saul's. Of course, he'd had years to get his working. I was still new to mine.

Miguel and Uncle Saul shook hands. I could see Uncle Saul's eyes narrow as he talked to Miguel. I knew he was assessing his personality. I was eager to find out what he thought.

Somehow, Uncle Saul got Miguel to put on a big white apron and had him cooking crawdads on the stove. I stayed at the oven making biscuits and then frying the biscuit bowls in the deep fryer. It was fun watching the three men make food. The diner was beginning to smell wonderful. I couldn't wait until the food was ready.

I could see Uncle Saul was making enough food to feed a small army. I told Marty he should bring the rest of the men down from the homeless shelter. "We'll have more than enough for everyone."

Marty smiled and thanked me. "Your uncle is amazing. I guess you take after him, Zoe. Why isn't he helping you with your business?"

"It's a long story. Mostly, he can't live in Mobile anymore. He had a popular restaurant here years ago. People still talk about eating there. From what I can tell, it was quite an experience. He helps me out when he can."

"Sounds like some of my crew." Marty grinned. "People need a break sometimes. I'm glad he didn't drop out of your life entirely. Maybe he could stay around for a while to help you through this other problem. From what Ollie has told me, I don't think you're safe here."

"I'll be fine," I assured him. "I'm going to find some plates and silverware for everyone. I hope all of you are hungry. I don't think I can store any more food in the refrigerator. We have to eat all of this or it has to go home with someone."

Marty agreed and walked back to the shelter. I found some old china plates and cups that had come with the diner. I'd washed them and stored them, though I'd had no intention of using them. This little party was more people than were legally allowed to eat here until I made other changes. But the zoning officer had said it was okay to have people there, so long as I didn't charge them to eat.

Ollie, Miguel, and Uncle Saul were busy laughing and cooking. I waited a few minutes after getting the tables set up for Marty to return. The food was going to be ready anytime. What could be keeping them?

"I'm going to check on Marty," I told everyone. No one replied. I wasn't sure if they hadn't heard me or were too busy to respond. "I'll be back with hungry men in a few minutes."

Crème Brûlée meowed. Otherwise, my announcement fell on deaf ears. With a shrug, I headed out into the night to see if I could help speed up the process.

I heard a noise in the back of the building. It probably

wasn't a good idea to go back there, but last month, I'd found a stray cat trapped in the trash container. I'd helped him get free and received three scratches for my efforts. Crème Brûlée had snubbed his nose at me for days afterward.

Knowing all of that, I went back there anyway. It was very dark behind the old shopping center that housed the diner, the consignment store, and the homeless shelter. There was another vacant storefront that had old sewing machines in it. Marty told me there had once been a tailor shop there. Now it was just creepy.

I'd asked the electric company a few times about repairing the streetlight behind the building. They'd told me it was on a list. It seemed to be a very long list.

Walking carefully around old car parts, broken bottles, and partial wood pallets, I searched the area, listening for the sound I'd heard up front. I didn't call out. I was hoping it was nothing more than another cat. If it was something, or *someone*, else, I didn't necessarily want them to know I was there.

I thought about Terry. He was killed back here. There was still crime scene tape fluttering in the slight breeze. Maybe this hadn't been such a great idea after all.

And what if Don Abbott wanted another crack at me? I began to feel all kinds of stupid for being there.

I also thought about the green Lincoln that had come from somewhere in the parking lot to pick up Delia on the night Terry had been killed. I didn't know who was driving that vehicle, but Delia did.

I knew she'd said the man in the Lincoln was someone important, and that she didn't want to bother him by asking questions about Terry's death, but maybe he'd seen something and didn't realize it. I decided to ask Delia about it again.

I heard the sound again, the one that had sent me exploring back there. It was a groaning noise. Someone was in trouble.

"Hello?" My voice quivered and cracked. I sounded like a woman in a bad horror movie. "Is someone out here?"

A groan came back to me, muffled, but definitely there. "Zoe? Over here."

I hesitated. It seemed like something someone would do to get my attention and then stick a gun in my face. I wanted to make sure no one was really lying on the ground, maybe injured. I just didn't want that to be me after I responded.

"If that's you, Don, my friends are inside and they'll come looking for me in a minute." I hoped that was true. Miguel, Ollie, and Uncle Saul had been having such a good time, I wasn't sure. Delia was busy trying on clothes.

"Zoe," the spectral-sounding voice called again. "Help me."

It definitely wasn't a cat. I ran toward the sound. There was a figure on the dirty blacktop. I didn't hesitate this time. I kept going until I'd reached my target.

It was Marty. He was injured, clutching his hand to his head and moaning.

"What happened?" I helped him sit up.

"I heard something back here. I was afraid it was someone trying to reach the shelter. It happens all the time. I looked by the trash bin, and suddenly, a man jumped out at me. He hit me in the head with something. I went down, and he started asking questions."

"Questions?" I immediately became suspicious. That attack may have been meant for *me*. "What kind of questions?"

"He wanted to know about you, Zoe. He asked me crazy questions about you and a stolen recipe."

FIFTEEN

Stolen recipe?

I helped Marty to his feet. "What kind of stolen recipe?"

By that time, I had been missed at the diner. I heard Ollie call my name from the front of the building. I answered, and told him I needed his help getting Marty inside.

Miguel, Uncle Saul, and Ollie ran into the alley to find us. Ollie and Uncle Saul supported Marty to get him back inside. Miguel stayed with me as we followed them.

"Are you all right?" he asked.

"I'm fine. Someone mugged Marty. He said the person asked a lot of questions about me, and a stolen recipe."

"You shouldn't have been out here by yourself. Don Abbott could've killed you. You have to be more careful until this is over."

"I didn't have much choice," I said. "Besides, it could've been a stray cat. As it was, we might never have heard Marty out there groaning if I had ignored it. I can't spend my whole life thinking that someone is out to get me."

"Your whole life, huh?" I could hear the smile in his voice. "It's only been a few days."

"Yeah, well, you know what I mean. Let's go inside. I want to know more about the recipe."

Ollie and Uncle Saul put Marty in a comfortable chair in the television room at the shelter. He'd never made it back to ask the men if they wanted to come to dinner.

"It doesn't look too bad." Ollie examined the wound on Marty's head after cleaning it. "I don't think you need stitches."

"Miguel can take you to the hospital, if you're worried." I wasn't sure about Ollie's diagnosis. "Or we could call an ambulance."

"No. No. I'll be fine." Marty smiled at Ollie. "Ollie had some medical training in the Marines. I'm sure he knows a nonlethal wound when he sees one. I trust him."

Ollie went to get a bandage with a smug smile on his face.

"If you don't feel like coming down to the diner to eat, I can bring a plate to you," I offered.

"I really think you and I should talk for a minute, Zoe," Marty said. "Everyone else can go to the diner. We'll be there in a few minutes."

He didn't have to say it twice. Miguel and Uncle Saul went with the men to get them set up with food and something to drink. Ollie stayed behind with me and Marty. He put the bandage on Marty's head and then sat down to hear what he had to say.

"Things have been crazy around here." Marty smiled and put his hand on the new bandage. "Thank you, Ollie. I think I might be able to shed some light on what's going on—at least as much as I understand from my attacker."

"What did he look like?" Ollie demanded. "I bet it was the thief again. He doesn't know when to quit."

"I'm not sure what he looked like. It was dark. I was

intent on getting back here. I should've been more aware of my surroundings."

"You said something about a recipe when we were outside," I reminded Marty. "What was that all about?"

"The man wanted to know your schedule, Zoe. He wanted to know what time you leave in the morning, and what time you get back. He asked me where you usually park your food truck. He said you have something that belongs to him. He said it was a recipe that was stolen from him, a valuable recipe."

Ollie snorted. "What kind of recipe? Does he think it will win a million dollars in a contest or something? That's crazy talk."

"Did he say what kind of recipe?" I thought it sounded weird, too, but we already knew Terry wanted to sell something that could fit in the pocket of his jeans. That could be a recipe.

I was with Ollie, questioning what kind of value someone could put on a recipe. It wasn't like it was a priceless diamond or a gold coin. Who would pay a lot of money for a recipe?

"He didn't say." Marty shook his head. "He seemed very sure that you have it. He wants it back. I hope he won't try and hurt you to get it."

"He'd be wasting his time," I replied. "My recipes are valuable to me, but I don't think anyone else would pay for them."

Marty shrugged and declared himself ready to eat. We went down to the diner, and Uncle Saul's eyes narrowed as we talked about the stolen recipe. "You know, I remember hearing something about a stolen recipe a few months back." He scratched his head, trying to recall exactly what he'd heard.

"You don't really think all of this—Terry's death and Don's threats—has been about a stolen recipe, do you?"

Miguel asked. "What kind of recipe is worth that much money?"

Delia came out of her makeshift room when she heard all the loud, excited talking. When she found out what had happened, she was upset. "You should have had one of the men with you, Zoe!"

"I would have if I'd known what was going to happen!"

I took out my laptop and looked up "stolen valuable recipe" on Google. My search returned a slew of information. I ate my dinner, and read what I'd found.

"Well?" Ollie asked impatiently. "What's worth attacking Marty?"

"How about a stolen recipe worth more than a million dollars?" I looked at my three conspirators over the laptop screen.

"No way," Ollie said. "No recipe is worth that much money. I don't care how good the chocolate cake is."

"It was someone famous who wrote it, wasn't it, Zoe?" Uncle Saul asked.

"I'd say so—Thomas Jefferson. Who knew Thomas Jefferson could cook?"

"That's even crazier," Miguel said. "What would Terry be doing with that kind of historic document?"

I read from the text on the screen. "Apparently, someone stole the recipe from a museum in Virginia where it was being displayed. It was written in Jefferson's own hand. That's what makes it valuable."

Uncle Saul snapped his fingers. "That's right! I remember now. The recipe was for crème brûlée. It was Jefferson that introduced that dessert to this country after he'd returned from France."

When Uncle Saul said crème brûlée, I heard my little Crème Brûlée meow loudly. He finally came out of the bedroom to see who was calling him. He walked right past all the other men and came to stand by Uncle Saul.

When Uncle Saul laughed and scratched his ears, Crème Brûlée bit him and hissed.

"I think that was a warning not to talk about him that way in public," I told him with a rueful apology.

"That's okay." Uncle Saul watched Crème Brûlée walk back into the bedroom, his head held high.

"I don't believe a taco truck driver from Mobile engineered the theft of an antique recipe in Virginia," Miguel said. "He must've gotten it from someone else."

Ollie was done eating and tried to look over my shoulder at the laptop. "Does it say anything about who took the recipe from the museum?"

"No. The police are baffled. The FBI was called in because the recipe was on loan from the Smithsonian. It's considered a national treasure."

"Okay, like I said, Terry didn't set this up and elude the police and the FBI," Miguel added. "Someone else must have done the hard work. Somehow Terry was unlucky enough to get his hands on it. That's probably why he was killed."

"You've got no real proof of that," Uncle Saul reminded him. "I don't see that information getting Delia off the hook for Terry's death. Or getting Zoe off the hook from someone believing she took the recipe from Terry."

Miguel agreed. "I can't even imagine telling Detective Latoure that I think this is what happened. I looked at Terry's file. As far as I could see, Terry had never left Alabama."

"Who else might be interested in a valuable recipe?" I asked. "It had to be stolen for a recipe collector."

Uncle Saul shrugged. "Or someone interested in Thomas Jefferson."

I had to give him that. I could see where this could go in many ways. Terry could've accidentally found the recipe and planned to sell it. It would be hard to say exactly where to look for a buyer.

"Well, at least we have somewhere to start, thanks to Marty." Miguel nodded to him. "I'm sorry we had to find out the hard way."

"That's okay." Marty looked embarrassed by the attention. "I certainly don't deserve any praise for being mugged. It's scary thinking that this person is out there searching for Zoe. I hope you can convince the police that she needs protection."

"Never mind the police," Uncle Saul said. "I'll take her back with me to my place. She'll be safe there."

When the four of them agreed this was a good idea, it was as bad as my parents wanting Uncle Saul to take me away and save me from my own poor choices. It wasn't happening, either.

"I appreciate the sentiment, but I'm not leaving my business. Maybe I could take out an ad in the paper, or on that old billboard right next door. I could tell everyone that I don't know what happened to Thomas Jefferson's recipe for crème brûlée."

Crème Brûlée, the cat, meowed another warning from the bedroom. We all laughed. Uncle Saul made jokes about Crème Brûlée protecting me—careful this time not to mention his name.

Everyone was done eating and had hearty appreciation of the cooks' efforts. Ollie walked with Marty back to the shelter, and the other residents followed.

That left me, Miguel, and Uncle Saul drinking my special blend of coffee, talking about what had happened with Marty that night.

"I guess they couldn't get you out there, Zoe," Miguel said, "so they decided to use Marty to send a message. You should really consider your uncle's offer to leave town until this blows over."

How many ways could I say no? If I waited a few weeks to come back to my business, I would've lost all the momentum I'd gained. People forget very quickly.

"I think it would be better to come up with a plan to find Terry's killer," I suggested. "Now that we know what he's looking for, all we have to do is find out who has it."

"That sounds like a tall order," Uncle Saul said.

"Maybe," I admitted. "I don't have much choice. You know what I mean about my food truck. I can't up and leave now. I've worked too hard."

"Is it worth your life?" Miguel asked in that sincere way he had.

"Probably not. But I think we can find the killer, and that will take care of it."

"What about the man who threatened to shoot Zoe?" Uncle Saul looked at Miguel. "Could he be responsible for all this?"

"I don't think so," Miguel said. "Abbott's file looks like Terry's file. Neither one of these men would think of a scheme like this. I think Terry fell into it, and might have told his partner about it. Abbott probably figures Zoe has the recipe since Terry was found dead in her food truck."

Uncle Saul nodded. "If what you're saying is true, Miguel, there is a mastermind behind the theft who passed it off to Terry, for whatever reason. It beats me how you're gonna figure out who it is without getting hurt."

"I think we both agree on that," Miguel said.

"I don't agree. We can figure this out." I challenged him and Uncle Saul. "We can do this—without abandoning my business."

We kind of agreed to disagree. Miguel and I exchanged good nights and shook hands. Uncle Saul hugged him.

That was the extent of my possible romantic dinner with Miguel. I watched him leave the parking lot and hoped it would get better.

"You like him, don't you, honey?" Uncle Saul observed me.

"I do. He seems like a nice person."

"He's good-looking *and* a lawyer. Even your mother should like that!" Uncle Saul waggled his crazy gray and black eyebrows up and down. "I like him better than Johnny Lee."

I didn't enlighten him as to my mother's opinion of Miguel.

"*Tommy* Lee," I corrected automatically. "Well, that egg has already been broken. He's like my parents. He thinks doing this business is beneath me. Not to mention that he's been seeing someone else on the side."

"The disagreement about the business, I can understand. All couples disagree about something. The other is bad news, Zoe. Better dump him quick. Pick up the smart lawyer instead."

"It's not as easy as all that." I explained while we made a chocolate raspberry cake for Marty. We both agreed that he deserved something for taking that lump on the head for me.

We cooked and talked, and drank too much coffee, until well after midnight. Uncle Saul gave me a recipe for a spicy fish stew with carrots and potatoes. I was excited about trying it out on Monday.

Understanding the nature of my situation, Uncle Saul had come prepared to spend the night. He'd brought a chaise lounge with him, which he set up in the kitchen.

"Good night, Zoe," was the last thing he said to me when we were both in our respective beds. "I hope you'll give more thought to coming back home with me for a while. If I'd known it was more than your daddy's passing fancy to kidnap you, I would've taken you there already. Don't be so stubborn that you're stupid."

I heard him but only answered with, "Good night." There was no way I was giving up what I'd built. I was the only one who knew what leaving my job and security behind had cost me. I was the only one who got to make that decision.

I sincerely hoped it would pay off and I wouldn't get killed.

Crème Brûlée licked my face and bit my nose as if to

tell me it was going to be okay. I whispered good night to him, too, and was asleep almost as soon as my head hit the pillow.

Two hours later, as Uncle Saul snored in the kitchen, someone tossed a concrete block through one of the plate-glass windows.

My new day began with flashing lights on a police car, and the sure knowledge that someone was sending me another warning.

SIXTEEN

Officers Schmidt and Gayner were at the scene again. I gave them coffee and some biscuit bowls while we talked. They took our statements, both of which kind of went, "We were asleep and suddenly heard the glass break in the front of the diner."

Delia didn't hear a thing until we woke her.

What else could we say? Everything else was speculation, even though Marty and Ollie both came outside to see what was going on. There was poor Marty with the cut on his head from the previous attempt to get my attention.

Marty had made it very clear that he didn't want to involve the police in his assault. Like everyone else at the shelter, it seemed he had a past he didn't want to explore with law enforcement.

I was thankful that the block hadn't come in through the window near where Uncle Saul had been sleeping. It could've been much worse. That made at least two people

I knew who could have been, or had been, hurt by my stubborn refusal to close the business and leave town.

Oh, but I hated the idea of giving up. My parents would gloat because they'd feel sure they were right. Tommy Lee would no doubt tell Betty at the bank.

It was more than that, of course. I was terrified of losing everything and having to go back to the bank with my tail tucked between my legs to ask for my job back. The chances were I would never build up the courage to pursue my dream again.

On the other hand, I didn't want my friends and relatives hurt, either. How could something like this happen to me now, of all times?

I took the official police report from Officer Schmidt, who thanked me for the coffee and biscuits. He warned me to be careful. "It's a tough neighborhood."

He had no idea.

After the police had gone and Uncle Saul was making eggs and pan toast, I called the insurance company and made a claim for the window.

"They said someone should be out later today to repair it." I yawned after I'd hung up and poured more coffee.

"That's good for today, honey. What about tomorrow, and the next day? If this person is determined to get this recipe, the harassment could go on for a long time. Or tomorrow, he might decide to personally try to get the information from you. Do you know what I'm saying?"

I did. It was depressing.

We sat at the counter together. He ate his food with gusto. I pushed mine around on my plate. I drank some coffee, and he finally ate what I'd left behind.

"What can I do, Uncle Saul?" I appealed to him. "I can't just leave. You know that. There has to be another answer."

He patted my hand. "I think maybe I have an idea. At least we might be able to get a few more answers about this recipe thing. I don't know if it will be what you need, Zoe, but we can try my idea and find out."

I hugged his neck. "Thank you. Whatever you have in mind is worth trying. Let me get dressed."

Delia was still asleep and had left a "do not disturb" sign on her door. I wasn't sure how she'd managed to get herself completely into the closet, but I admired her tenacity.

After putting on some jeans and a top, I asked Ollie to keep an eye on the diner. The broken window was an open invitation. I didn't want to share everything I had with the people who lived around me.

"Do you need to close your cat in a closet or something so he doesn't get out of the diner?" Ollie asked as he agreed to keep watch.

"I think he'll be fine. He probably won't even notice the window is open. He usually doesn't walk that far from the bedroom. Thank you so much for doing this. I'll let you know what we find out."

Uncle Saul had many contacts from his former life in Mobile. He explained his plan as we drove his old, wood-paneled station wagon through town.

"I figure some of my friends who are in the antique business might know more than your Internet about the Jefferson recipe. They won't only spout facts at us—they'll know the gossip, too."

"What a great idea!"

"Thanks. You know, my brother didn't get *all* the smarts in the family."

"I never thought he did."

We got to the first antique store on South Water Street. The neighborhood was old, full of iron lace balconies and window treatments. Mobile was famous for its elaborate scrollwork, like its sister city, Charleston, South Carolina.

Most of the old work was gone, lost to time, and even being used to support the city. Mobile had sold off a ton of iron during the bad years after the Civil War.

It was Saturday, and the weather was fine. The rain had cleared out all the humidity and left behind some sweet breezes. Uncle Saul's friend, Ben Weathers, was stacking furniture and knickknacks on the sidewalk for folks to admire as they waited to catch a cruise ship.

Uncle Saul and Ben shook hands.

"It's been a dog's age since I've seen you, buddy," Ben said with a wide grin.

Ben Weathers was a short, thin man with a crown of white hair fluttering around his pink face. His keen blue eyes were mostly hidden behind glasses—when those weren't perched on the tip of his nose.

"You don't make it out to the swamp very often," Uncle Saul chided him.

"Man, you ain't got no tourists out there. I get 'em coming and going off the cruise ships every day. I don't have to wait for Mardi Gras or the Azalea Festival anymore."

Both men laughed at that. Uncle Saul introduced me. Ben shook my hand and told me I was welcome to park my food truck at his place anytime.

We went inside the small shop together. There was so much merchandise packed in there, I could hardly tell one thing from the other. There were old grandfather clocks, desks, rocking chairs, and thousands of smaller items.

Ben tried to sell me some antique kitchen utensils. I refused, telling him I was just getting started. He gave me an old silver spoon, black with tarnish, for good luck.

Uncle Saul finally explained why we'd come, and asked Ben if he'd heard any rumors about the Jefferson recipe.

Ben invited us to sit down on some furniture he said had been salvaged from the Southern White House during the Civil War. It was in pretty good condition, though I suspected the velvet was new.

"Rumors? Saul, there's a full-blown hurricane of innuendoes and dark intentions about that thing. I wish I had it. I could probably get at least a million and a half for it."

"Any ideas on who might've taken it?" Uncle Saul asked.

"I've heard a few names mentioned. You're probably thinking someone close to home. That would be Art Arrington."

"Chef Art from the old Carriage House Restaurant?" Uncle Saul looked surprised to hear that name. He explained to me, "Chef Art had a great little place over on South Royal Street. They said the governor used to come and eat there every weekend. Anybody who was anybody liked to be seen there."

"Was the food good?" I asked.

"Good?" Ben kissed his fingers. "It was like the angels themselves brought the food to Chef Art fresh every day. The man was a genius!"

"What happened to him and the Carriage House?" I wanted to hear the whole story. Of course I knew who Chef Art was. He was part of Mobile history.

"He got too big for his britches," Uncle Saul said. "Some men from New York City came and offered him a deal to open a restaurant there. He did, and it did real well for a while. He tried to keep the original open, too. That didn't work out so well."

"Then the Carriage House in New York closed. By that time, Chef Art had lost his place here, too," Ben supplied. "Still, he came back home with a pile of money. Bought that old mansion, over on Spring Street, I think."

"You think he could be involved?" Uncle Saul asked Ben.

Ben put his head close to Uncle Saul's. "Chef Art has his fingers in a lot of different pies. There's been some talk that he tried to get that Jefferson recipe at an auction before it went to the Smithsonian. A friend of mine said Chef Art probably hired someone to steal it when he had the chance."

I had to admit, I'd been reluctant to believe that a recipe could be worth that much money. The way Ben explained it made a believer out of me. By the time Uncle Saul and I left the antique store, I was ready to go and ask Chef Art for it.

"I don't think it's going to be as easy as all that," Uncle Saul cautioned as we climbed back into his station wagon.

"We could at least tell Detective Latoure about the recipe and Chef Art. Maybe she could take it from there."

"Maybe. I don't have much faith in the police."

"Or the government. Or any other institution." I'd heard his opinions many times on those matters. "That's why you went to live in the swamp."

He pinched my cheek. "You're getting a smart mouth on you, girl. I have one more stop I'd like to make. I'd like to get a second opinion, so to speak."

Since I'd confined my food truck business to downtown, five days a week, and the occasional weekend festival, I had nothing better to do than hang out with my uncle. Trying to figure out whatever we could about the stolen recipe could be worthwhile.

We drove toward Mobile Bay and met up with another antique dealer who was an old friend of Uncle Saul's. Danny Butcher was sitting at an outdoor antique festival. His tables were packed full of the odd and unusual.

Danny was a little odd and unusual himself. He was dressed like a pirate from his tricorn hat to his knee-high boots. He looked like Captain Hook from the old Peter Pan movie.

He laughed when I took several pictures of him with my cell phone. "Us pirates don't like having our pictures taken, even by a bonny lass such as yourself. Makes it too easy to create wanted posters."

He growled at me, and I took another picture. "I promise not to help the authorities catch you."

"Nice getup," Uncle Saul said. "You've come up in the world since I saw you last, Danny."

"And I heard you've been sinking out there in the swamp,"

Danny retorted. "What brings you away from the gators and snakes?"

Uncle Saul explained that we were looking for the person who'd stolen Jefferson's recipe. "Any ideas?"

"Not really. A man came by a couple of weekends ago. He said he had the recipe and wanted to know if I'd buy it from him. I figured either it wasn't real, or he was crazy. You can clearly see I don't have that kind of money."

"What did he look like?" I asked him.

"Kind of tall, greasy red hair, wearing a hat that said Tacky Tacos," he supplied. "Sound like your man?"

It sounded exactly like Terry. "Did you see the recipe?"

"Nah. He told me he had it on him and kept fiddling with something in his pocket." Danny laughed. "If it was the real recipe, you'd have to take some money off for mistreatment. An old document of that sort needs to be preserved and cared for. You can't shove something like that into your jeans and take it around town trying to sell it."

Uncle Saul nudged me. "Danny was a museum curator when we were young. He gave it all up for this sweet business he has going here. Good choice, huh?"

"*Arhh.* Ye better be careful how you speak of me youth." Danny closed one eye and put his hand on the pommel of his sword. "You know I had reason to get out of that business."

"Yes, you did." Uncle Saul turned to me. "The museum accused Danny of trying to steal an artifact. What was that again?"

"Nothin' you need worry about," Danny said. "I was cleared, anyway."

"But they never found the artifact, did they?" Uncle Saul seemed to be joking. I wasn't completely sure about that. Who knew he had such disreputable friends?

"Can you think of anyone with the kind of money it would take to buy Jefferson's recipe? It would have to be a collector, right?" I asked.

"I can think of a half-dozen people who'd covet that kind of thing." Danny squinted at me. "You mean to tell me you think that was the *real* deal? Where would someone like your taco friend get a valuable, historic recipe?"

"I'm not sure yet. Thanks for the information. Could you write down the names of those people you think might want the recipe?"

"Don't need a list. Only one man would have the money for something like that—and be willing to pay it—Chef Art Arrington."

We had to move away from the tables full of antiques as a large group of tourists descended on Danny's wares. Uncle Saul and I went back to the station wagon.

"Looks like Chef Art is our man," he said.

"Maybe we should pay him a call."

"Maybe not. At least you shouldn't see him with me, honey. Art and I go back a long way—none of it good. It would be best for you to take Ollie or Miguel out there. Better think of a good story, though. You can't go up to a man like that and flat out ask him if he has the recipe."

On the way back to the diner, I tried to think of a good excuse to put Chef Art at ease. It didn't come right away. I wasn't even sure I could get Miguel or Ollie to go with me.

We made a detour so that Uncle Saul could visit another old friend while he was in town. This stop came with lunch in the kitchen of one of the most popular restaurants in Mobile. I wasn't complaining.

The Laughing Goat was housed in a two-story, redbrick, Queen Anne–style commercial building. A plaque on the outside said it was on the Historic Register and had been built in 1891.

The inside was classic, with hardwood floors and white linen tablecloths. There were colorful flowers everywhere. Large ceiling fans gracefully kept the air circulating, probably the same way they had for the last hundred years.

Chef Paul Dismukes was a jolly, bearded man with a

broad chest and broader belly. He was tall and strong, almost lifting Uncle Saul off the floor with his bear hug.

"Saul, you old devil! You must be looking for lunch. Sit down and let me feed you." Chef Paul caught sight of me and kissed my hand. "And who is this lovely creature? Are you married again and hiding her out in the swamp?"

"No, you fool." Uncle Saul laughed. "This is my niece, Zoe. You remember her. She was a mite scrawnier back then. She was always eating at my place."

"Of course! I remember." Chef Paul moved in to give me a bear hug.

I was pretty sure a few of my ribs were cracked when it was over. He'd also managed to give me a pat on the butt. No more close contact for him.

"As a matter of fact, I have your brother and his . . . er . . . *lovely* ex-wife eating here right now," Chef Paul said. "Let me go find them."

"No! I mean . . . not right now." I really didn't want to see my parents. I was glad they had a good relationship after the divorce. It made things easier for me. But I didn't want to be part of that right now.

"Okay." Chef Paul shrugged. "Well, sit down, you two. I'll have someone bring you something."

The large kitchen was covered in stainless steel appliances and counters. Dozens of fast-moving servers and cooks jumped at Chef Paul's commands. Fresh herbs were growing in pots everywhere with special lights, or in windows. The aromas coming from the big pots and skillets on the massive stoves were enough to set my mouth watering.

Being a guest of a chef, and eating in his kitchen, was a high honor. We were seated at a small table in a corner. One of the servers laid a white linen tablecloth for us, and a small pot of rosemary was placed in the center of the table with a lighted candle.

"You're gonna love this, Zoe." Uncle Saul tucked his

napkin in under his chin and picked up his fork as the first course arrived.

We had salmon cakes and wild greens, which included dandelion leaves. They were tender and delicious. The salad dressing was a house secret, but I tasted a hint of honey in it.

Next came black-eyed peas, cooked until they were firm, but soft. There were shallots with them, and fresh mushrooms.

After that, we had macaroni and cheese with spicy pimento cheese instead of the regular cheese variety. Right after came brown sugar–glazed pork roast that was melt-in-your-mouth good. It was followed immediately by hush puppies, shaped like dolphins, that contained hot peppers.

Dessert was mango pie, the restaurant's signature dessert. Chef Paul sat down with us for this last course, slurping coffee from a big mug as we finished eating.

I was so stuffed, I felt like I was going to pop. I had plenty of good ideas for the Biscuit Bowl tucked away for the future, too.

"What did you think?" Chef Paul asked us.

Uncle Saul wiped his mouth with his napkin. His eyes narrowed. "The salmon cakes were a little dry. The macaroni and cheese was a little too spicy. The pork roast was cooked too much. The pie was excellent, if you don't count the crust."

The two men faced each other. Chef Paul's face was a blend of horror and amazement. The servers and cooks in the kitchen stopped running back and forth. They appeared to be holding their breaths as they waited for Chef Paul's response.

"I can't believe you liked the black-eyed peas." Chef Paul started laughing and the tension broke. "You're an old buzzard, Saul. Lucky for you, your place is closed so I can't come and say what I think about *your* food."

Uncle Saul laughed, too. "You did that plenty of times

before I closed. And you stole that brown sugar glaze from me, Paul. You better be giving me credit on the menu for it."

Both men laughed so hard that tears were rolling down their cheeks. Activity in the kitchen picked up again—so much so that no one noticed when one of the guests from the dining room came into the kitchen to say hello.

"Zoe? Saul?" My father's face was distressed. "What the hell are you doing here?"

SEVENTEEN

Chef Paul scurried away like one of his cooks, supervising a big pot of dumpling soup being made on the stove.

"You said you'd take her out of town." Daddy faced Uncle Saul.

This was the only time—when the two of them were close together—that I could see the family resemblance between the two brothers.

Uncle Saul was the eldest. He'd long ago given up any idea of trying to tame the Chase family curly hair. It looked like a bird's nest sitting on his head. His idea of good grooming was to smell a shirt he'd worn the day before to see if he could wear it again.

My father never let h   is hair get more than an eighth of an inch long. That disguised his curls and kept them under control. I was pretty sure he dyed his hair, too. Usually people with truly black hair start getting gray early.

I knew that was true. I had my first gray hair when I was eighteen!

Daddy's blue suit was impeccable. He worked out regularly and had the polished air of a successful businessman.

"I got her out of the hospital," Uncle Saul said, defending himself. "She's not in any danger now that we know about the Jefferson recipe."

"Danger? What are you talking about?" Daddy ran his manicured hand through his crisp hair. "Anabelle wants her out of this food truck business. She wants Zoe back at the bank and married to Tommy Lee. What part of that didn't you understand in the kidnapping plan?"

"Daddy, I'm not giving up my business."

"Hush, Zoe. You don't have a say in this. It's all about what your mother needs you to do. You're lucky she didn't come back with me to see Paul. Neither one of us would ever hear the end of it."

My father and Uncle Saul argued a little more before Chef Paul threw them out of his kitchen. We went out the back door, the way we'd come in. My father went out front to lie to my mother, no doubt. I felt sure he wasn't going to tell her that he'd seen us in the kitchen.

Uncle Saul started the old station wagon. "Zoe Chase, you're gonna have to learn to stand up to that woman."

"I thought I was doing that already. How many ways can I say, 'I want this business' and 'I'm not marrying Tommy Lee'?"

"I don't know, but next time, your parents might hire a real kidnapper who'll take you to one of those camps up in Birmingham where they brainwash you. You better make peace with your mother fast."

I agreed with him but didn't know what else to say or do. "Maybe I should go ahead and move to Birmingham and change my name. They have a good food truck business going up there."

"You have to take a stand in a seriouslike manner," he explained as he started back to the diner. "You want to be your own woman? You gotta stop being their little girl."

"How do I do that?"

"Search me. I've never been anyone's baby. You better find out fast if you *ever* want to have your own life."

I put that on my list of things to think about, right up there with trying to figure out what Terry did with the Jefferson recipe. Finding out that second part seemed more immediate, since people were threatening me with guns and throwing things through my windows.

Or was it just easier to handle the idea of being murdered for some old recipe than it was thinking about facing my mother?

The insurance adjuster had come and gone when we got back to the diner. Already, a truck with a small crane was putting in a new window.

"I hate insurance," Ollie said. "That little insurance dude said to tell you that you only get one of these replacements a year. He said you need to put up some iron bars or get out of this neighborhood unless you want your insurance payment to go up."

With his message delivered, Ollie shrugged and went back to the shelter. I thanked him as he walked away.

"I gotta go, too," Uncle Saul said. "It's been fun, Zoe, but I have to get home and feed Alabaster before she gets it into her head that she should eat the neighbor's chickens again."

Alabaster was Uncle Saul's albino alligator. He'd kept the alligator as a pet for years. Occasionally, Alabaster wandered off and caused some problems. It was lucky Uncle Saul's nearest neighbor was five miles away.

"I'm sorry you have to go." I hugged his neck, standing on tiptoe. "Thanks for taking me to see your friends. I hope I can do something with the information."

"If not, come on out and stay with me. This will all blow over as soon as someone finds that recipe. Until then, watch your back. I have an extra gun with me, if you need it."

"No, that's okay. I think I might get into more trouble if I start shooting people."

Uncle Saul got in the station wagon and drove away. My heart sank a little as I watched him go. I wished I could live in the swamp with him, but there wasn't much call for a food truck out there.

- - - - - - -

I was working on making some macaroni with pimento cheese when I saw Miguel's Mercedes pull up. My heart did a little dance that he was there and maybe we could go back to the idea of that possible romantic dinner.

Then I saw him get out of the car on the driver's side with Delia getting out on the passenger side. This was obviously not a romantic visit.

"Hi, Zoe," Delia greeted me. "Miguel took me to talk to the DA. I don't think it did much good."

Miguel came in after her and asked how everything was going. I wanted to tell him about the cement block through the window, and what Uncle Saul and I had learned.

I was nervous, though, and fell back on what I knew best. "Would you two like to try some macaroni and cheese?"

It turned out neither of them had eaten lunch, and they were both hungry. They sat down at the counter and I ladled some pimento cheese macaroni into bowls. I had some cans of soda left and put those out.

Delia praised my macaroni and cheese. She tried to laugh off the part about her not needing a strategy for court because she was innocent. I could tell she was scared.

I glanced at Miguel. He shook his head. "It's all going to depend on the jury she gets. This could go either way. The police certainly don't have a rock-solid case, by any means. We'll have to find ways to insert some skepticism into the jury. Or find the real killer before then."

Speaking of finding the killer—or at least the reason Terry was killed—I quickly changed the subject and told him about the broken window and the information Uncle Saul and I had received from his friends.

"Art Arrington, huh?" He sipped his soda. "I haven't heard his name in a long time. We used to eat at his restaurant. Good food."

Without thinking, I asked, "We?"

His face changed. I was immediately sorry I'd asked. I was so anxious to hear about him that I'd put my foot in it.

"My mother and me. She was a big fan of Southern cooking. The spicier, the better. The Carriage House was one of the first places I took her when I started making some money. We never ate out much when I was a child. She loved it!" He frowned. "It wasn't long after that she died. She was very young."

Trying to get my foot out of my big mouth, I forged ahead. "What about you? How is the spicy mac and cheese?"

"Good." He smiled. "Delia is right. You're a wonderful cook, Zoe. I'm sure when you get everything up and running here, there will be lines waiting through the parking lot."

"Thanks." I hoped there was no damage done. I'd seen the gray cloud settle over his features. I hated that I'd caused him pain.

I was too young to really remember the Carriage House Restaurant. I figured Miguel was maybe six or eight years older than me. He must have been fresh out of law school when his mother had passed.

"I think we should talk to Detective Latoure," Miguel said. "She might not know about the Jefferson recipe yet. It could give her another direction to look in for Terry's killer."

"If you think that will help, I'm all for it." I grinned to show him I was willing to work for the team.

"Then let's go," he said.

"I need to get rid of some of this food that I've been making. Maybe the two of you could help me take it down to the shelter."

The three of us went down that way. The consignment shop was open and had dozens of bargain shoppers inside. It was odd to see so many new and expensive cars in the parking lot. Bargain shopping apparently appealed to people who could afford much better. The shop was probably a must-see on some tourist website.

I was glad we were able to go down and check on Marty, too. The men living at the shelter were thrilled to see us bearing food. I promised them there would be more later as I worked on new dishes for the food truck.

Marty seemed to be doing fine. "I have a little headache still, but otherwise, no side effects. Thanks for asking."

The men at the shelter were very appreciative of seeing Delia. There was plenty of whistling and "hey, baby" comments while we talked to Marty.

They'd been the same way with me the first time I'd gone inside. Now it was my food that they found attractive. That was fine. Better my food than me.

"Any news on the recipe?" Marty asked before we left.

I didn't want to go into everything Uncle Saul and I had unearthed. It would be better to share it with Detective Latoure first. Uncle Saul always said, loose lips sink ships. I wasn't sure exactly what that meant, but I knew it had something to do with telling secrets to more people than was necessary.

"We're still working on new leads," Miguel said in a professional tone.

Marty smiled. "Well, I wish you luck. Stay out of dark places, Zoe. I'd hate for you to end up like me, or worse."

We talked for a few minutes about the concrete block, and having the diner window replaced. There wasn't much to say about the incident. Either the killer was trying to send me another message, or the police were right and it was part of being in a bad neighborhood.

"If you're ready, we could go ahead and talk to Patti."

"That's fine," I added quickly.

"Great."

"Unless you had something else planned." Miguel seemed a little nervous.

"No. That would be fine." I threw in a little hint. "I don't even have plans for dinner."

"Good. That way if the interview goes a little long, it will be all right."

"Sure. That would be just fine." It seemed that Miguel wasn't good at taking hints. "I'll freshen up a little and get my bag."

When we got back to the diner, I excused myself, threw Crème Brûlée out of my office/bedroom, and rapidly changed clothes to go out with Miguel. I had a beautiful wine-colored dress that was a little on the short side for me. The neckline was kind of revealing. I decided maybe Miguel needed more of a hint.

I crept into the bathroom with my cosmetics and hairbrush. Miguel and Delia were talking about the case. That gave me a few extra minutes to put on my best face.

Before I could work on my curls, there was a light tap at the door. I peeked out—it was Delia. She quickly came into the bathroom with me.

"You could do so much more with your eyes." She took my cosmetic bag from me. "You have such pretty eyes, Zoe, with that pale blue iris surrounded by the dark blue ring. And you have great skin. Let's try a little dark shadow on your lids to bring them out."

I wasn't sure exactly what to say. We were face-to-face in a very small bathroom. It struck me that I had nothing to lose.

"That dress is a knockout," Delia said as she did my eyes. "I hope you have a little darker lipstick to go with it. That pink you usually wear is nice, but you need something more dramatic with your coloring."

I didn't have any other lipstick. Delia fished her own lipstick out of her bag. It was a close match to the dress I was wearing.

It was like being in school again. Delia finished my new look, chattering the whole time about various things I could

do to make Miguel notice me. She pulled down my bodice
to make the neckline even more revealing, and took off the
tiny gold cross she wore.

"Let's get something shiny in there." She grinned. "We
have to flaunt it if we want it to work for us, right?"

I looked in the cracked mirror and approved the job she'd
done. With a little more highlight on my cheeks and eyes, I
looked very different.

Delia held her head to one side and studied my hair. "You
know, I think we could do something with these curls, too."

"Thanks, but there's always a price to pay for messing
with the curly hair. I know my limitations. I like the rest of
the look. You're very good at this."

"I have to be good at something besides waiting tables."
She shrugged. "Go get him, Zoe. From what I've heard,
Miguel has been alone too long."

"You're a good person, Delia. You've only begun to
scratch the surface of who you are, I think." I dropped the
wine-colored lipstick she was letting me borrow into my
bag. "Thanks for your help."

Delia looked at the green paper beads she'd given me the
night Terry was killed. They were still in my bag, of course.
I hadn't even thought about them again.

"Do you want those back now?" I asked.

"No!" She recoiled as if I'd asked her if she wanted to
hold a snake. "You keep them, Zoe. I—I can't."

EIGHTEEN

- -

"What's wrong?" I thought that was a weird reaction.

"Nothing." She bit her lip. "Terry gave them to me. I—I don't want to think about it."

She abruptly left the tiny bathroom. I followed behind her.

What was bothering her about the beads? Maybe bad Mardi Gras memories? People gave out beads, kind of like these, along the parade route every year. These were paper instead of plastic, and they were bigger, but there was nothing unusual or particularly offensive about them.

Miguel and Ollie were standing there, watching us. No doubt wondering what we were doing in the bathroom together.

"Ready?" Miguel asked.

I smiled. What was I thinking? Both of these men had been married. They were used to the ways of women. "Yes. Let's go."

Delia's cell phone rang again. She stepped outside to answer it.

"I'm going to hang around the diner awhile," Ollie said. "Delia might need some help."

"Okay. I'll see you both later." There was the proof I needed that Ollie was interested in Delia. I was happy to see it.

Miguel and I got into his Mercedes. He pulled out into the Saturday afternoon traffic.

I was wondering if I should throw out a few more hints or let him pick up on it by himself. I decided it would be a waste of my great dress, and Delia's makeup talents, not to try sending a few ideas his way.

"I didn't think I'd be going to police headquarters again until Monday with the food truck," I told him. "Lucky for me I don't have to dress up when I'm making biscuit bowls."

"I suppose so." He glanced at my dress. "That could be a mess if you had flour all over it."

Okay.

"Delia is a good person. I appreciate you representing her. She wants to be a hairdresser when this is over. She did my eyes. Good, huh?"

"Very nice." Miguel didn't even look at me that time.

Maybe he wasn't ready yet. Or maybe I wasn't very good at this anymore, like I had been in college. I used to be good at catching a man's eye. Probably all of that skill had deserted me while I'd been safely dating Tommy Lee. *Use it or lose it.*

When we reached police headquarters, Miguel parked the car and came around to open my door. I decided to try one last time to get his attention.

Carelessly, I dropped my handbag on the ground at his feet. "Oops. Sorry." I bent over to pick up everything that had spilled out.

Being a gentleman, Miguel helped me. It was still daylight, the sun shining off the car and windows in the building. I knew he had to be on eye level with my neckline and the little gold cross Delia had let me wear.

"No problem." He politely handed me my bag.

That was it for me. Miguel wasn't into it. Better to focus on what I had to say to Detective Latoure.

The police station was less crowded than the last time I'd been there. The officer at the desk called Patti Latoure for us. A few minutes later he told us to go back to the office on the right.

Dismally, I regretted wearing my good dress. I wasn't sure if the chairs we'd sat on were grimy or had gum on them. If Miguel had noticed me at all, it wouldn't have been so bad.

"Miguel." Patti shook his hand as we walked into his office. "Zoe. What brings the two of you in on such a nice Saturday?"

"We have some information about Terry's death," I told her. "It could make a difference in the case."

Patti gestured toward the two chairs in front of her desk. She sat down in the worn leather chair behind it.

"I thought I'd made it clear that you should be glad to be off the hook, Zoe. Why are you still pursuing this?"

"Let me explain." I told her about the cement block in my diner window, and about Uncle Saul's friends. "We know that Terry was probably killed because of this recipe. I know it sounds absurd, but I think that's what we're after."

Patti smiled, almost despite herself, from the wry expression on her face. "Good work, Zoe. You're right. Bannister and the man who took the Jefferson recipe have something in common. They're both dead."

"What?"

"We received word that the police in Atlanta were looking for Terry Bannister in relation to another homicide there. They think Terry Bannister took the recipe from the man in Atlanta who'd stolen it and then killed him."

I glanced at Miguel and then back at Patti. "So you've known the whole time?"

"Not the whole time. I congratulate you on finding out

about the Jefferson recipe. And I'll say it again—stay out of it. You can guess from your broken window that you're not in the clear as yet. As long as the recipe is out there, you're not safe."

"What about my client, Delia Vann?" Miguel asked. "I assume charges against her will be dropped in light of this news."

"Don't assume anything." Patti shuffled through some papers on her desk. "You know how this goes. If we drop the charges against your client, the real killer will know something is up. We want to keep him guessing. I hope we're one step ahead of him."

Miguel nodded. I could see he wasn't happy with that verdict, but he understood after years of being a prosecutor.

"Do you have any idea where the recipe is, or who paid to have it stolen?" I asked.

"We're working on that," Patti said. "It's too soon to tell. We have a person of interest we're following."

"Is that Chef Art?"

Patti frowned. "This isn't a guessing game! Stay out of it!"

"What about Don Abbott?" I ignored her. "I'm pretty sure he came after me because he knows about the recipe. I don't think he's smart enough to be the one behind all of it, do you?"

"You're very good at interrogation, Zoe. Maybe you should consider a career in law enforcement."

"I don't think so, although I'd be happy to have all of you come down to the Biscuit Bowl for lunch during the week."

Patti frowned. "Let me repeat my warning. I can't say this strongly enough. Two men have already died because of this stolen recipe. Don't make me have to explain your death to your parents."

"I appreciate the warning. Believe me, I won't be part of this anymore." I smiled, and shook her hand, after getting to my feet. "Thanks for your time."

"My pleasure." Patti nodded at Miguel. "I'll be in touch."

As we walked out of police headquarters, Miguel said, "I'm glad you're going to stay out of the investigation, Zoe. I think you've come close enough as it is."

"She didn't tell us much. At least I didn't get much out of it, besides her confirming what we already knew. Did you get more out of it than that? I mean—maybe your old DA instincts kicked in?"

He laughed. "I think you're giving Detective Latoure too much credit. She knew about the recipe and how it was stolen because the Atlanta police told her. A person of interest means she doesn't have much real proof. She's fishing for something right now. Probably hoping she can find the recipe and it will lead her to the buyer, and the killer."

"Which probably means she could use a little help." I waited for Miguel to unlock the car door and then scooted inside. "It sounded like a cry for help to me."

"Which part of what Patti said made you think she was asking for help?" Miguel put on his seat belt and started the car. "I think she was telling us to stay away from what's been happening. Just because we know about the recipe doesn't mean we have to be involved in the search for it."

"Did you see that poor woman's desk? She's so underwater, she's like a lobster! I don't think she could ask outright, but I think she could use a hand."

"Not from you." Miguel backed out of the parking space. "I think she made that very clear."

I shrugged. "I guess we heard two different things."

"Zoe, I don't want you to be on my client list again. Trust me on this. You'll only get hurt if you get involved any further."

"I won't do anything illegal," I promised. "I'd like to see that recipe, wouldn't you? And like Patti said, having the recipe in police hands would mean that I'd be safer. Delia, too. The killer won't have to go after us anymore."

"I want to go on record as being against this idea."

It was very formal, but he *was* a lawyer, after all. They tended to be a little formal—at least the ones I'd met. Believe me, my mother had thrown enough of them my way to see if any of them were marriage material.

I realized that was the downside of breaking up with Tommy Lee, too. Once I was on the market again, I'd be fair game for every relative and friend who had a single man in mind for me.

"I appreciate your help, Miguel."

"But you won't leave it alone, will you?"

"I guess we'll see. Right now, I don't have any idea how to pursue this. If something comes up . . ."

Traffic had been light on the roads back from police headquarters. We'd made the drive very quickly. Miguel parked his car outside the diner. I was ready to say good-bye and go inside. It seemed obvious to me that my romantic notions about him were only fancy.

"Zoe, anything you do could put you back on the killer's radar," Miguel argued. "If you find out anything, promise me you'll give the information to the police."

"I will."

He didn't look like he believed me. "Be careful."

I got out of the car and went around to the driver's side. I could see, through the new plate glass, that Delia and Ollie were cooking something. I thought I might as well ask Miguel if he wanted to stay and eat.

He didn't seem to even think about the question before answering. "I'd love to, but I have a desk full of paperwork that needs to be done. I'll talk to you later, Zoe."

I watched the Mercedes pull back out into traffic, feeling properly rebuffed. Maybe I thought Miguel was cute, but I was beginning to feel that he didn't share my view of a possible relationship between us.

Maybe what people had said about him—that he was still grieving for his wife—was true. It was depressing thinking about it. Since I didn't want to share those feelings with Delia and Ollie, I put on a big smile and went into the diner.

The aromas from the cooking food were heavenly. Delia and Ollie suddenly seemed to be very close. They were laughing and working on dinner. Ollie snaked one long arm around Delia, supposedly to get the cayenne. I'm sure Delia and I both knew better.

"Zoe!" Ollie finally noticed me. "We thought we'd start dinner. I hope that's okay. Delia is a wonderful cook."

"That's fine," I told him brightly. "What is it? It smells great."

Delia's face was flushed from the heat of the stove. I thought she'd never looked prettier, even without all the makeup she wore when she was working at the bar.

"It's an old recipe my granny used to make," she explained. "You had all the ingredients. I wanted to do something for you. You've been so kind to me. I didn't expect you back for dinner, but that's okay."

"I can't wait to try it. I'm going to change clothes. I'll be right back."

I felt a little out of place. I could hear Ollie and Delia laughing and talking while I was in the bathroom putting on jeans and a blue tank top. Clearly, they were interested in each other. I didn't want to intrude.

On the other hand, it wasn't like I had someplace else to go. I was happy for them. I let go of my disappointment with Miguel and joined them.

By the time I'd fed Crème Brûlée, dinner was sizzling on the plates. We sat down to eat together. Delia and Ollie asked what I'd learned from the police.

"It wasn't exactly a give-and-take of ideas," I explained.

Delia nudged Ollie with her elbow. "You can tell she hasn't spent much time with law enforcement. It's never a give-and-take with them, Zoe. They pump you for information and then send you on your way."

Ollie agreed. "It's the nature of the beast. They don't want you to know what they're doing. You're supposed to tell them everything *you're* doing."

I chewed and swallowed some of the spicy peppers, sausage, and onions. "At least I know that what my uncle's friends told him was true. There *is* a stolen Jefferson recipe, and it's valuable enough to make someone kill for it."

"What's it for, the recipe?" Delia asked.

"Crème brûlée," I explained. "It seems that Jefferson brought that recipe, and others, back from France when he went there in 1784. The recipe is written in his own hand."

"And that's what makes it valuable," Ollie said. "Valuable to some people, anyway. Collectors, I imagine."

I told them what Uncle Saul's friend had estimated the value of the recipe to be. Ollie let out a long, low whistle. Delia smiled and shook her head.

"I'm not sure exactly where to go from here." I explained about Chef Art Arrington. "I was thinking I could go out there and ask him, see what his response would be."

"No!" Delia said loudly.

Ollie also disagreed. "I remember him. He sounds like bad news to me, young 'un. Let the police take the risks. That's what they get paid for. Besides, they know what they're doing. You stick to making food."

I was surprised that they didn't think it was a good idea to circumvent the system. After all, they had both lived outside the system for a long time. Their responses made me rethink a plan to get in to see Chef Art.

Ollie hung around until after midnight, regaling us with his funny stories. He had to be doing this for Delia. Mostly, Ollie didn't have so much to say.

I enjoyed their company. Watching the two of them together, I could see a new romance budding. I loved seeing friends find each other. It made me feel a little lonely, in this case. I knew I'd get over it, and I was happy for them.

Delia quickly burst that bubble after Ollie went back to

the homeless shelter. We were talking as we got ready for bed. I teased her a little about her and Ollie.

Her pretty face became dead serious. "Women like me don't have happily ever after, Zoe. That's a Hollywood myth. We don't suddenly meet good-hearted eligible bachelors who decide to marry us and take us away to a new life."

I sat next to her on the rollaway bed while she brushed her long, dark hair. "Are you saying that you can't fall in love with someone like Ollie?"

"I'm betting we're only a few years apart in age, Zoe. But we're a lifetime apart in experience." She smiled at me a little sadly. "I'm not saying it can't happen. They say miracles happen every day. But even men who aren't so eligible, like Ollie, don't want to marry women like me. I've got no prospects except this body and this face. It's just a fact of life, girl. Don't get all blue about it. I'm okay. When this is over, I'll go back to my life. You'll become a famous restaurant owner. It's the way the world works."

We finally said good night. I thought about her words for a long time after I lay down with Crème Brûlée.

I didn't agree with her. I couldn't agree. Dreams had to be able to come true. Delia was only saying what other people had said to her. I decided right then and there that she would never go back to waiting tables in a smoky bar again.

Was working in a food truck any better?

I wasn't sure. I fell asleep with the question on my mind.

- - - - - - -

The next day was Sunday. Normally, this was the day I had dinner with my family. I'd hoped that since I was supposed to be with Uncle Saul, I might get away from what was sure to be a depressing event.

No such luck.

I was cooking eggplant—cubed and fried—in a delicious caramel sauce when my mother called and requested my presence.

I guessed my father told her what happened. He wasn't ever good at keeping things from her.

I didn't want to go but I knew I didn't have much choice. My father was footing the bill for Delia's legal work, after all. I took a shower, changed clothes, and called a taxi to take me to my mother's house on Julia Way.

The big, old-fashioned houses in this part of Mobile were wonderful examples of Southern house art, circa 1800s. Nothing was spared from the architecture and design. The houses were like elegant old ladies, dressed in their iron lace and clapboard finery. They weren't as colorful as some of the other areas around the city. They were far too refined to be gaudy.

The house I grew up in had been in my mother's family for generations. It was grand and elegant. The grounds took up more than an acre on Julia Way. The gardens had been featured in *Southern Living* magazine more than once. There was a private, walled courtyard, and a guesthouse in the back.

The green lawn was smooth and well kept, and the large oak trees dripped with Spanish moss. Flower beds were carefully cultivated for the season, nothing too provocative. My mother wanted a little color, but nothing that would call extra, unwanted attention to the house.

I walked up to the wraparound porch where I'd played as a child. June, my mother's housekeeper, greeted me at the door. There was never a cobweb at the top of the twelve-foot ceilings, never a dust bunny in a corner.

It had been a fun place to grow up with all the little places to hide, and even a secret passage that came out at the triple back-to-back fireplaces. When my mother got mad because I quit violin lessons without telling her, I hid for hours in there. Uncle Saul finally found me.

Dinner was almost as much fun as going to the dentist. There were outbursts followed by long moments of icy silence between courses.

I applauded my mother's chef, Wesley, on his choice of rhubarb and pork ragout. It was inspired.

He bowed his head and thanked me. "Do you catch a hint of something different?"

I closed my eyes. "Nutmeg?"

He had a satisfied expression on his face when he left the room. It was always wonderful to talk to someone who loved food as much as I did.

I followed Uncle Saul's advice and stood my ground through the arugula salad with caramelized onions and goat cheese. I wasn't going to marry Tommy Lee, and I wasn't giving up my food truck.

"Reason with her," my mother demanded of my father while we ate bisque of tomato soup made from fresh tomatoes.

"What am I supposed to say? She sounds like she's made up her mind, Anabelle."

I'd pretty much been a disappointment all my life, except for a few brief years after college. Why change now?

My mother even pretended to cry as I enjoyed my lemon sponge cake. I'd never seen her actually shed a tear—talk about steel magnolias. When she went through the effort to appear as though she was crying, I knew how serious the matter was.

Of course, the botched kidnapping attempt should've given me a heads-up. I guess I was too wrapped up in everything else that was happening to really take offense at it.

My father, bless his heart, kept trying to find a compromise, smooth the way, as he always did. It seemed as though we were too far apart on this one. I was refusing to give up my dream, and they were adamant that it had no place in my life.

After a few painful hours of being together, I said good night and left the house.

It was pleasant to draw my first deep breath since I'd arrived there as I waited for the taxi I called. I was glad that ordeal was over.

I heard a footstep in the darkness, and had turned to see if it was my father, when someone dropped a smelly cloth bag over my head, picked me up, and put me roughly into the back of a car.

Again.

NINETEEN

I couldn't believe it. Were my parents so desperate that they'd try the same thing *twice*?

I could only assume my kidnapper wasn't Uncle Saul this time. I felt sure they'd learned their lesson about using friendly relatives to get the job done.

It scared me a little, even though I knew they wouldn't let someone hurt me in the process of trying to change my mind. Had they hired a mercenary, or some professional brainwasher, to get me to give up my dream?

The car started moving. The interior smelled like those big, stinky cigars, brandy, and expensive leather.

I tried to get my thoughts together. The best way to combat this was to demand to be released—and to offer more money to my abductor than my parents had offered.

The hood was snatched off my head. At that point, I didn't even care how badly my curls were mangled. I put on an angry, defiant face as my eyes adjusted to the dimly lit interior of a limousine.

What?

They'd hired a really expensive kidnapper who apparently provided limousine service. That took me back an instant. Who drives a limousine and kidnaps young women who disagree with their parents? The trade must be very lucrative.

"Good evening, Miss Chase."

I focused on the cultured, very Old-South voice. I looked across and saw the face of my abductor.

"Chef Art?"

I would've known that face anywhere. He was like Colonel Sanders and Emeril rolled into one—my first cooking idol.

Art Arrington was a big man, not so tall, it seemed, as very round. His gray beard was closely clipped on his large face. His hair was a snowy wreath around his head. He wore a white linen suit and a red string tie.

This was the face of restaurant success to me. If I hadn't been so angry, I would've asked for his autograph. He was more myth than man. What I wouldn't have given to be able to stand side by side cooking *anything* with him.

It was hard, but I had to put aside all that hero worship. The man had abducted me and was driving me around in his limousine—I had no idea where. I was pretty sure I knew why.

"I'm glad to see you recognize me." Chef Art smiled and offered me a glass of wine. "I have some lovely chocolates that pair delightfully with this vintage. Would you care to try some?"

"I don't think so. Thanks." It was all I could do to keep from grinning at him like a kid. "Why am I here?"

"I think you probably know the answer to that, Miss Chase. May I call you Zoe?"

"No, you may not. Don't play games with me. Tell me what you want."

He sighed heavily, as though his words were a burden on

him. "I want what every man wants. Life, liberty, and the pursuit of happiness. That doesn't seem like too much to ask, does it?"

"Not to mention the handwritten copy of a recipe for crème brûlée that Thomas Jefferson brought to this country in the 1700s."

Smiling like a possum caught in the trash can, Chef Art agreed. "Why, yes. What an astute young woman you are."

"Thanks." I wasn't sure where this conversation was leading. The limousine kept driving through the dark streets. I realized this could get ugly if Chef Art thought I was standing between him and the Jefferson recipe.

I waited, heart pounding, for him to make the next move.

"Did Terry Bannister give you the recipe?"

"I barely knew him. Why would he give me anything?"

"Good point." He made a pyramid of his fingers and studied me across them. "Now that I have a good look at you, I don't think you killed anyone. You're from a good family, with deep roots in the community. You've lived an ordinary life—until recently. What was that all about? I confess that I originally thought you had to know about the recipe, and that's why you'd quit your job."

Though the first part of his assessment was true, it was also irritating. How many people were going to tell me that I had lived a very ordinary life?

The last part was so far from what was happening that I thought he must be delusional. "And now?"

"Now that I see what you're doing—the food truck and that terrible greasy spoon—I realize you've simply made a mistake in your life track. It happens all the time. You'll do a course correction, and go back to your trivial life again soon. Don't worry."

"Thanks for that. I don't see this as being a mistake. I can't believe *you* do." I glared at him even though it may have been lost in the dim lighting.

"All of my life, you've been my idol. I've always wanted

to be like you. You loved food before it was fashionable. You took big chances, like opening the Carriage House restaurant in New York. I thought for sure, if anyone would understand, it would be you."

He smiled. "Flattery will get you everywhere. Would you like my autograph?"

I crossed my arms against my chest. "No. You said terrible things about me and my dream of opening a successful restaurant. You thought I killed Terry for the recipe. You're not who I thought you were."

An expression crossed his broad face that I can only explain as regret. *Probably nothing to do with me.* I had convinced him that I didn't have the recipe. I'd interfered with his dream.

"I'm truly sorry, Miss Chase."

I wasn't about to give in that easily. I glared back at him, my breath coming fast.

"How can I make it up to you?" His eyes roamed the interior of the car as though it would give him inspiration. "I could make a public appearance at your food truck. Would that help?"

I was a little excited about that idea, if the offer was real. Chef Art's personality still meant a lot to the people of Mobile. I might get some TV or radio coverage from it.

When I didn't answer right away, he said, "How about if I invite you to one of the benefit dinners at my home *and* make a public appearance at your food truck?"

That was even more exciting.

Chef Art's benefit dinners were famous. People came from around the world to eat the food he, and his guest chefs, had created. They paid a hefty price for the meal and the chance to mingle with celebrities. I could never hope to get into one of those dinners on my own.

Along with the public appearance, I was pretty sure I could forgive him almost anything. "Deal. You invite me to the dinner, and make an appearance at my food truck, and I'll forget this ever happened."

He stuck his hand toward me, gaudy rings on every finger. "You drive a hard bargain. I may be wrong about your potential. Forgive me for thinking you had the Jefferson recipe."

"That's quite all right. How about Wednesday at noon for the appearance? I don't know why, but Wednesday is always a big lunch day."

"Wednesday is hump day. People want to think about the coming weekend and eat well for a change," he explained. "Wednesday it is. Where will your food truck be?"

"I'm working the parking lot outside police headquarters on Government Street. You can't miss my food truck. It's the only one with the spinning biscuit on top."

He laughed loud and long. "Brilliant! I'll be there. I'll have my social secretary get in touch with you about the benefit dinner. It was wonderful meeting you, Zoe Chase."

The driver had already stopped the limousine and was opening the door for me. We were parked outside the diner. I hadn't even thought to look out.

I thanked Chef Art—even though he'd kidnapped me. My disrupted ride home in a taxi was nothing compared to what he'd promised.

Hundreds of ideas ran through my mind as the limousine pulled out of the parking lot and I went into the diner. I'd spoken to the woman on the local radio station that did food truck announcements during the week. I couldn't remember her name, but I knew her business card had to be in the diner somewhere. I could tell her about Chef Art's appearance.

I told Delia about what had happened. She wasn't as impressed as I was with the unexpected turn of events.

"Zoe, if Chef Art thought you had the recipe, so do other people."

"I know. But he's going to make a personal appearance at my food truck Wednesday, and he invited me to his benefit dinner! This is much bigger news. We already knew people think one of us has the recipe."

She took my hand as though she wanted to say something. I waited and let her gather her thoughts.

"I hadn't realized Chef Art was involved in all of the things that are going on right now." Delia frowned and her bottom lip trembled. "He was my date the night Terry was killed."

"What are you saying?" I thought back to that night. I remembered the big green Lincoln that had picked her up at the corner. The car had come from the back of the parking lot. "You think Chef Art killed Terry?"

Delia shushed me as though someone else was in the next room spying on us. "I've kept it a secret this whole time because I know he's a wealthy and powerful man. I didn't want to say anything. Terry's dead. I'd like to stay alive a little longer."

I sat down on one of the stools at the counter. All of my exciting new dreams were starting to crash. I couldn't believe Chef Art would kill Terry for the Jefferson recipe. But then, I couldn't believe *anyone* would kill Terry for it.

I had to consider that Chef Art had been desperate enough to risk kidnapping me to ask if I had the recipe. He could've been motivated enough to kill Terry.

"This is terrible," I whispered back. "He could change everything for me. Just him being at the food truck could get a lot of publicity. It would be like the seal of approval from a man everyone here knows and loves."

"You should keep it that way," Delia said. "Let's get through this in one piece, Zoe. Let the police handle it. If they catch him, fine. If not, oh well. I'm not testifying against him in court. I don't want the police to know what I just told you."

I stared at her beautiful face, which I had envied since I'd first seen her. "We have to tell Detective Latoure. What if he killed Terry for the recipe? He could kill someone else."

"That's *their* problem. I'm not repeating what I told you. You can go to the police if you want to, but I'm not going to be part of it."

"You could go to jail for killing Terry. Surely it's worth that much of your life to turn Chef Art in to the police."

She shook her head. "From what Miguel told me, the police are looking in another direction now. It may be that they're looking at Chef Art, for all we know. Anyway, I don't think they're gonna want me for much longer. I'm going to keep my mouth shut and ride this storm out. You'd be smart if you did the same."

There wasn't much else to say on the matter. I cooked my savory biscuit bowl filling for the next day, and made my sweet fillings. Even after the setup was done, and Delia and I were in bed for the night, I still thought about what she'd told me.

I couldn't prove anything if she wouldn't cooperate. It would be my word against hers—and hearsay at that. I knew enough about the law from my mother to know that it was less than useless.

I couldn't say it to anyone else, but I whispered my fears and misgivings to Crème Brûlée that night. He seemed to understand. He bit my finger as I stroked his soft fur—then he licked my whole hand. It seemed to make us both feel better.

- - - - - - -

The alarm clock went off early the next morning. I dragged myself out of bed without my usual enthusiasm. Ollie was knocking on the door before I finished dressing. Together, he, Delia, and I got everything out to the food truck and set up for what I hoped would be a busy day. I put Crème Brûlée in his bed last after he'd finished eating.

Ollie sat beside me as we drove to police headquarters. Delia rode in the back. I thought about telling Ollie what Delia had told me last night. I wanted someone to convince Delia to tell the police about Chef Art.

Ollie clearly wasn't the best choice for this. He talked about how wonderful Delia was almost nonstop. The rest of the time, he was asking me questions about her. He wouldn't be objective. With his major crush on Delia, it seemed unlikely that he'd take my side in the matter. I didn't say anything to him about my meeting with Chef Art or my talk with Delia.

I wished Miguel were there. He might be able to convince Delia to help the police. I knew he wouldn't like it that I was trying to interfere again, but Chef Art had been the one who'd come to me. Why wouldn't Delia tell Patti Latoure about him?

The parking area at police headquarters was quiet and empty when we reached it. I claimed my spot and prayed for good weather. The weatherman was calling for sunshine and moderate temperatures. It was a perfect day to grab lunch outside and enjoy the sun.

Ollie set up the tables and chairs. He swung open the doors and erased Friday's menu from the chalkboard. "Are we selling eggs again today?"

"No." I was trying to get things set up inside. "Spicy sausage gravy in a biscuit bowl for breakfast. The savory filling is pimento macaroni and cheese. Sweet filling is a choice of cinnamon apple with a slice of cheddar, or custard with nutmeg."

"Okay."

Delia stopped me as I was getting ready to deep-fry the first load of biscuits. "You didn't say anything to Ollie, did you?"

She looked worried. I felt bad for even thinking of telling him. "No. I won't say anything to Ollie."

"Thanks, Zoe." Delia seemed relieved. She started right in by taking out the apples and slicing the cheese.

Outside, our first customers of the day were ready for biscuit bowls with sausage gravy. I'd put a little extra cayenne into the gravy. One man was surprised when he tasted it, raising his eyebrows and fanning his mouth with his hand.

"Hot!" He bought two more to take upstairs with him. He told Delia that he was a lawyer representing a man the police were questioning for robbery that day.

"Well, you'll need all the extra spice you can get then, won't you?" She smiled and winked at him as she gave him his biscuits. "Don't forget to stop by for lunch. We have some really good pimento cheese and macaroni."

"Will do. Thanks."

"Don't forget to say thank you," I murmured after he was gone.

"Sorry. I felt like we had a connection. I didn't want to waste it. I'll say thank you from now on."

The rest of the day was a repeat performance of the early morning. We were swamped with customers until about ten. That slowdown gave us enough time to get ready for the eleven-thirty crowd.

The Dog House was there again, late. I wasn't giving up my prime spot today. Suzette's Crepes was missing, but Charlie's Tuna Shack showed up. There was also a food truck I hadn't seen—Yolanda's Yummy Yogurt. Yolanda offered fresh fruit mixed into homemade yogurt. I saw people walking over there after leaving our food truck. Some went straight for the yogurt.

Yolanda's food truck was decorated with fruits that hung from the sides like fish in nets. They also played Bob Marley music to attract customers.

"Maybe we should play music," I suggested.

"Nah." Ollie didn't like that idea. "It would probably throw off as many people as you'd get from it, Zoe."

"I don't know," Delia said. "Maybe something jazzy and cool might be good."

I tabled all of the music ideas as the lunch crowd got busy.

It was all we could do to keep up with the customers waiting at the window. I was seriously worried about running out of macaroni and cheese. The food was bulky in the small container I had for it. The soupier savories went further.

Around twelve thirty, I took out my last bowl of macaroni and cheese. There were plenty of biscuits today. It was hard getting the exact number right without knowing how many people would show up. If I made too much of any food, it could go to waste and cut into my budget. If I didn't make enough, my customers would go somewhere else.

Things started slacking off again at about one thirty. Good thing, too, because I saw my mother seated at one of the café tables. She was staring at the food truck with an occasional angry glare at the spinning biscuit on top.

"I think that woman out there may be an unhappy customer." Delia pointed to her. "If I didn't know better, I'd think she was giving us the evil eye."

I took off my apron. "That's my mother. The only thing she can do is stare at us until we catch fire. Could you two handle the truck for a few minutes?"

"Sure," Ollie said. "Take all the time you need. I'd feel better if you sit so she can't see us."

I laughed at that. That stare my mother was giving us was a winning technique for her in the courtroom. She was famous for it, but I hadn't been afraid of it for a very long time.

TWENTY

"Mother." I sat opposite her with my back to the food truck to hide Delia and Ollie from her angry eyes.

"Zoe."

"Nice day, huh?" I looked around at the sunshine and the blue sky above us. "If you're hungry—"

"Do you *really* think I'd eat food from a truck in a parking lot?"

"It's *my* truck," I reminded her. "I made the food."

"That doesn't change my feelings on the matter."

I tried not to get angry or offended by her attitude. Sometimes it was hard.

"Then why are you here?"

She took a deep breath. "I wanted to talk to you, alone—without your father. I was really hurt when you sneaked out of the restaurant and left us there with Tommy Lee and your engagement ring."

"I was very hurt that you thought Uncle Saul should

kidnap me and drag me into the swamp with him so I'd lose my business."

"I don't think that's the same thing at all. I'm talking about *family*. You still remember that word, don't you? You're talking about this crazy thing that you're doing that's ruining your life."

"I won't ever forget that you're my family. I love you and Daddy. But you can't tell me how to live my life anymore. I love my business, too, and I'm starting to be successful at it."

She made a hissing noise, not unlike the one Crème Brûlée makes right before he bites. I'd never noticed the similarities before.

"You're selling greasy food that you make in an old diner, out of a motor home that scares me when I look at it. Why would you consider this to be successful?"

I knew I could never explain it to her. I wasn't even going to try anymore. When she was standing in line outside my fabulously famous restaurant, hoping to get a table, she'd understand. *Maybe*.

"And I'm not marrying Tommy Lee. I know you love him. I know his parents love me. We're not right for each other."

"If it's about that girl from the bank, men sometimes lose their way, Zoe. We have to make allowances for them."

"Seriously? Did Daddy—?"

Her normally pale face turned a little red. She glanced away, as though she didn't want to meet my eyes.

I took that as a yes.

"I'm sorry." I think it was the first time in my life that I empathized with her. I loved my father, but I suppose I always knew something was up with the many scenic vacations that he took alone.

"That's neither here nor there. And if you don't want to marry Tommy Lee, I'm certainly not going to try and force you to do so." She took my hand and leaned forward across the table. "But Zoe, look at the people you're making friends with now. Who is that tall man with the tattoo, and the woman in the tight shorts with too much eye makeup?"

"I hired them to work with me." I didn't plan to help make her point about the quality of my friends.

"And that lawyer you've been hanging around with." She scowled. "I hope you aren't seeing him as a replacement for Tommy Lee. He's a lawyer, so that's in his favor. But he dropped out of the real world. He actually represents a lot of felons—at least that's what I've heard."

"Like *me*?" I felt the argument coming and tried to keep it from happening. "There's nothing between us, Mother. He was there the night the police found Terry in my food truck. He was nice to me. That's it."

"Except that you're having your father pay him to represent your friend, the cocktail waitress." She nodded at Delia.

She'd known all along. She probably knew Ollie lived at the homeless shelter, too. I had no doubt that she'd made it her business to know everything that I was doing.

"It's true. It doesn't mean anything about me and Miguel. I wish you and I wouldn't always go between not talking at all and arguing. We used to talk, when I was in school."

She smiled in a superior fashion. "That was back when you were willing to listen to reason."

I got up. "I have to go. Once lunch is over, it's time to go home. I'll talk to you later."

"Everything doesn't have to be good or bad between us." She stood up, too, and hugged me. "Let me help you. I know you're in debt for all of this. Let's move on, okay?"

"I'm not done with *all of this*. This is my life. You can be part of it, or we can live in the same city and never see each other. I agree about moving on, but not in the direction you want."

I went inside the food truck and hid, knowing she'd leave. Ollie and Delia looked at me like I was a stupid kid. I'm sure they were listening. Both of them were so far removed from having arguments with their parents. It made me feel young.

"She's gone," Delia said. "I'm sorry you're having family trouble."

Ollie snorted as he laughed. "I haven't seen anyone in my family in over ten years. At least you still *have* a family, Zoe. You should work it out with them—except that she's totally wrong about Miguel."

I thanked them and got busy cleaning. Delia and Ollie were laughing and joking as they were outside cleaning the tables and chairs.

Looking at the cash drawer, I could see we'd had a great day. I wasn't crazy enough to sit there and count it, but the drawer looked pretty full. We'd still have a few people who'd stop on their way home after work. There were still biscuit bowls to sell.

Miguel stopped by on his way into police headquarters. He told Delia that the police were going to drop the charges against her.

"Thank you so much." She hugged him in response. "You're the best."

"I appreciate that. Try to stay out of trouble. The police, and whoever killed Terry, are still looking for the Jefferson recipe. I don't know that they won't have another go at you."

Delia and I exchanged looks. I wanted to urge her to tell Miguel about Chef Art being in the parking lot the night Terry was killed.

"I'll watch my back." Delia didn't mention it. "I've done it for a long time."

"Are you going to look for another place to live and work?" he asked.

"I don't know yet." She smiled at me. "I've really enjoyed working with Zoe. I'd like to stay on, if she'll have me."

"Of course. You're a lot better at the window than Ollie. Customers aren't crazy about his mean look."

Ollie wasn't happy with that. "I'm good at the window.

I kept that jerk from taking your money, didn't I? But if you want to keep me making savory fillings, that's okay, too."

"You can always scare off thieves," Delia said. "You're close enough to put your big, handsome face in the window when I give you the signal."

"Handsome, huh?" Ollie viewed himself in the stainless steel plate on the food truck wall. "You're right. I can keep the biscuit bowls coming, and still scare off people I don't like."

He made his mean face, obviously knowing exactly what I'd been talking about. We all laughed. Miguel said he had to go inside and talk to Detective Latoure.

I accompanied him out of the food truck. I wouldn't give away Delia's secret about Chef Art, but I could keep Miguel up to speed by telling him about being kidnapped.

"Are you okay?" he asked when I told him about what had happened.

"I'm fine. He didn't try to hurt me, or even threaten me. He wants the recipe. I think he may be involved with what happened to Terry. Maybe even before that—to Terry's friend in Atlanta."

I'd already walked up the stairs to police headquarters with him. At the large concrete landing, we stood and talked for a few minutes.

"Without proof, there's nothing Detective Latoure can do," he told me. "I'll tell her about Chef Art. She won't like it. Nobody wants to go after a beloved icon. Still, it would be worth her knowing so she can keep an eye on him."

"I might be able to help with that proof." I hadn't planned on saying anything to Miguel about the benefit dinner, but I needed a date for that night, and he sprang to mind. I figured the worst he could say was that he was too busy.

"That sounds a little risky, Zoe," he said after I'd explained about the dinner.

"Maybe not as much if I'm not *alone*," I hinted. "I could bring someone with me."

He frowned. "I don't know about Ollie in a group like that."

I wondered if he was *completely* obtuse. "I was thinking about *you*, Miguel. You know all about the recipe. You'd be good to have there as backup."

"Let me know about the date, and I'll try to go," he said. "I still don't know if that's a good idea. It could be dangerous if Chef Art is involved in this."

"He's not going to be able to do much. There will be a ton of famous people there, and chefs making all kinds of food. It might be hard for him to step out and kill someone."

Miguel agreed. "Keep me updated."

I watched him walk inside the building. It was a little victory—he hadn't entirely blown me off. He didn't seem very excited about it.

Ollie, Delia, and I sat around playing cards for a while. Business was very slow until about four thirty. A trickle of late lunch customers stopped by then and took food home with them for dinner.

I wrote a supply note. I was quickly running out of to-go boxes. I hadn't planned on using so many. They weren't cheap, either, but if customers wanted them, I'd have to keep them in stock.

By five thirty, the building seemed to mostly be empty. The other food trucks were leaving. We were securing everything so we could do the same. It had been a good day in many different ways. I knew Delia was happy not to be under suspicion for Terry's death, and I was happy that Miguel might go with me to the benefit dinner.

We drove back to the diner. Nothing seemed to be out of place, or broken. I hoped whoever was responsible for hurting Marty, and throwing the cement block through my window, was busy looking in another direction.

I thought about Chef Art again. I knew Miguel was right. The police wouldn't want to confront him. Still, the timing, and his motivation for killing Terry, seemed to make him a perfect suspect.

I figured he thought Terry had the recipe with him. Maybe he'd planned to buy it from him. Something went wrong, and Terry died. Now, the Jefferson recipe was lost again. If Chef Art had killed these men, he probably wouldn't be satisfied until he found it.

There wasn't a lot of food leftover to take to the homeless shelter. Ollie and I took what we had. All of the men seemed grateful for it. I talked with Marty for a while to see how he was getting on after being mugged on my behalf. I made sure he got biscuit bowls with sweet and savory before anyone else.

"I'm fine," he told me. "Still worried about you, Zoe. People have been killed for this recipe. I don't want that to happen to you."

"I don't, either," I agreed. "I think the person looking for the recipe may understand that I don't have it."

"Why do you say that?"

I told him about my conversation with Chef Art. "I think he believed me about not having the recipe. I guess we'll see if things get quiet again around here."

"I guess we will. But be careful in case it isn't true."

We talked about how things were going at the shelter. I finally said good night and went back to the diner. Crème Brûlée was cranky because he hadn't been fed immediately when we got back from police headquarters. I endured his love bites and let him lick them. Afterward, he settled down, purring, and I went in to make a little something to eat.

Ollie had stayed at the shelter. Delia was making herself a grilled cheese sandwich. I let her make one for me, too. We ate them with only coffee to drink. Every meal doesn't have to be elaborate. I was too tired to do anything more than get ready for the next day.

Delia helped me with the dessert fillings. I made another

batch of Ollie's gumbo, since that had gone over well last week. We didn't talk much. I guess we were both tired.

Once the food was ready for Tuesday, Delia yawned. "I love working with you, Zoe. But these hours are killing me. Who gets up before noon?"

"People who want to sell breakfast biscuit bowls and have the best spot for lunch." I yawned, too. It was contagious.

"I guess so. I appreciate you paying me today. Working with you is the first money I've made during daylight hours in a long time."

I had been happy to pay Delia and Ollie fifty dollars each for their help that day. I'd been surprised by how much money we'd brought in. At that rate, I'd have some savings put away toward my restaurant in no time.

"I was glad to have you there." I started to ask her again about Chef Art, and if she might change her mind about taking that information to the police. Really, I was too tired to argue about it again. Tomorrow would be another day.

Nothing unusual happened that night. It gave me the sense that I'd been right about Chef Art being behind the theft of the Jefferson recipe, and possibly Terry's death. I wasn't sure why he'd believed me when I'd told him that I didn't have the recipe, but I was glad of it. Trying to get my business up and running was hard enough. I didn't need the extra strain of dealing with those other problems.

- - - - - - -

I got up right away when the alarm went off at four A.M. Crème Brûlée protested my moving him on the bed by clutching my arm in his two little paws. It would've been sweet, except for his slightly extended claws. They left tiny red imprints in my arm, not quite breaking the skin.

"Why do I put up with you?" I stared into his unhappy face.

He licked my nose to apologize, and I forgave him.

"I'm going to feed you right away, and I want you to use

the litter box before we go." There had been a minor potty accident yesterday. I knew he'd needed more time before I rushed him out of the diner.

He looked like he understood. When I put his food down, he ate right away. I left him there, and went to take a shower and get dressed. The weather forecast looked good again for that day. It was supposed to continue to be clear until Thursday. That would give me a nice day for my Chef Art event. I planned to call everyone I could think of to come out to the Biscuit Bowl tomorrow.

I was a little worried that I might tell everyone that he would be there, and then he wouldn't show. On the other hand, if no one knew he was coming, my publicity would be limited to the people going in and out of police headquarters.

It seemed to me that I was better off taking a chance that he wouldn't stand me up.

He probably wouldn't, I thought as the water from the shower sluiced down over me. After all, I could still press charges against him for kidnapping. I didn't want to do that. I wanted Chef Art as my friend, not my enemy—unless he was a killer. That was yet to be seen, as my mother always said.

I put on a clean pair of jeans and a Biscuit Bowl T-shirt. I'd had dozens of the shirts made when I first started out. It was too bad the company I ordered them from hadn't done a good job sewing them. I could only wear each one a couple of times before it began to fall apart.

I still had a few new ones for Wednesday. I knew the sizes I had would fit me and Delia. I wasn't sure about Ollie. I had to remember to have him try one on so I could be pre-pared for tomorrow. My plan was to go out and buy him a plain blue T-shirt, if nothing else, so at least the colors would match when we were on TV.

I dried my curls as I was thinking about adding sage to the savory biscuits. I was making glazed strawberries for my sweet biscuit bowls.

I realized I hadn't seen or even heard Delia since I got up. Maybe her alarm clock wasn't working or she needed an extra nudge. Like she'd said, she was used to going to bed at this time and not getting up until noon. It was quite a time shift for her.

I went over to her bed and put my hand down to shake her. There was no one there.

TWENTY-ONE

I turned on the big light. Maybe she'd walked around me in the dark to the bathroom.

No.

I searched the diner, even the back part that I didn't use. She wasn't anywhere inside.

I turned on all the lights and went back to the roll-away bed.

Delia wasn't there, but something else was.

Chef Art had promised me an invitation to the benefit dinner at his home. The invitation, printed on harvest yellow stationery, in flowery script font, was on the bed in her place.

I called the police.

It only took a few minutes for Officers Schmidt and Gayner to respond.

I met them outside. "My roommate, Delia, has been kidnapped."

Officer Schmidt nodded and yawned. "You know, another hour and we would've been off duty."

"What makes you think she's been kidnapped, ma'am?" Officer Gayner asked.

"You know the kind of things that have been going on here." I didn't feel like I needed to brief them. "I got up this morning. She was gone. All I found in her place was this invitation."

Officer Schmidt looked at the invitation. "You're a lucky lady. My wife would kill to be invited to one of these dinners." He smiled at his partner. "I'd kill not to have to go with her."

"Was there a disturbance during the night? Did anything out of the ordinary happen?" Officer Gayner at least tried to be responsive. "Was the diner broken into? Any sign of a struggle?"

"I don't think so." I tried to think if I'd heard anything last night. I was so tired, I wasn't sure I would've heard any noise, unusual or not. "Maybe you should look around. I don't know what I'm looking for."

The two officers went inside and examined the area where Delia had been sleeping. I noticed that her few personal belongings were gone, too. Maybe she'd left. Maybe she'd decided that working with me was too hard.

"I don't see any sign of a struggle," Officer Gayner observed. "Have you tried to call her?"

"I didn't think of that." I took out my cell phone and called her number.

All three of us heard her phone ring. It was on the floor under the rollaway bed.

"She wouldn't have left without it." I tried to make a point. "Her whole life is in that phone."

Officer Schmidt took out a notebook. "What does she do for a living? What's her name?"

"She works with me here in the diner and on my food truck. Her name is Delia Vann."

The officers exchanged knowing glances.

"She's good-looking, light brown skin, long hair?" Officer Schmidt asked.

"Yes. That's her," I agreed.

Officer Gayner said, "Yeah. We know her. She's working with you now?"

"Yes. Can you call something in so everyone will look for her?"

Officer Schmidt put away his notebook. "We can't file a missing persons report for forty-eight hours anyway, unless there are extenuating health issues. Sorry."

"But she's not just missing." I stopped Officer Gayner from leaving the diner. "She wouldn't leave without saying anything. And why would she leave behind the invitation to Chef Art's benefit dinner and her cell phone?"

I could tell Officer Gayner wanted to believe me. He was sympathetic. "I'd like to help you. My hands are tied. If she doesn't turn up in forty-eight hours, go to the police station and file a report. The chances are she's decided not to work with you anymore, and didn't know how to say it. It happens. As for her cell phone, she'll pick up another one—one where you won't be able to reach her. Sorry."

I couldn't believe it. They walked out of the diner and got back in their car.

"What's going on?" Ollie frowned when he saw the police car.

"Delia's gone. I think someone took her. I know she wouldn't have left on her own without saying anything."

I went through the whole thing again with Ollie. He looked through the diner, and even in the food truck. There was no sign of her.

In the meantime, I called Miguel to let him know what was going on. He was there when Ollie and I were done looking around the outside of the diner.

"I'll make some coffee," Ollie volunteered. "There has to be another explanation for Delia going missing."

We sat down at the counter with mugs of coffee, Delia's cell phone, and the invitation to Chef Art's benefit dinner.

"Tell me again what Chef Art said to you in the car when he picked you up." Miguel pulled out a notebook and a pen.

I repeated my conversation with Chef Art. "I didn't want to mention this yesterday. Delia swore me to secrecy, but I think things have changed."

I told him and Ollie what Delia had said about dating Chef Art and that he had picked her up there the night Terry was killed. "I remember seeing the green Lincoln pull out of the back parking lot. I was standing on the corner, talking to her. She got in the car and it took off."

"Why didn't Delia say something?" Ollie asked.

"She didn't want to make an enemy out of Chef Art," I told him. "She said the police wouldn't go after him and she'd be stuck with him being angry for no reason."

Ollie jumped to his feet and slammed one fist into another. "I'll show him an enemy. Let's go out to his mansion right now and drag him out. He'll tell us where she is."

"I think she went with him," Miguel quietly said.

"What?" Ollie turned on him. "She wouldn't take off like that. She liked being here. She told me so herself."

"I'm not saying she didn't like being here," Miguel added. "I'm not even saying she went of her own volition. She may have agreed to go with him to spare Zoe any further problems."

"That's stupid," Ollie fumed, walking from one end of the room to the other.

"Look around. The door wasn't smashed. Delia walked out without saying anything. The fact that she left behind the invitation Chef Art said he'd send Zoe tells us he was here. That doesn't mean he had to hurt her to get her to go with him."

"You're speculating," Ollie said. "I still think we should drive out there and demand to see him. Then we can ask him some questions."

"Chef Art probably has security people," I told him. "They won't let us in."

"What about the police?" Ollie demanded. "Delia's missing."

I told him how the police had felt about that. "They won't help for at least forty-eight hours."

"We have no demands, just the invitation," Miguel argued. "We have no proof that she didn't go of her own accord."

"Chef Art is supposed to come to police headquarters tomorrow and help me promote my food truck." I realized as I said it that the chances were that he wouldn't show up now. There was no point in calling anyone and telling them about an event that wouldn't happen.

It was depressing. I was also afraid for Delia. I may have been part of making Chef Art feel that he had to kidnap her. Maybe he hadn't really believed me about not having the recipe after all. If he hurt her—I didn't even want to think about it.

It was eight A.M. by this time. I would've missed the breakfast crowd but could've still driven the Biscuit Bowl to police headquarters for lunch. I probably would've been there before most of the other food trucks anyway. My heart wasn't in it that day.

Ollie stalked back to the homeless shelter. Miguel told me he had a few friends who might know something more about Chef Art and the Jefferson recipe. I asked if I could go along. Otherwise, I was bound to sit and eat all the food I'd made for that day. I'd end up five pounds heavier and still depressed.

"That's fine," he said. "I can't guarantee anything. Since the theft of the Jefferson recipe has also involved at least two murders, we have to assume Chef Art is playing this close to the chest."

"How will he announce that he has the recipe? Won't the police want to talk to him?"

"Probably," Miguel said. "If he uses the benefit dinner to announce that he's found the recipe, he can't keep it. The only way it could help him would be with publicity. If he wanted to keep the recipe in his personal collection, he'd have to keep his mouth shut about it."

"Of course, we're only speculating that Chef Art took Delia to keep it a secret that he has the recipe." Miguel and I got in his car after I'd locked up the diner. "It makes more sense that you'll go to the dinner and Delia will be there on his arm, wearing an expensive dress. I didn't want to say that in front of Ollie. I think he likes her."

"In other words, she was protecting him because they might have a relationship." I nodded, thinking about what the two policemen had said earlier. "I really thought she liked Ollie, too."

"She probably does." He pulled the Mercedes into traffic. "But Chef Art is a wealthy man who lives in a mansion and travels the world. Why wouldn't she want to be with him?"

I could see how she could feel that way. What else did she have? My offer of working in my food truck and sleeping on a rollaway bed in a pantry didn't seem like much compared to it.

"I'm going to make a quick stop at my office, if that's okay," Miguel said. "I left my briefcase there last night." He parked the car and I went inside the building with him. It was part of the shabby-chic area of Mobile. The buildings were older but had a flair to them that came with age and money being spread around to make them popular.

I liked the area, especially the little cafés and restaurants that had opened on the ground floor of some of the buildings. They were too pricey for me to rent, which was how I'd ended up being in the old shopping center that should probably have been torn down years before. There was also a problem with higher crime rates here.

"This is nice," I said as we walked into his office. It was

very low-key, nothing extra. Only one painting of Mardi Gras on the wall.

We heard a noise outside the closed door. It sounded like someone was trying to get in.

"Do you think that's Delia?" I whispered.

"I don't know. Let's not take a chance."

Miguel and I hid behind a partial wall that separated the main part of the office from the small area that held a fax and copy machine.

I was hoping he might have a gun. I knew he didn't when he picked up a baseball bat. I grabbed a toner cartridge and crouched down behind the wall with him.

The front door opened. All the muscles in my body tensed. My heart was slamming against my chest. We watched as Don Abbott walked right by us. He seemed intent on going through the papers on Miguel's desk.

I stared into Miguel's face and mouthed, *"What now?"*

I wasn't embarrassed to admit that I was afraid. Unlike us, Don probably had a gun, and wouldn't mind using it if he found us.

The way he was going through every drawer and every tiny scrap of paper made me think it would take him a while to reach the area where we were hiding. He'd get there eventually. I wished we had some kind of plan.

Miguel did. He walked boldly out of the room with his hand in his jacket pocket. I wished he'd told me what he'd planned. I didn't know what to do.

"Mr. Abbott!" Miguel got his attention.

Don turned around sharply, an angry look of surprise on his face. "I thought you weren't here. Let me have it, Miguel. I figure you have the recipe. It won't do you any good unless you know who the buyer is."

I was relieved to see that Don didn't seem to have a gun, either. He put his hands up, like they do in the movies. Did he really believe Miguel's hand was a gun in his pocket?

"Tie him up, Zoe," Miguel said in a harsh voice.

I knew he was trying to get the upper hand with Don before he discovered the trick. I wouldn't have guessed it would really work.

I didn't waste time thinking about it. I found a curtain sash that was loose. Don sat down on a chair, and I used the sash to tie him to it. He smelled awful. I held my breath as I pulled the sash as tight as I could. I didn't know how long it would hold him. I hoped Miguel had a second part to this plan.

Once Don was secure in the chair, Miguel took his hand out of his jacket pocket and frisked him. No one had a gun. That was a relief.

Don shook his head. "Man, that's one of the oldest tricks in the book. I really thought you had a gun!"

"And you fell for it," Miguel said. "Why are you here?"

"I guess for the same reason you two are here—the recipe."

"Why do you think I have it?" Miguel stared intently at him.

"You're the only one I could think of that I haven't searched. I was thinking Biscuit Girl gave it to you."

"Biscuit Girl?" I couldn't believe he called me that.

"Yeah. I was pretty sure that Terry slipped it to you."

I started to correct his assumption.

Miguel stopped me. "We want part of the money."

Don laughed in his greasy way. "I *knew* it. Nobody's above a million dollars. We could split it, you know? You give me the recipe, and I'll tell you who we're supposed to take it to."

"You start," Miguel insisted.

Don didn't look happy about that. He launched a colorful protest, but Miguel ignored him.

"Okay. Fine." Don looked around the room. "I didn't know where Terry hid the recipe. But I knew he wrote the location down for me to find in case he got in trouble. He had some girl make it into beads."

"Beads?" Miguel scoffed. "How could he write it down in beads? Do you think I'm kidding about what I'll do if I don't get the truth from you?"

I grabbed Miguel's sleeve. As soon as Don said beads, I knew what had happened. "Green paper beads, right?"

TWENTY-TWO

Both men looked at me.

"Terry gave Delia some beads in the parking lot the night he was killed. She gave them to me. She said she didn't want to see them."

"So you've been holding the information the whole time?" Don threw back his stringy hair and laughed out loud. "I'm losing it."

Miguel took my arm and we walked behind the partial wall again.

"What beads are you talking about?" he whispered with as much intensity as he'd used questioning Don. He was still holding my arm. "How can anything be written on beads?"

"The beads are made from paper. I guess Terry had someone use the beads as a place to hide information about the recipe. I hope he didn't have the recipe made into beads or it will be worthless."

"You didn't mention the beads to the police?"

"Is this an interrogation?" I jerked my arm away from him. "I didn't think it meant anything. I almost threw them in the garbage."

"Sorry." He smiled. "This may be the break we've been looking for."

"But why would Terry write down where the recipe was hidden? He must've been the one to hide it."

"He probably did it in case he needed someone to back him up, like Abbott said. Sometimes, thieves hide what they've stolen and give that information to a friend. If their lives are threatened by the buyer, they have some leverage. In this case, Terry knew one man had already died. He probably wanted to use Don as a backup but was afraid to give him too much information."

We went back to question Don again.

He was gone. I wasn't as good at tying someone up as I'd thought.

"He's probably gone to your place to find the beads," Miguel said. "Let's go."

I smiled at him. "No need to rush. I have them with me. I keep forgetting to take them out of my bag."

To my surprise, Miguel kissed me quickly on the lips and grabbed my hand. "Let's take a look at them."

I almost couldn't move. All the time I'd spent wondering if he had any feelings for me. Surely this was a sign. Maybe he wasn't ready to date yet, but his response was genuine in his excitement.

"Are you okay?" he asked when I didn't start out of the office with him.

"I'm fine."

He frowned. "Was that too much too soon?"

"No. Not at all." I gazed into his dark eyes. "My bag is in your car."

He squeezed my hand, and I ran out of the office with him. He locked the door behind us, and we went quickly out to the car.

We got in and Miguel drove away. "Let's go somewhere public where Don will be less likely to bother us."

I was surprised he didn't want to take the beads to the police, and said so.

"There have been so many twists in this case. I don't want to give anything to Detective Latoure until we're sure of it. It ruins your credibility if you're constantly giving the police unimportant information."

That was good enough for me.

We drove to a small coffee shop. I found a table in a dark corner while Miguel got coffee for us. It was exciting thinking we might be on the right track for the recipe—almost as exciting as Miguel kissing me.

It wasn't a big kiss, but that was okay. It was a beginning.

He came back with my double shot mocha and his plain coffee. We sat across from each other, and I took the beads out of my bag. I felt the seating was strategic. We could see people coming toward us and hide what we found in the beads.

It was difficult taking the beads apart. There was tough string holding them together. Miguel used the knife on his key chain to cut the string so the beads would be separated.

As he cut the first string, I started unwinding the paper that the beads were made of. It was tightly wound and difficult to pull apart without tearing. Eventually, I got the paper strip unwound from the first bead. It took me ten minutes. Miguel was done cutting the string between the beads. He watched me as the green paper opened under my fingers.

There was nothing written on it. I sipped my coffee, and looked up at him. "I guess we'll have to unwind all the beads until we find it."

"Or Don lied to us."

"We won't know until all the beads are unwound."

Miguel began unwinding the strips of paper, too. "Why would anyone want to do this?"

"It's good for the environment. Usually, they're made from recycled paper. They look pretty, don't they?"

Miguel looked at the bead that was half unwound in his hand. "Yes. Beautiful."

I laughed at him. "Well, when they're done right, and you're not taking them apart, they look great. And there's no plastic."

"How does anyone even think of doing something like this?"

"I don't know. I'm not crafty. I cook. That's about it."

"You're very good at cooking, Zoe." He unwound the rest of his bead. "I'm sure your dream of owning an important restaurant will come true."

There was nothing written on his bead, either, or the next bead I unwound.

"Would you like me to take those cups for you?" a coffee shop employee asked.

"No!" Miguel and I both barked. The waiter went away quickly.

"I hope he wasn't traumatized by our response." Miguel started on another bead.

"He might never be able to pick up trash from tables again."

I started on another bead, too, and glanced from under my lashes at Miguel. I knew I'd already asked him about going to the benefit dinner. He hadn't responded. Was it too soon to ask him again?

"Have you had a chance to think about going to the benefit dinner with me?"

"Not really. It's not the kind of thing I normally do." He smiled at me as though to ease the pain. "I'm not much of a party person."

"I can understand. I'm not usually a party person, either." I was lying. I loved parties. Combining that with all the excellent food, and the chance to see Chef Art's mansion, was irresistible. But it looked like I might be going alone.

"Are you still sure you should go? You might not like what you find out about Delia and Chef Art."

I shrugged. "The dinner may not happen at all if what we find on one of these beads leads us to Chef Art as the killer."

"That's true." Miguel finished another bead. There was nothing written on it. "If anything is *really* on one of these beads."

It wasn't much of an answer to my question about Miguel going with me to the benefit dinner, if it happened. I guess it was his way of saying no. He was trying to be nice.

Maybe it wasn't me, though—he had kissed me, even if it was only a peck. Maybe he didn't like being out in Mobile society after giving up his job at the DA's office.

We were forty-five minutes into unwinding beads. String and green paper littered the table between us. None of the waiters came over and asked if we needed anything else. Not that I blamed them.

Our fingertips were green from the dye in the paper. There was one bead left for each of us. If there was nothing there, we'd have to look elsewhere for more information.

"Choose your bead," Miguel said. "Let's hope there's something on one of them."

Each of us quickly unwound the paper. We were getting to be experts by this time.

Mine was still blank, but there was writing on Miguel's last bead.

"Chef A. Green chili. Food truck. Watch your back." Miguel looked up at me when he was done reading. "I guess that says it all."

"If this was meant for Don, we'd better figure it out before he guesses what it says."

We threw our trash into a can as we walked out of the coffee shop. Miguel kept the single strip of paper from the last bead and put it in his pocket.

"Food truck? It has to mean the taco truck," I guessed.

"Probably."

"Maybe the recipe is in the taco truck. What if we find it?" I asked him as I got into his car.

"We take it to Detective Latoure and let her deal with it from there."

"That way we may never know who killed Terry," I reminded him. "Maybe we should show it to Chef Art first, and get his take on it."

"I know this is the first time you've done anything like this," he said. "Trust me, if we find this recipe, we need to get out of the game. We've come pretty far across the line already. It doesn't take a lot to charge someone with impeding an investigation."

I didn't say anything else about it. I knew Miguel was totally looking at the problem from a lawyer's point of view. I also knew, from my mother, that wasn't always the *right* way to look at things.

Miguel had Terry's home address since he and Delia had been involved. He lived a little outside the city in a rental house that looked almost as bad as the area where my diner was located.

We were at the right place. Terry's Tacky Taco truck was in the drive. Miguel and I got out of the car after he'd parked behind the food truck.

Both of us cautiously looked around. That's what comes of people holding guns on you, and beating up your friends. You constantly expect bad things to jump out at you.

Miguel opened the back door to the food truck. It wasn't even locked. It was hard for me to believe Terry would've stashed a recipe worth a million dollars in the truck without at least trying to protect it.

Maybe it was one of those things where it's the last place you'd expect to find anything valuable so he felt it was safe. I would've put it in the bank.

Well, since it was stolen, maybe not. But I would've found somewhere more secure than this.

"Green chili," Miguel said when we were inside the taco truck. "This place is such a mess. I don't know how we'll find anything. How did he work this way?"

It wasn't only that pots, pans, bowls, and spoons were thrown everywhere. There was a heavy layer of grease on everything, too. I hated to touch any of it. I should've brought gloves. No wonder cops on TV wear them.

"I wish we'd brought a flashlight." I looked at the serving window that was shut. "Maybe we should open that so we can see in here. Green chili could be something that holds green chili. Or it could be a can of green chili. Or a green chili pepper, although I hope it's not inside a real pepper."

"I'll open the window," Miguel volunteered. "Take my cell phone. The flashlight app is on it."

I looked at the mess with the light from the flashlight as Miguel went outside.

He was right. Everything was such a jumble of food and cooking and serving utensils—I wasn't sure if we'd find anything without emptying the entire truck. Maybe this was why Terry wasn't worried about anyone else finding the recipe.

Opening the serving window helped—even though it made the interior of the truck look even worse. The smell was awful, too.

"I'm never eating anything from a food truck again," I said.

Miguel laughed. "Your food truck doesn't look like this."

"No, but I can't ask for a tour of the food truck before I order. I hate to think what kind of germs are in here. It doesn't look like he'd wiped anything down for weeks. I think these are rat droppings over here, too."

"You don't ever have to worry about that since you take your cat with you."

I didn't go into what a coward Crème Brûlée was. I didn't like to say bad things about him all the time. I loved him the way he was—hissing, biting, and cowardly.

We started picking things up off the floor. A quick scan of the upper areas where the food was made didn't show anything green, chili or not.

"I wonder if someone else already had this idea and that's why the truck is such a mess," I said. "I don't see how he worked this way. He'd have to pick this up every day while he was working. I don't think he was that ambitious."

"The police probably went through this, too." Miguel picked up the pieces of several broken spice bottles. "We don't even know what size this recipe is. It could be anywhere."

I was under the area where Terry would've taken orders and handed out food. There was a little bit of everything down there. I found an empty salsa box and started filling it so I could look through it when I got up. The light wasn't much better than before we opened the serving window, at least not where I was.

"Do you think this could be what he was talking about?"

I bumped my head on the counter as I tried to get up and see what Miguel had found.

"Careful." He took my hand and helped me off of the greasy floor. "If you cut yourself in here, you'll probably need a tetanus shot."

"What did you find?" I rubbed my head ruefully.

"It's green." He held up a small canister. "It says chili on it."

I opened the canister. The lid was pressed down so hard that it opened with a popping sound. We both looked inside. There was nothing there, not even chili peppers.

"I don't know. Maybe someone already found it." I was greasy and disgusted with being there. Turning the whole thing over to the police was beginning to sound pretty good.

"You may be right. We could be looking for anything. Green chili could be a code used between Don and Terry for all we know. I think we should call Detective Latoure and tell her what we've found so far."

I thought that was a bad idea. I put the box of items I'd picked up from the floor on the cabinet and continued surveying the walls, shelves, and counter.

"I guess you're right. I don't know what else to do. Keeping information from the police could be worse than impeding an investigation."

"Agreed. Shall I call or do you want to?"

— — — — — — —

We waited at Terry's house until three police cars pulled up. Detective Latoure was in one of them. The other two were from the local police department.

"This better be good." Patti Latoure shook hands with the other officers who were from Fairhope, outside Mobile. "We don't really like to go into one another's territory, if you know what I mean."

Miguel gave her the piece of green paper from the necklace and explained the situation. "We thought you should know."

She smirked. "You mean after the two of you couldn't find the recipe."

"It's not just the recipe," I said. "Delia has been taken, too. We think she might have been kidnapped."

"Or she's working with the killer," Patti said. "Have you reported her missing?"

I explained the problem I'd had with that. She sympathized but agreed that it was police policy.

"Don Abbott knows about the recipe," I told her. "I had the beads, so he couldn't find it. We wanted to beat him to it."

"And did you?" she asked.

"No. We couldn't find anything except a million reasons to call the health department," I confessed.

"We searched this food truck already." She peeked inside the taco truck. "Did the two of you make this mess?"

"No. It was this way when we got here," Miguel said.

"Then someone else has been here looking around, too.

I'll have the taco truck towed back to Mobile and forensics will go over it again. Have you been in the house?"

"No. We looked in here because the note said food truck," I said.

Patti looked at the green note, already sealed in an evidence bag. "Are you sure Terry meant *his* food truck?"

"Where else would he hide the recipe?" I asked.

She raised her brows. "You said in your statement that Terry had been inside your food truck the day he was killed. And you said Miss Vann gave you the beads, telling you that Terry had given them to her."

I couldn't believe it. "You think he put the recipe in *my* food truck?"

TWENTY-THREE

"I don't see how he would've had time to hide anything in my food truck when I was trying to throw him out."

I said this as Miguel was following behind Detective Latoure's car. We were headed back to the diner with the lights and sirens blaring on the front police car that was our escort.

"He could've planned to do it this way." Miguel kept his eyes on the road as the speedometer crept up to eighty miles an hour. "You were distracted by what he was doing to you. You wouldn't have noticed that he left something behind."

It was hard for me to believe. Even if I'd missed him leaving a green chili item behind in the Biscuit Bowl, I would have seen it since. I thought I knew every inch, every item in my food truck. It shook me a little to think that I might be wrong.

"Why would he leave it with me? He didn't even know me."

"He probably didn't care if he knew you. He could always

break into your food truck later and retrieve the recipe. Maybe that's what he was planning to do when he was killed behind the diner."

"I guess so." It was a little hard to take in when I thought about it. I looked out the side window at the trees and houses that were rapidly flying by as we approached Mobile. "He wasn't killed in the Biscuit Bowl, but it might have been close."

Miguel squeezed my hand where it rested on the seat between us. "This is all speculation, Zoe. It might not have played out this way. We'll see when we get there."

I was sure it was getting to be commonplace for my neighbors in the old shopping center to see police cars pulling into the parking lot near the diner. It would be humiliating if the other shops filed complaints against me and I was forced to leave, especially in this neighborhood.

Detective Latoure was out of her car and walking toward the back of the Biscuit Bowl truck as Miguel was parking. I quickly took out my key—I never left my food truck unlocked.

I realized as we got closer that no one needed the key. The back door was open.

"Looks like Don beat us here," Miguel said.

I let out a little screech when I saw the door had been pried open. There were utensils and serving trays strewn into the parking lot. Couldn't people search for things without making a mess?

Running to the food truck, I noticed Ollie, Marty, and some of the other men from the shelter coming to see what was happening.

Then I focused on the wreck that was waiting for me. I could see through the open door that nothing was where it belonged. Jars of spices had been emptied and plastic serving trays smashed.

"Zoe!" Ollie called my name.

He was standing beside the front door to the diner. The glass had been smashed open. It looked like Don hadn't given up his search for the recipe after he'd finished with the food truck.

My first thought wasn't for anything I owned. "Crème Brûlée!" I yelled as I ran past Ollie and into the diner.

Everything was ripped open and smashed in the diner, too. I ran to my bedroom area. The bed was torn apart. I couldn't find Crème Brûlée anywhere. His bed had been tossed, too. Even his kitty litter box had been emptied on the floor.

I walked slowly through the diner, calling his name. I knew Crème Brûlée would be in a bad mood, anyway. I hoped he wasn't hurt.

There was no answering meow to greet me and give me some idea of where he was. Where was he?

"What a mess." Ollie was looking around when I came back up to the front of the diner. "I'm sorry, Zoe. I didn't see anything going on. Whoever did this must've walked up or parked in back."

"You can't keep track of everything." I wiped tears from my eyes. "If I can find Crème Brûlée, I'll be okay."

"I thought you said he wouldn't run out."

"I did. He wouldn't, except that a stranger made a mess of his home. I don't know what he'll do now."

Ollie smiled. "Too bad he wasn't a little bigger. He could've stopped whoever did this. I think you might need a tough dog instead of a cat with an attitude."

"Don't even say that! He has to be here somewhere."

Detective Latoure came inside to talk to me. I told her about Crème Brûlée. A few minutes later, everyone, including Miguel and Marty, was looking for him with me. They searched behind the stores and in the Dumpsters. He seemed to have disappeared.

"I hope Abbott didn't take your cat with him," Patti said.

"He wouldn't have kept him for long," Ollie said. "Believe me, that's one mean cat."

I kept looking. Where would Crème Brûlée hide if he

was threatened? If we were still living back at the apartment, I'd know where to find him. Anytime a repairman showed up there, Crème Brûlée hid in my bedroom closet.

I wondered what he'd equate with that closet?

I glanced into the makeshift pantry I'd built to keep the rats away from my food. Usually, it was closed and locked. Don had cut the lock from the metal pantry. The door was still open.

Carefully, I opened the door and peeked inside. The first thing I saw was a rapidly swishing yellow and white tail. That movement was followed by a warning hiss.

"There you are." I reached into the pantry and got a small nip on my arm for my trouble. I didn't care. I hugged Crème Brûlée until he started growling at me. Then I kissed his little face and put him down.

"You're safe now. I wish you could talk and tell me who did this."

I found a comfortable place for him until I could get the bed put back to rights.

"I'm glad he's okay," Patti said.

"Can you pick Don up and arrest him?" I asked. "I want to press charges for all of this."

"I'm sure we can find him. We'll need some proof. I'll have my team go over the food truck, and your diner. I'm sorry this happened, Zoe."

"Me, too." The full realization of how much I'd lost—and how much would have to be cleaned up before the Biscuit Bowl could go out again—hit me with a hard thud right in the chest.

It was just as well that Chef Art wasn't really planning to join me tomorrow. There was no way I'd be ready to roll in the morning. Even if I could make do with what was left of my food supplies, I'd never get things in order before then.

I felt like going home and crying. Only this *was* home now, and crying wouldn't do much good. Somehow, I'd get through this. I'd start again. I wouldn't let this beat me.

Miguel offered to take me out for lunch. I knew it was probably because I looked as lost and pathetic as I felt. He was being kind—giving the police some time to start working on the food truck and the diner without me watching them.

I appreciated his sweet thought. I didn't want to watch whatever the police were going to do. I accepted his invitation. This time, I didn't even think of the lunch being romantic. I didn't care. I only wanted to get away from the destruction.

Miguel was even nice enough to let me put Crème Brûlée and his bed in the backseat of his car. Not everyone can handle a cat in their car. Tommy Lee certainly couldn't. Neither could my mother.

Miguel was wonderful about it. He didn't even complain when he tried to stroke Crème Brûlée and my evil cat bit him.

"He does that when he likes you." I showed him the mark on my arm where Crème Brûlée bit me as I was searching for him. "See?"

"That's . . . *nice*." Miguel smiled and closed the back door. "Where would you like to go for lunch?"

I knew there wouldn't be a lot of choices. I couldn't leave Crème Brûlée in the car while we ate lunch. The only place I could think to go was Happy's Drive-In. Visions of roller-skating waitresses serving comfort food as they flew by on the smooth pavement captured my thoughts.

I liked Happy's. I'd always asked to eat here when I was a kid. The answer was always no. My mother didn't eat at curbside restaurants.

As soon as I started driving, I came here for lunch, and after school for snacks. Everything was made fresh when you ordered it. Even the milkshakes were made with hand-dipped, hard ice cream.

"What's good?" Miguel asked as he looked over the huge menu.

"I always have a milkshake. It doesn't matter what flavor. All of them are delicious. Their cheeseburgers are awesome, and so are their hush puppies. They actually make them with their own batter, not frozen."

"Sounds good." Miguel ordered cheeseburgers, hush puppies, and milkshakes for both of us. I had the blueberry orange sky milkshake. Miguel had chocolate, not even chocolate delight. It suited him.

"Let's go inside for a minute so I can say hello to Happy. Crème Brûlée will be fine."

"There really is a Happy?"

"Sure. He opened this place when he got out of the navy in 1981. He was a cook on a ship for years. He started right out cooking professionally."

We went inside. There was only a narrow aisle between the deep fryers, grills, and other food appliances. The roller-skating waitresses zoomed in and out past us, holding trays of food above their heads.

"Happy!" I hailed my old friend who'd given me my first summer job.

"Zoe!" Happy was dressed in white pants and shirt, as always. He looked almost the same as he had the first day I'd met him. Maybe he was a little rounder, and a little older. "It's good to see you. I hope you got milkshakes. They're really good today."

We hugged, and I introduced him to Miguel. The two men shook hands.

Happy nudged me. "I like this one. And he's a lawyer. You better hold on to him, Zoe. What happened to Mr. Perfect? I hope he ran that expensive piece of junk he drives into a telephone pole."

Happy's only experience with Tommy Lee wasn't a good one. Tommy Lee had my mother's dim view of eating at fast-food restaurants. I'd brought him inside to meet Happy. Tommy Lee had spent the whole time on his cell phone, brokering some stock deal.

What made it even worse—Tommy Lee had called Happy's food greasy and had refused to eat lunch. We never went back again.

"I've heard about your food truck, Zoe," Happy said. "It's been on the radio a few times. You need to get on that website that tracks the local trucks."

"I know. I can't figure out how to contact the person who runs it."

"Why didn't you say so? Darnell Weaver runs that site. He worked here awhile before he found his thing on the Internet. He does interviews, and reviews of restaurants and food trucks, too. Maybe he could get you set up. I have his number here somewhere."

Happy gave me Darnell's phone number and email address. I hugged him and said thanks. "I can see our food is getting cold outside. Thanks for the information. I'll see you later."

Happy hugged Miguel, too. Miguel looked surprised to begin with, but he kind of rolled with it. That seemed to be the type of man he was. Maybe it was because his life had been a series of ups and downs. He'd learned to roll.

We got back in the car. Miguel had to get in from the passenger side because the food tray was already attached to his side of the car. I got in after him, and he passed me my food.

Crème Brûlée smelled the food—especially the burgers—and started looking pitiful. He flipped on his back in his bed and put his paws up in the air. He laid his big head back and let out a few pathetic meows. All the while his nose was sniffing the air.

"You know this will make you sick," I told him. "Quit looking cute. I'm not feeding you."

His meows got louder. I realized he was probably stressed by everything that had happened to him. I gave in and handed him the tuna treat I always carried in my bag for him. He was satisfied with that and went back to sleep. I could hear him snoring over the sound of traffic going by, and the sixties music Happy always played.

"This is a really good burger." Miguel smiled at me "Food means a lot to you, doesn't it?"

That question made me feel a little strange. Was he saying I talked too much about food?

"I suppose good food, and its preparation, is important to me because I'm involved in the industry."

It sounded like a sound bite I might have given Happy's friend, Darnell, for an interview. I smiled, and drank some milkshake to mitigate it.

"You're definitely involved in the industry, Zoe. You have a real passion for it. I could see it on your face as you were cooking the other night."

"Thanks, I guess. I know making food for people isn't as important as being a lawyer and getting people out of trouble. It's just what I do."

He swallowed what he'd been chewing. "Don't ever say that. You make people happy, and they feel better, even if they're going through a bad time. I think that's as important as anything else."

After a bad day, his words were very nice. I wasn't going to wait for a better invitation. I leaned toward him and kissed him lightly, as he'd kissed me at his office. "Thanks. That means a lot."

He turned serious after that, and didn't finish his lunch. We didn't talk, either. I wondered if he felt guilty about his dead wife, or was afraid we were getting too close.

Whatever it was, I didn't push myself on him. I didn't finish eating, either, and the waitress came to get our tray. I thanked Miguel for taking me out and saving me from watching someone else plunder my belongings.

"You're welcome. I guess we should be getting back. I have a client to depose this afternoon."

And that was the end of my lunch with Miguel.

I was still contemplating what I'd done or said wrong as

we drove back to the diner. I didn't want to apologize. It seemed like he could take that the wrong way, too. It was a good thing I wasn't thinking about romance with lunch. I would've been disappointed. This way, I was just confused.

The police were packing up as we were getting out of the car. Detective Latoure was gone. The crime scene team said they were finished getting fingerprints and whatever evidence they could find.

I thanked them for their help and told them the Biscuit Bowl owed them a free lunch—redeemable anytime they wanted to visit me outside police headquarters during the week.

They seemed happy about that. I felt better. I thought about what Miguel had said about me making food. I knew he was right, despite what other people in my life thought. It made me happy to see people enjoying my food. Why shouldn't it make them happy, too?

Miguel said he had to leave. "I'll be glad to come by later and help you get this mess sorted out, Zoe. Will you be able to work tomorrow?"

"I hope so. Thanks for all your help."

I waved to him as he left the parking lot. Marty and Ollie walked down from the shelter. I could see the consignment store employees nervously looking out of the front window to see what was going on.

"We have lots of free hands to help get this cleaned up for you," Marty said when he reached me. "You've fed us better than we've eaten for a while. Let us help you get set up again."

I was happy to let them help. All those extra hands could make quick work of the cleanup. I got Crème Brûlée set up in our makeshift bedroom and went to get things started.

We worked for a few hours. Half of the men were in the diner. Another smaller group, led by Ollie, was in the food truck. Things were really starting to get back in shape. I thought I might even be able to go back out tomorrow. I made a list of the supplies I would need to do so.

As I was taking stock of the ruined food, I heard Ollie shout from outside.

"Zoe! You have to see this. I know what happened to Delia."

TWENTY-FOUR

Everyone crowded around as Ollie showed me a note he'd found duct-taped to the trash bin in back.

"I was bringing the trash out of the truck when I saw it," Ollie said. "This proves Delia *was* kidnapped. I knew she wouldn't leave on her own."

The note was short and to the point. *I'll trade you the recipe for Delia. Meet me here at midnight. No police.*

"We don't have the recipe. Why does everyone think we do?" I threw the note on the ground. "How are we going to help Delia?"

"Didn't Miguel say you had the directions to find it?" Marty asked.

I wished Miguel *wouldn't* have said that. "Not really directions. It was more a vague idea of where the recipe *could* be. As you can see, it's not in the diner or in the food truck."

"I'm gonna strangle that Chef person when we find him." Ollie growled and twisted his hands in an imitation of wringing Chef Art's neck. "What about giving him everything you and Miguel found? Maybe he'll understand what it means and give Delia back."

"We gave it to the police," I explained. "Miguel thought it would be bad not to."

Most of the men from the shelter had issues with law enforcement. They groaned and muttered about Miguel's decision to give up something that could have saved Delia's life.

It occurred to me that this whole ordeal had become like a soap opera for them. It was something to take their minds off of their situations.

"I don't have the paper anymore, but I know what it said. Maybe that would be enough to get Delia back." I looked at the hopeful faces of the men around me.

"Maybe," Ollie agreed. "Chef Art is bound to be pretty well connected. He's got money and he's got Delia. I don't know if he'll be happy with further instructions."

"It could still be a trick. We don't know for sure that Chef Art has her," I disagreed. "It could be Don Abbott, or someone else who knows about the Jefferson recipe. Maybe he got his hands on an invitation. We have to be ready for anything."

"But not with the police," Ollie argued. "Calling them would be a surefire way to get Delia killed."

"We have to tell the police," Marty said. "Many of you are on parole. Getting involved in this could send you back to prison."

Marty's voice of reason was drowned out by the negative reaction from Ollie and his friends.

I didn't know what to say. I wasn't versed in hostage negotiations. I didn't even have what the kidnapper wanted. I could tell Chef Art what I'd read on the paper. That was about it. If that wasn't what he wanted, he could kill Delia.

"What did the strip of paper say, Zoe?" Marty asked as the men discussed plans for setting up an ambush for Delia's kidnappers.

They sounded like they knew what they were doing—even if it *was* from a kidnapper's point of view. Some of them had experience with that type of thing.

"Not much," I told him. "It said, *Chef A. Green chili. Food truck. Watch your back.* I think it was supposed to be for Don Abbott. Miguel and I were thinking Don was Terry's fallback in case he got in trouble."

Ollie was listening. "Maybe it was in the taco truck."

"We tried there. It looked about the same as my food truck. The police had it towed to go over it again. I'm glad they didn't feel the need to look over mine again."

"The police already looked through the Biscuit Bowl a few times," Ollie said. "Maybe whoever has Delia doesn't want to keep looking."

"I don't know." I went back inside and sat down on a stool at the counter. "I want to get Delia back, too. But what if her kidnapper isn't happy with the directions? He could kill her."

"He won't know you don't have the recipe," Ollie reminded me. "It's not like he gave you a number to call in case you don't have it. We'll have to fake it. He's coming tonight at midnight. Either we're ready for him, or we could lose Delia for good."

The men from the shelter had a plan of action. I knew we needed a cooler head. Marty and I were trying to persuade them not to try this alone. It wasn't working. I thought about calling Miguel. He'd know what to do.

In the midst of what was quickly getting out of hand—too many mentions of baseball bats and tire irons—my mother pulled up in the parking lot.

Great! That was *exactly* what I needed.

I struggled through the loud group of men who were offering suggestions for terrible things that should happen to the man who trashed my place and kidnapped Delia. I'd hoped to head my mother off before she could get into the diner. Usually, she didn't even get out of her car when she stopped by. Today, she was stalking right toward the door.

"What's going on?" Her voice would have made a drill sergeant envious. It cut right through the voices of the men around me.

They all turned and stared at her in her pale mauve suit.

"It's nothing, Mother," I told her with a nervous laugh. "We were talking about doing some things. Nothing serious."

"Not if you call beating the man who kidnapped Delia down tonight serious," Ollie said.

"Kidnapping?"

I couldn't believe my mother was even listening to him. "Let's talk outside."

"I think I should hear what's going on with these men, Zoe. Why don't you make some coffee?"

What was happening? Why was my mother sitting in my diner that she previously wouldn't even enter? Why was she talking to these men who were obviously wearing threadbare clothes and boots with holes in them? I was beginning to wonder if I'd stepped into an alternate universe.

Then it became obvious. One of her assistants—Sam or Dan, I couldn't remember—was videotaping the whole thing from a discreet distance.

Was she seriously thinking this was going to help her campaign to be a judge?

"What's going on?" I asked Sam. Or Dan.

He handed me a flyer. It had my mother's picture on it with the caption *Anabelle Chase—the judge who fights for you*. "Voters are gonna eat this up. She's right there in the trenches with the common people who need her."

It wasn't the craziest thing I'd ever heard, but it was right up there in the top ten. My mother certainly didn't look the part of a woman who was in the trenches, wearing her expensive designer suit and shoes. No one was going to fall for this.

But I was wrong about that part. Ollie, and the other men from the shelter, bought into it. The next thing I knew, Sam or Dan was putting an appointment into my mother's calendar to negotiate with Delia's kidnappers at midnight.

"Don't worry about a thing," my mother told them. "I'll take care of this for you, my constituents."

All of the men, except for Marty, seemed happy with this. Marty was still arguing to call in the police. His words were falling on deaf ears as they walked back to the homeless shelter, each of them carrying a *Vote for Anabelle Chase* flyer.

When we were alone with only Sam or Dan, I confronted her. "What are you doing, Mother? You've never negotiated with kidnappers in your life."

"Negotiating with the kind of sharks I'm used to will get me through it. Don't worry, Zoe. I can swim with the barracudas and not get bitten." She smiled at me. "I knew if I came down here, I'd find something that would make good press. You live in the perfect area for me to bring in some new voters. I'm going to have Sam start registering your friends tomorrow."

"Some of them may be convicted felons who can't vote."

That didn't faze her. "We'll find ways around that, Zoe. That's what's good about the American election process."

I gave up trying to talk her out of it. With a promise to be back at midnight, my mother left with Sam at the wheel. I tried to put the whole thing out of my mind and concentrated on getting back to work tomorrow.

Ollie and the other men had done a great job cleaning the back of the food truck. It was as if it had never happened. I walked through and checked everything. Once the food was ready tomorrow, I'd be ready to roll.

It was therapeutic shopping for the food items I needed. I drove the Biscuit Bowl on that kind of excursion. It was a good chance for people to take a look at it. I always had a few menus to give out if anyone commented on it.

It was about the cheapest promotion I could do, yet it had yielded results. People who'd bought food from me had told me they'd seen my food truck parked somewhere, and thought they'd try me out. That was about the best anyone could hope for.

Uncle Saul had told me I had to break the ice first and then my food would do the talking for me.

I missed him. I wished he'd stayed in Mobile a little longer—at least until the craziness was over. I wished he was going to be at the diner that night instead of my mother. He would know what to do without panicking or calling the police.

He couldn't be around all the time. I understood that. He loved his swamp, and all the creepy-crawlies that went with it. Don't ask me why.

I ended up giving a few menus to people at the grocery store. They promised to stop by at police headquarters, or whenever they saw the Biscuit Bowl open for business. I thanked them and said I would give them a free sample if they told me they'd seen me there. Just another gimmick I'd worked out.

Traffic was heavy on my way back to the diner. Driving the big motor home was much different than my Prius had been. It was really like driving with your house on your back. I couldn't imagine how big truck drivers did it all the time. It was a little scary.

I parked the food truck by the diner. Miguel's car was there. He was standing outside, talking to Ollie. I had no doubt what that conversation was about. I was glad to have the help bringing in the supplies. I take it where I can get it.

"So your mother is going to negotiate with a man who probably killed at least two other people to get the Jefferson recipe." Miguel shook his head. "Why didn't you call me?"

"You were the first person I thought of." I explained about how all the men from the shelter had reacted when they'd heard about the killer trying to exchange the recipe for Delia. "My mother walked into that. She couldn't have done it any neater if her assistant, Sam, had thought it up."

"It's crazy," he said. "Your mother doesn't know anything about hostage negotiation. You're all likely to get hurt."

"One man can't get all of us." Ollie walked into the last part of our conversation with a box of beans. "At least there's something to do besides sitting around."

"I know you don't think the killer will come alone," Miguel chided him. "They'll have guns, Ollie. Not baseball bats and tire irons."

"I can see someone ratted us out." Ollie frowned at me. "I thought you were all for this, Zoe."

"No. Not at all. Marty and I were both trying to convince you that it was a mistake."

"Whatever," Ollie said. "I think we can get this done, and get Delia back. I'm going down to the shelter and getting everyone ready. You want in on this, Miguel, or not?"

"Not the way you're doing it," Miguel answered.

"Fine. We'll take care of it ourselves. See you at midnight, Zoe."

After he was gone, Miguel and I talked about the problem.

"I suppose we could call in the police," I said.

"That could be worse," he surprised me by saying. "The killer might not be worried about your mother and the men from the shelter. If the police are here, he could kill Delia."

I shook my head as I started a large pot of red beans. "Have you heard anything about the police catching up with Don? I have a feeling he's the one who trashed my truck. He's probably going to be the one here at midnight, too."

"You think he kidnapped Delia and killed Terry?"

I thought about it. "I don't know. Chef Art is involved in this somehow. I don't think he'd get his hands dirty or mess up his reputation. He could've hired Terry, and then Don, to do the dirty work for him."

"True. But if that's the case, why did Chef Art take a chance on kidnapping you himself? He could've sent Don.

There was no way for him to know that you wouldn't report him after he let you go."

"True." I handed him three large Vidalia onions to peel. That was probably my least favorite part of cooking. Miguel had asked if there was anything he could do to help.

"Maybe, if nothing else, we'll get some answers about Delia tonight." He rolled up his shirtsleeves. "Maybe Don will show up with Chef Art looking on from behind him."

I laughed. "Nothing is ever that easy."

"You're right about that."

Miguel stayed for dinner after helping me get my food ready for the next day. I was pleasantly surprised. I didn't know what to expect after that uncomfortable moment when I'd kissed him in the car.

He acted like nothing unusual had happened at all. We didn't talk about it, which I thought was unfortunate. I would've liked to know what I was dealing with. I gave him a few little hints during dinner, but he never said a thing. It was growing ever clearer to me that Miguel was not a hinting kind of person.

I made the spicy peach filling for my sweet biscuit bowls, and we shared one of them to see what it was like. There was a hint of spiced rum in the filling that gave it an unusual flavor.

"What do you think?" I was trying to be more proactive.

He nodded and smiled. "Really good. I like the spicy part. I like the whole biscuit bowl idea, Zoe. It's clever."

"Thanks." I licked a little peach filling off my finger. "And the kissing? Where is that going?"

He looked at me like I'd just told him there was a bomb in the oven. "You come right to the point, don't you?"

"Well, I've been hinting around at things with you, Miguel, and it doesn't seem to do much good. I thought the direct approach might be better."

He looked down at his empty plate. "Zoe—"

"Don't worry about it. You won't hurt my feelings. But

you kissed me first at your office. I admit it wasn't a big kiss, but neither was the one I gave you in the car. If that's not what you had in mind, now's a good time to tell me."

"It's been a long time for me." He took a deep breath. "I'm sure you know about my wife and daughter. Everyone knows about it. For a long time, I never looked up from my work. I didn't want there to be a world outside that was still turning. I pretended I was alone."

"And now?"

"Now, I'm starting to look up again." He smiled and took my hand in his. "It has something to do with you. Maybe it's because you're such a good cook."

"But? I hear a 'but' coming."

"Zoe, you just broke up with the man you thought you were going to marry. I think you should give yourself some time."

"You're worried about being Tommy Lee's rebound?"

"Not exactly. I think you should be sure. At this point, I don't think you are."

I knew my deeds of the past few months were going to haunt me. Hadn't my mother warned me of it? I didn't think it would happen this way.

"That's fine. I understand." I got up and took our dishes to the sink. "For the record, Miguel, I like you a lot. I don't plan to waste any more time on Tommy Lee. I guess we'll see what the future brings."

"I like you, too, Zoe. I guess we'll see how that goes."

Miguel helped me get the food truck restocked with food containers and other items that had to be replaced. We didn't talk about our possible relationship. We were both very careful to stay away from that subject.

Really, I was glad that he wasn't still working out his grief about his wife. I wasn't worried about how I felt. I could see where he might feel uncertain about me. I might even seem a little flighty to him. After all, he knew everything about me quitting my job and upsetting my otherwise *ordinary* life. That could make someone wonder if they were only a fad.

I was tired by the time midnight rolled around. The thought of getting up at four A.M. wasn't something I was looking forward to. I was excited about going back to work, a lot more excited than I was about the ordeal to come.

My mother and her assistant, Sam, along with a TV news crew, got to the diner a little before midnight. I couldn't believe she expected to negotiate for Delia's life with a camera crew watching. She'd exchanged her pretty suit for black pants and sweater with a black flak jacket on top.

Ollie and his friends were all in place with their baseball bats, tire irons, and other creative weapons hidden about them. The clock in the diner struck midnight.

"Here we go." I added a small prayer for everyone's safety.

TWENTY-FIVE

Nothing happened.

We all sat around for an hour, drinking coffee and eating donuts that my mother had thoughtfully brought with her. She didn't touch them, of course. I wasn't sure if she'd ever eaten a donut. That waist didn't stay tiny without sacrifice.

"Do you think they're still coming?" one of the TV newsmen asked with a yawn.

"Criminals aren't known for their punctuality," my mother said. "Why don't we go outside and shoot another promo for the piece?"

"We've already shot three promos for it, Mrs. Chase," the reporter said. "If the killer doesn't show up, there won't be anything to promo."

My mother was a little put out by his attitude. She walked over to where I was sitting on a stool at the counter. "Isn't there someone you could call, Zoe? You know this criminal. I'm sure if you told him we were ready, he'd come."

"I don't really *know* him. It's not like we're friends. I'm not even sure who it is."

"He must know we're ready for him," Ollie said. "We should've kept this covert. The enemy has lost the element of surprise. Once he loses the high ground, he won't take any chances."

"What's he babbling about, Zoe?" my mother muttered.

"He doesn't think he's coming, either," I interpreted.

"I think we're going, Mrs. Chase." The reporter began to round up his crew. "Next time, maybe you should get an RSVP from the kidnapper."

"Wait!" My mother ran after him. Sam ran after her. They were all in the dark parking lot.

"Might as well head back," Marty said. "It's just as well this happened. At least no one got hurt."

"Delia might not feel that way about it." Ollie walked out the front door, his baseball bat on his shoulder.

After that, it was only a few minutes before everyone was gone. Miguel was the last to leave. "Are you still going to go out tomorrow?" He glanced at his watch. "Today, I mean?"

"Yep. I'll manage. Thanks for all your help tonight."

"Are you okay?" He studied me for a moment. "I mean, with this thing between us?"

I smiled. For a lawyer, he was remarkably ill at ease sometimes. The lawyers I knew, admittedly friends of my mother's, were glib on every subject. "I'm fine."

He shook his head, raked his fingers through his hair, and started to speak. "Good night, Zoe."

After he was gone, I locked up and turned off the lights. The smell of coffee had managed to overpower the spicy red beans, onions, and tomatoes I'd made with okra and corn for my savory biscuit bowls.

I dressed for bed and snuggled with Crème Brûlée, who heaved a loud sigh and snuggled back without biting, for once.

"I'm not worried about it," I told him. "Everything is going to be fine. It has to be. This is my whole new, messed-up life. It has to work out."

– – – – – – –

I got up with the alarm buzzing and my heart pounding. I was glad to be awake after having a terrible dream about my mother trying to save Delia and failing. There were cameras taking thousands of flash pictures with my mother's smiling face near Delia's dead body.

It was gruesome. I was glad to concentrate on the coming day. Maybe it wasn't going to be the big promotional boost I'd hoped for with Chef Art's help, but at least it was something to do, and another day to do it.

I said a little prayer for Delia's safety as I showered and dressed. I hoped she was staying somewhere decent and eating well. She deserved a new life, too, like I had. I wanted her to have that opportunity.

I fed Crème Brûlée early, which gave him plenty of time to use the litter box before we left for the day. My savory dish was hot, and biscuits were baked. Everything was ready to go in the food truck.

Ollie tapped at the front door. I opened it, happy to see him.

"I didn't expect you to be here this morning," I told him.

"I thought I'd try it again today. We'll see about tomorrow. What needs to go out?"

Between us, we had everything set up in the truck within thirty minutes. By six A.M., we were out on the road, headed for police headquarters. They were already talking on the radio about where food trucks were supposed to be that day.

I slapped my hand on the steering wheel. I'd totally forgotten about sending my information to the website again. With all the other things going on, and worrying about Delia, it had slipped my mind.

"Looks like we're the first ones here," Ollie said as I pulled the Biscuit Bowl into a parking space.

"Good. The weather is supposed to be nice today. I have spicy eggs and cheese for breakfast. All we need to do is start the coffee."

"You're real good at this, young 'un." He patted me on top of the head with his big hand and wiggled his fingers. "What's that stuff on your hair?"

"Gel," I said, a little self-consciously. "You don't think these curls stay like this by themselves, do you? Not in this humidity. It dries after a while."

He laughed. "That's good. I was having these thoughts about you and Miguel playing kissy face and him getting his hand stuck in your hair."

"That's not even funny. And we won't be playing kissy face for a while. He doesn't think I know what I'm doing. I guess no one thinks I know what I'm doing."

"I do. You're doing what's right for you. Don't worry about it. I never do."

Somehow, that didn't make me feel any better.

I got things set up in the kitchen and started the first batch of fried biscuits. Ollie put out the chairs and tables and wrote the day's menu on the board as he lifted the window covers.

I was amazed to see five people already in line, waiting behind Ollie. It was barely seven thirty. Not that I wasn't thrilled to see them—just surprised.

By eight A.M., there were fifty people in line. Where were they coming from? I was out of spicy eggs before eight fifteen. It drove me crazy that there was no way to plan what I needed. I might have made all those eggs and sold none of them.

I hated to tell people that we were out of eggs. They didn't seem to care. There were people lining up on the sidewalk as far as I could see. I started serving my lunch savory and sweet menu. I wasn't sure what I was going to do when I ran out of that.

It was exciting to see so many people wanting to eat my food. It was scary, too. I hoped they weren't going to be disappointed that they had to eat lunch food.

I thought about sending Ollie to the nearest store to buy more supplies. The problem with that was making the supplies into food. I could get by with something that I could put in a biscuit bowl that only needed to be warmed, but I couldn't make more biscuits. When I ran out of those, I would have to head back to the diner, and the rest of the day would be lost.

"Where are they all coming from?" I asked Ollie, wishing this had been the day Miguel and Delia had been with us.

"I heard a few people saying they saw some information on the Internet and came by." He stuffed more money into the cashbox. "We're gonna have to dump this or get a bigger box."

On the Internet? I knew I hadn't posted anything. It seemed someone else had posted for me. I didn't mind. I was thrilled with the result. It was everything I'd been dreaming about.

By nine A.M., there were two TV station trucks there—also two policemen who said we had to move the Biscuit Bowl to the parking lot. The crowds were keeping people from getting in and out of police headquarters.

"Maybe that will slow them down some," Ollie said. "I don't know how much more of this we can handle."

I moved the Biscuit Bowl carefully around the crowd of people as the police held them back. I couldn't believe how many people there were. These couldn't only be employees going in and out of police headquarters.

The crowd followed as I parked my food truck in the lot next to police headquarters. I noticed Suzette's Crepes took my spot in front as soon as I'd moved away. I couldn't begrudge them that space. I also couldn't believe people were running to be at the Biscuit Bowl when we reopened. What had gotten into everyone?

After we were resettled, the back door opened, and one of the nearly famous TV personalities came inside with a cameraman following close behind her.

"Are you Zoe Chase?" she asked in a pleasant voice. "I'm Renee Reynolds. I'm sure you recognize me from the six o'clock news. I'm here to cover your big event."

I was flustered and uncertain. What big event was she talking about? If she meant my sudden popularity, I was totally without answers to explain it. I stared at her, and the camera behind her, not knowing what to say.

"Renee!" A booming male voice followed her into the food truck. Nearly everyone in Mobile recognized Chef Art's voice. Renee certainly did.

"There you are." She smiled and hugged him, mindful of her hair and makeup. "I was wondering when you were going to show up."

"Well, I'm actually a bit early." Chef Art pushed his large form into the back of the food truck. Renee shifted to one side, kind of flattened against the wall—and Ollie.

"What are you doing here?" I'd forgotten about his pledge to help me with promotion. He was a kidnapper, possibly a murderer. How brazen could he be?

Chef Art smiled his famous smile. "Renee, could you give me and Miss Zoe a few minutes to discuss our strategy for lunch?"

I noticed he didn't move out of the way. He expected everyone else to find their way around him. I guess that was one of the perks of being famous.

"Zoe, do you want me to stay?" Ollie's big face was as dark as a thundercloud. He gave Chef Art such a mean look, it would have made anyone else quail in fear.

"Yes." I folded my arms across my chest and glared at Chef Art. "You have a lot of nerve showing up here."

Once the TV crew was gone, Ollie added, "Yeah. Where's Delia?"

"Delia?" Chef Art looked confused.

"Delia Vann," I explained. "Where is she?"

"Oh." Chef Art grinned. "I don't know. I love to visit with her, but not during working hours."

Ollie put his big hands on Chef Art's neck. Even though his hands were very large, they couldn't quite meet above Chef Art's white jacket. "Stop playing around. We know you kidnapped her to get the recipe."

Chef Art's gaze darted between us. "I swear, the closest I've ever come to kidnapping anyone was Miss Chase here. And that was even more like a conversation than a kidnapping. Why would I think Delia would have anything to do with the Jefferson recipe?"

Ollie and I looked at each other. I could tell we were both thinking the same thing—was Chef Art for real?

"I don't believe you," I finally told him. "If you came to look for the recipe, your people have already searched everything I own. I don't have the recipe. If I did, I'd give it to the police."

"I think we've gotten off on the wrong foot," Chef Art said in a congenial tone. "Yes, I want that recipe. I've offered to pay several people for it since I heard it was back on the market. I don't ask questions about how these things happen. But I haven't kidnapped Delia—although the idea is quite appealing."

That was enough for Ollie. He couldn't get his hands around Chef Art's throat, but he did shake him a little. "Where is she? What have you done with her?"

"I assure you, my dear boy, I haven't done anything to her or with her that she didn't fully participate in. And even that hasn't been in a while. I last saw her on the night my unfortunate contact for the Jefferson recipe was murdered."

"So you're saying you didn't kill Terry Bannister?" I asked.

"No. Why would I? A man could get a bad business reputation that way. Terry was supposed to procure the recipe for me. I would have paid him the sum we had agreed upon. Nothing more, nothing less. Definitely not murder. I don't do that."

"You hire other people to do it," Ollie said. "Admit it. You're the one behind all of this."

Chef Art righted his snowy white chef's hat. "If you mean that I wanted the recipe, you're right. I'm a collector of old recipes. The Jefferson recipe for crème brûlée would be a jewel in that collection. However, I didn't authorize a theft, or a murder, or even a kidnapping to get it. You're looking for someone else."

"Then why are you here?" I demanded.

"To honor a debt. We had an agreement, Miss Chase. My motor home is outside. My publicity team is working at full capacity. I'm ready to help you cook and serve some of your delicious food—and pose for photo ops with you."

It was overwhelming thinking about the response his presence and publicity had brought about. It was a little depressing, too. I guess I must've looked disappointed.

"Oh, I'm so sorry. You thought this was all *you*." Chef Art pinched my cheek. "Be patient. It will come. For now, let's give the public what they want, shall we?"

Chef Art and I did interviews with Renee Reynolds and another TV personality I didn't recognize. There were suddenly hundreds of balloons, with the names of the Biscuit Bowl and Chef Art emblazoned on them, being given out to children.

He wasn't kidding about his PR people working overtime. It was like a circus. Unfortunately, it was a circus that was running out of food. I was down to my last tray of biscuits, and we weren't even close to the end of the large crowd I could see from the open windows.

Ollie was taking orders outside to speed up the process while Chef Art and I cooked and bantered for the radio station that had set up shop right outside the Biscuit Bowl.

"I'm going to have to close." I couldn't believe it. "No more biscuits."

"Don't be absurd," Chef Art said. "You can make more biscuits in my motor home. I'm sure I have plenty of supplies, and there's a double oven onboard. Ollie and I will hold down the fort here while you work—if he can keep from killing me while you're gone."

"Sorry. He kind of has a crush on Delia."

"Really?" He looked absolutely surprised. "She's a beauty. Does he think he has a chance with her?"

I thought about that as I left the Biscuit Bowl and stepped out into the sunshine to look for Chef Art's motor home. It wasn't hard to find. His face was colorfully painted on the side of the fifty-foot-long motor home. It was so big, I could've driven the Biscuit Bowl right into it.

Once I reached it, two of Chef Art's assistants greeted me. They took me into the huge, stainless steel kitchen that was equipped to feed massive numbers of people. They asked what I needed and took out flour and vegetable shortening. There wasn't enough they could do for me.

When I was set up, and baking four trays of biscuits (love that double oven), the two assistants left to take pictures, sending them to Twitter and other social media outlets. It was awesome what could be accomplished with enough people and money.

I set the timer for the biscuits and prepared the next four trays. This was like being on a reality TV show where your fondest wish came true. I wasn't sure about Chef Art being the innocent party in what was happening with Delia, and I felt guilty enjoying the spoils of his largesse knowing she was still out there in danger.

Still, I couldn't help wallowing in the success a little, and dreaming about someday attaining Chef Art's following for my food.

The ovens made a chiming sound, letting me know the biscuits were ready. I got up to take out the pans and put the next four in.

The sliding glass door to the motor home opened, and Don Abbott stepped inside.

TWENTY-SIX

"You!" he said with a sneer.

"You!" I looked for the rolling pin I'd seen in one of the drawers.

"Where's Chef Art?"

"He's in my food truck. What do you want?"

"I guess now the two of you are in cahoots." Don looked around the kitchen.

"I'm not sure what that means." *Who says cahoots, anyway?* "He's helping me promote my business today."

"Yeah. Like I care."

"Well, I don't care what you think, either. You can go find him."

"I have the recipe," he said with a wide grin.

"Good for you."

"You better believe it's good for me. I've worked hard for this piece of paper."

"How much is he paying you?"

"Not enough. Why? I'm not cutting you in, if that's what you're thinking."

"That's fine." I didn't wait any longer. I took the biscuits out of the oven, thankful that none of them had burned. I couldn't help it anyway. I was distracted. "You can give Delia back now."

He looked blank for a minute. "I don't have her."

"Don't pretend you didn't try to set up a meeting to swap her for the recipe."

"I didn't set up a meeting. I don't have her. I don't need to swap anything for the recipe. It's mine now."

"You know that's stolen property, right? If you sell that to Chef Art, you'll be selling stolen property that was involved in two murders. You could go to prison for life."

I hoped I sounded knowledgeable. I wasn't sure I had any ground to stand on with those charges, but he didn't know.

"With the money Chef Art is going to pay me for the recipe, I'll be going away for life, but not to prison." He stroked his dirty, stubbled chin. "I'm thinking Tahiti, or one of those other islands that don't have extradition."

I acted like it was nothing to me as I put in the four new trays of biscuits. "Fine. Go on then."

"All right. I will."

But before he could leave, I had to ask about Delia. "If you don't have Delia, who does? It must be part of this whole thing. Someone wanted to trade her for the recipe. Who else is involved in this besides you and Chef Art?"

He shrugged. "I don't know. You should ask Chef Art. He might've hired more than one person to find the recipe."

It seemed like a good answer. He left the motor home. I took a deep breath, glad to see him leave. At least he wasn't brandishing a gun this time.

Someone else knew about the recipe—and what it was worth—if Don was telling the truth. I was probably a fool to believe him. He might've killed Terry. What was a lie to him?

When the biscuits had cooled, I took the first four trays to the Biscuit Bowl. It was surrounded by people. They formed a sea around it that made it tough to get inside. Chef Art's security people created a path for me.

"Glad you made it back in time," he quipped when he saw me. "I was afraid these people might turn on me if we completely ran out of biscuit bowls. Any thought on replacing the fillings?"

I put down the trays of biscuits. This had to stop.

"I just saw Don Abbott at your motor home. He said he has the Jefferson recipe. He also said he has no idea where Delia is, or who could have her."

His eyes lit up when I mentioned the recipe. "That's good news."

"For *you*," I reminded him. "I know you don't think much of Delia, but she's my friend. I want her back."

"I want her back, too. And I never said I didn't think much of her. She's a wonderful companion."

The whole time he was talking, he was taking orders from Ollie and filling biscuit bowls with amazing speed. He worked like he'd done this exact job all of his life. Somehow, it made me even angrier.

"Look, if Delia was ever good to you, you owe her something for getting her caught in the middle of your hunt for the recipe. She's a person, too. She has dreams and goals, just like you do. Think about it. Did you hire more than one person to bring you the recipe? If so, who was it?"

"I think you need to talk while you fry up more of those bowls," he reminded me. "As for Delia, let me check into it. You're right. I hired a few people for the operation. As I said, I'm a collector. The Jefferson recipe means a lot to me."

"That's fine. Just come up with an answer or I'm going to call the police, and you'll have company when you get that recipe from Don."

His eyes widened comically. "You *wouldn't*! After all

I've done for you today? I've put you on the food truck map in Mobile."

"And I didn't tell the police that you kidnapped me to ask me about the recipe. I think we're even."

"There's that," he admitted. "Trust me. I didn't mean Delia to be involved in this. I knew she was dating Terry, but that was only a point of interest. We'll find her. Now, get to frying."

I did as he said. I wanted to help Delia. I wasn't sure what to do except make sure that the people who seemed to be the players in the theft of the recipe knew that she wasn't forgotten. I planned to have another talk with Detective Latoure before the end of the day.

What a day it was. We ran out of everything, including serving boxes and plastic forks and spoons. There was nothing left to eat or drink when we finally closed the doors to the Biscuit Bowl.

I felt like a limp rag, just waiting for someone to come and put me in the hamper. I'd done three interviews by myself and five with Chef Art. I had to empty the cashbox five times and had more credit card receipts than I'd ever seen before. It was amazing what publicity could do.

"*Whoo-eee!*" Chef Art was still full of energy. His white jacket was as clean as when he'd stepped into the food truck. He'd done plenty—I couldn't have done it without him. His white hat was still at the jaunty angle on his head.

I could tell he loved all of this. I was a mess and wanted to go home and take a nap. Ollie had taken orders and passed out menus until they were gone. He looked as exhausted as I felt.

"I don't know what to say," I admitted. "It was wonderful. I never knew people could eat so many biscuits in one day."

"And that's just the start for you, Miss Zoe Chase," Chef Art said. "Unless I'm very much mistaken, you're on the rise. Your business will continue to grow. Don't do anything stupid, now, hear?"

"You mean like *you* did?" Ollie asked.

"You could say that. Still, I live in a thirty-six-room mansion with three guest cottages, a swimming pool, and tennis courts. I travel around the world on my own private jet, and my yacht is anchored out there in the bay. I think it worked out all right, don't you?"

Even Ollie, who wasn't a fan of Chef Art, had to admit he lived a good life, despite his mistakes. Ollie kind of growled his agreement. He left the Biscuit Bowl to get the chairs and tables from outside.

"Now, what are we going to do about Delia?" Chef Art tapped his chin. "And where is Don Abbott with my recipe? That was hours ago that he told you he had it. I didn't want to draw attention, but I have my limits of patience."

"I don't know. He was at your motor home when I was there. He left before I did. Maybe he decided to sell it to someone else."

His eyes narrowed a little in his always pleasant face. That was the only hint of any anger about my words. "Let's go take a look around, shall we? You don't have to bother taking those biscuit pans back. One of my assistants will get them."

I decided to go with him. If nothing else, I'd be a witness to Don selling the Jefferson recipe to Chef Art. I could use my cell phone to record it. Maybe I could use that as some kind of leverage to get Delia back. What else could you expect when you offered so much money for something? There were bound to be people who would do anything to win the prize.

As Chef Art and I left the Biscuit Bowl, it was starting to get dark outside. The parking lot was almost empty at police headquarters. There was no sign of the crowds that had been there that day.

Suzette's Crepes and the Dog House were closing up, too. I had no doubt some of that business Chef Art's promotional team had generated went to them, too. Their owners looked pleased, even if my food truck had been the hit of the day. We all knew it was staying in the game that mattered. It didn't hurt that people would associate the Biscuit Bowl with Chef Art from now on. It was what I did with that valuable association that would affect me in the long run.

"I don't see him," I said to Chef Art. "I was only kidding about him selling the recipe to someone else. It seems odd that he knew there was a big payday coming when he sold you the recipe, and didn't stick around."

"Yes it does." He scratched his beard. "Maybe he's feeling shy of you watching our deal, my dear. Maybe you should wait in your food truck."

I wasn't happy with that idea, but I knew it probably wouldn't do any good to argue. I figured I could tell him I was going back to the Biscuit Bowl and then wait outside his motor home until Don made his appearance.

I knew Chef Art wouldn't stand around waiting for Don. He'd want to go inside and relax. Despite his vigor, he had to be tired.

"Okay. I guess I'll take off. Thanks again for all your help." I shook his hand.

"You're very welcome. You're coming to the benefit dinner, right? I assume after that we'll be square?"

"That's right," I agreed. "I'll see you then."

Chef Art made a few more friendly remarks about the dinner and our association. I noticed he was looking around the whole time, like a cat stalking a mouse. He might not have appeared to be aware of what was going on, but he was alert to every movement.

I left him at the sliding glass door to his motor home. I started to walk briskly back to the Biscuit Bowl until I knew the coming darkness and the scattered vehicles left in the parking lot would obscure me from his gaze.

Then I doubled back to the side of his motor home where I could watch the door.

I was standing at the back end of the motor home, the

beginning of Chef Art's giant face painting. There were
large propane tanks attached here, as well as miscellaneous
scooters and a few pieces of lawn furniture. It was a big,
rolling house for an important man, as he'd pointed out to
Ollie earlier.

I saw two of Chef Art's assistants carrying the biscuit
pans and other items that had migrated to my food truck
during the day. They were talking and laughing as they
walked through the parking lot.

I moved back a little farther into the shadows, not wanting them to see me spying on their boss. My foot came down
on something squishy that I prayed wasn't dog poop. How
bad would that be in my surprise showdown with Chef Art
and Don Abbott if I smelled like doggy doo-doo?

I lifted my foot carefully and smelled. No poop odor. I
looked to see what I had stepped on and gasped.

There in the shadows of Chef Art's motor home was the
lifeless body of Don Abbott.

TWENTY-SEVEN

I didn't scream, though I had to bite my lip not to. I'd seen quite enough dead bodies in the past few days. I hoped this would be the last one.

Calmly, I dialed the number for police headquarters, instead of 911, and asked for Detective Latoure. When she got on the phone, I told her about Don.

"Where are you?" she demanded. "I told you not to get involved any further in this, Zoe."

"If you call 'getting involved' walking to the back of Chef Art's motor home, I guess I'm guilty. I'm out in the parking lot. You can't miss Chef Art's giant face. I'll be waiting for you. Is there anything I should do?"

"Anything like what? What did you have in mind?"

"I don't know. Cover the body with a tarp, or something. Direct traffic away from it."

"No. Don't touch anything. Don't move. I'll be right out. Just keep Chef Art from leaving, if you have to."

"You don't have to worry about that."

Patti Latoure was true to her word. She was downstairs with two uniformed officers in five minutes. They brought floodlights with them and lit up the area where I was standing like it was part of a Christmas pageant.

"Zoe." She shook her head, her face very grim in the sudden bright light.

"Patti."

"You seem very calm about all this."

"Well, you know how it is. When you've seen one dead body outside a coffin, the next one isn't such a big surprise."

"Whatever you say." She took out her notebook. "How did you find the victim?"

I described walking back there to wait for Chef Art to finish his business with Don. "I didn't realize he was right here, and probably wouldn't meet with Chef Art tonight."

She grimaced. "Could we have a little respect for the dead, please?"

"It seems wrong to accord him respect now that I didn't give him when he was alive. He held a gun on me and threatened to hurt people I care about. He probably kidnapped Delia, and I think he trashed my diner and food truck."

"We have a missing persons report out on your friend, Delia Vann. I have no reason to suspect Abbott of kidnapping her. Do you?"

"No reason?" I put my hands on my hips and stared up at her. "He was involved in stealing the Jefferson recipe. He planned to sell it to Chef Art tonight. That's why I was standing over here. I wanted to witness that transaction so I could use it against him."

"And I think I heard something on TV about your mother looking into a ransom note for Miss Vann. No one else told me anything about *that*." Patti raised one brow. "Is that your idea of not getting involved in this mess? I should arrest you right now for being an accessory. You were supposed to come to me if you so much as heard or saw anything related to Terry Bannister's death or this recipe."

Good thing I had Miguel on speed dial. "I was only wait-ing and watching. And I would've come to you as soon as Delia was safe."

"And I'd arrest you except that it would mean another visit from your mother and father. Not a good thing for me."

Patti crouched down close to Don's body and checked his pockets, pulling a wallet, and something else, from them. She opened the piece of paper she'd found carefully and read it before she handed it to me.

"Is this what you're talking about?"

I couldn't believe she was giving it to me. I had no gloves, no training to handle what might be an important piece of evidence.

Instead of taking it from her, I looked at it closely. The scrawling handwriting at the top of the page said, *Crème Brûlée by Thomas Jefferson. A man who used to be president.*

"Well, that's not it!" I was very clear on the subject. "That has to be the worst forgery of anything in the world."

"What's going on back here?" Chef Art's voice broke up our conversation.

"Chef Arrington." Detective Latoure was courteous and careful in her handling of him. "I'm afraid a man has been murdered right here at the back of your motor home."

"You've got to be kidding." Chef Art took a step forward and peered at the man on the ground. "Did you . . . uh . . . find anything unusual?"

Before Detective Latoure could speak, I jumped in. "She found a really bad forgery of the Jefferson recipe. We both know that's what you're looking for."

Chef Art held his head high and straightened up. "I'll admit to having an *interest* in a certain recipe. I've done nothing illegal. The recipe is a collector's item, and I am a collector."

I could tell Detective Latoure didn't want to get involved in that issue. With me speaking up about it, she had no choice.

"Did you know that recipe—the real one—was stolen from a museum in Virginia?" she asked. "The man who took it was found dead in his motel room in Atlanta— without the recipe."

"I had no idea." Chef Art managed to look completely innocent. He was as fine an actor as he was a cook. "I'd heard that the recipe was up for sale. I arranged with a man I'd never met to sell it to me. That's it."

Before Detective Latoure could answer, Chef Art sent one of his assistants to fetch his lawyer.

"That could be a logical assumption on your part," Patti finally said. "There was no way for you to know the recipe was stolen."

"True," Chef Art agreed. "I haven't seen it as yet. I would've authenticated it right away. If I'd learned that the recipe had been stolen—heaven forbid—I would've *immediately* turned it in to the police."

It was the biggest load of hogwash I'd ever heard. I couldn't believe Detective Latoure was buying it, but she was nodding and looking serious, as though it made perfect sense.

"We think this man, Don Abbott, might be a part of the theft. His partner, Terry Bannister, was murdered. Whoever is interested in owning the Jefferson recipe, not an upstanding businessman like yourself, of course, has gone to extreme lengths to get their hands on it."

The medical examiner arrived. We were forced to move away from the motor home. The area was blocked off just in time. A TV crew arrived to see what all the fuss was about.

"Did you see the recipe?" Chef Art whispered to me while Detective Latoure was talking to the medical examiner.

"It wasn't the real recipe." I told him what it said at the top of the paper. "I'm no expert, but I don't think that was even remotely close to an antique document."

"So it's still out there, somewhere." He sighed as though in relief.

"Did it ever occur to you that you could be a suspect in this murder? In Terry's murder, too, for that matter? It looks like Terry was killed because he wouldn't hand over the recipe. He hid the location of it in some beads that he gave Delia. Maybe when Don showed up with this impossible forgery, you killed him, too."

"Looks can be deceiving." Chef Art dared a quick glance at Detective Latoure. "I definitely didn't kill Don Abbott. You're my alibi for that, Miss Chase. Do I need to remind you that I haven't been *anywhere* without you for the last eight hours?"

He was right. We'd either been doing interviews or cooking since I'd seen Don last. I wasn't sure about what had happened to Terry, but Chef Art was clear of Don's death.

"Sorry."

"That's all right." He sniffed and looked away, as though he was hurt by my supposition. "You young people. No matter what anyone does for you, you turn on them like a snake."

I started to remind him again why he'd helped me today, and that he was probably the catalyst in the deaths, if not the actual killer, of both men. His willingness to pay top dollar for the stolen recipe made him the accessory Detective Latoure was looking for.

Detective Latoure finally came back toward us. Chef Art gave me a warning look. He didn't have to worry. What could I say that I could prove?

"It looks like Mr. Abbott may have been killed with the same weapon used on Terry Bannister, a .22 pistol." She shrugged. "That is to say that they were both shot with the same caliber, anyway. We'll know more once the ME has some time to examine the body."

Chef Art shook his head. "Bless his soul."

Patti turned to me. "You didn't notice anyone else around the back of the motor home when you got there?"

"No, but it was dark already. I saw Don earlier today when I was making biscuits in the motor home. He told me he had the recipe Chef Art was looking for and asked me where he was."

"He didn't threaten you again, or act aggressive in any way?"

"No. I guess he thought he had what he needed. He didn't need to threaten me."

I could tell the way Detective Latoure turned to Chef Art that she disliked questioning him. Her brow was deeply furrowed, and there was a cautious tone to her voice.

"This recipe you wanted to buy—you say you didn't know it was stolen. How did you come to hear about it?"

"An antique dealer told me about it," Chef Art said. "He always keeps a lookout on that kind of thing for me. He knows I collect antique recipes. I had no idea we were dealing with the criminal element, Detective. Believe me, I would've immediately told the police if I'd been aware."

Patti's smile was hesitant as her pen hovered over her notebook. "I'm sorry to have to ask you this, Chef Arrington, but can you remember your whereabouts last Tuesday night?"

"I can indeed," Chef Art said readily. "I was in the company of a beautiful young woman. You can certainly check with her."

"And her name?"

"Miss Delia Vann."

Patti glanced at me. "I was afraid of that."

"I know Miss Vann has been kidnapped," Chef Art said in what seemed like a last-minute attempt to clear himself. "I had nothing to do with it, and even offered my assistance to Miss Chase in trying to find her."

"Chef Arrington, I'm going to have to ask you to accompany me inside and answer some questions."

"What? That's ridiculous!" Chef Art's flair for the

dramatic brought his voice to a feverish pitch. "I won't stand for being treated this way, Detective. You know who I am."

Patti's expression was one of long suffering. "I know. Believe me, if there was any other choice, I'd take it."

"You're not arresting me, are you?"

"No, sir. We need to verify a few things, that's all. I'm sure you'll be free to go in no time."

Chef Art seemed to accept his fate. He walked alongside Detective Latoure toward police headquarters.

"What's going on?" Ollie asked as a huge wave of reporters followed Chef Art toward the building. "Are they arresting him?"

"Probably not. He already called his lawyer." I looked back at where the crime scene people were doing their job. I realized that finding Don's body had affected me more than I thought. "Let's go home, Ollie. I think that's all I can do today."

I felt a little guilty leaving Chef Art that way. I reminded myself that he probably had a dozen lawyers on retainer. He didn't need my help. If Detective Latoure had questions about me being with Chef Art all day, I could answer them when they came up.

We drove back to the diner, with Crème Brûlée making terrible sounds. He was hungry and tired. It had been a longer day than usual for him. I hoped he'd get used to staying at the diner while I was out in the food truck. He was better off at home with his food and litter box.

"That was one awful day, Zoe, except for the biscuit sales. You kicked butt on those!" Ollie said as I parked the food truck in the space by the diner. "There isn't any food left. Everyone is gonna be disappointed about that."

Another thing for me to feel guilty about. I had an answer for this one. As tired as I was, I didn't think I could sleep yet. Cooking something would make me feel better. I decided to make some biscuits and sausage gravy for everyone.

Ollie and I got the food truck cleaned out, and I locked

it up for the night. I'd taken Crème Brûlée inside first. By
the time we were done, he was asleep on my bed, his little
white paws sticking up in the air. I stopped for a moment,
and rubbed his soft tummy. He didn't even wake up enough
to do more than hiss at me.

I laughed and went into the kitchen. Ollie had gone to
the homeless shelter to gather the group and tell them I was
making food.

Is it over now?

I thought about the whole series of events that had led to
Don's death today. I knew it was more than possible that
Chef Art would convince Detective Latoure that he had no
idea that the Jefferson recipe was stolen. Maybe he was even
telling the truth.

Detective Latoure obviously didn't want to charge Chef
Art with anything. That would probably be the end of that
aspect.

Still, three people had died, and Delia was still missing.
The recipe was out there, too. I wasn't sure where it would
go from there.

I had nothing to trade for Delia. If the killer had her, he
probably also knew the recipe Don had was a fake. What
else could I do to help my friend?

Miguel stopped by. He'd heard about what had happened
to Don. "Did you get a look at the recipe?"

I told him it was a fraud. "I don't know how we'll find it."

"I don't, either." He sipped the coffee I'd poured him.
"And I don't see any way to get Delia back safely without it."

I thought about it while I took out one pan of biscuits and
put in another. I stirred the sausage gravy. "What if we could
make the killer *think* we have the recipe? He must be thinking the same thing we are—the recipe is there, but he doesn't
know where. If we assume he knows the recipe Don had
wasn't real, it could work."

"Let's say you could convince the killer that you have

the recipe," Miguel began. "First of all, your life would be in danger again. Second, how would we get word to him? We don't know who or where he is."

"That's true," I agreed unhappily.

"Maybe the police already have the killer in custody, anyway. Chef Art may be the one behind all of this. We may have been right in thinking he kidnapped Delia. Don't let that happy Santa face and white hat fool you. Chef Art can play hardball. He knew the recipe was stolen, yet he still offered money for it."

"I don't think he killed anyone or kidnapped Delia, though. I think the person who took her put that invitation to his benefit dinner on her bed to mislead us."

"You're not seriously buying into his whole good-guy routine, right?"

I shrugged. "I told you, I have a feeling for people. Call it intuition, but it's more than that. Chef Art isn't exactly a good guy, but he's not a killer, either. I don't think he would've come out like that today to help me if he wasn't basically a good person."

"Except that you threatened him," he reminded me.

"I think if Chef Art was the killer, or even kidnapped Delia, he would've done a better job kidnapping me. Believe me, his heart wasn't in it."

"So, what's the plan?"

"I don't know yet. I'm hoping something will come to me." I smiled at him. "Feel free to make suggestions. You probably know more about this kind of thing than I do."

He smiled back at me, and I was caught in his sweet brown eyes.

"What do your instincts tell you about *me*?" Miguel asked.

"That you're one of the good guys. Maybe one of the *exceptional* guys." I leaned in close to him across the counter. "What do you think about *me*?"

Before he could answer, Ollie, Marty, and the rest of the group walked into the diner with hearty greetings and appreciative sniffs of the biscuit and gravy smells that perfumed the air.

"Later," Miguel whispered.

TWENTY-EIGHT

For a while, there was good conversation involving all different types of sports, fishing, and old times the men remembered with fondness. The biscuits and gravy disappeared like Alabama snow. There was nothing left to show for it after a few minutes.

Marty and Ollie took me aside and pledged their help finding Delia and the Jefferson recipe.

"There has to be some way to catch this killer before he does away with Delia," Marty said. "Any ideas?"

"I don't think he's going to stop until he gets the money from Chef Art. That's what started this whole chain of events," I said.

"Yeah," Ollie agreed. "But without the recipe to trade for Delia, what can we do?"

"That's the part I'm stuck on," I admitted. "Chef Art doesn't have the recipe. I'm sure of that. He was too excited about getting it from Don. On the other hand, the killer must not have it, either, or there was no reason to kill Don. I think he was probably angry that Don's recipe wasn't real."

"Or he just wanted to get rid of him." Marty shrugged. "The man was a nuisance."

Ollie shook his head. "I agree with Zoe. I don't think anyone has been able to find the recipe. Those clues Terry left on the beads were useless."

"You're right. I think that's what we need to do—find the recipe." I warmed to my subject. "We have to look back at the clues, and find it to trade for Delia."

"But you already searched both food trucks," Marty said. "Where else are you gonna look for it?"

"I don't know—yet. But we have to find it." I thanked Ollie and Marty for their help. "I'm sure we can do this."

"What are you three whispering about over here?" Miguel joined us.

"Finding Delia," Ollie said. "I've heard of long-distance romances, but this is ridiculous."

"I *knew* you liked her," I teased him.

"What's not to like? She's hot." Ollie waggled his eyebrows.

"But what does she see in *you*?" Marty wondered with one eye closed, examining his friend.

"I'm tall. I'm brown sugar through and through." Ollie's face puckered up, as though he was searching for another good trait.

"And you're a good cook," I added. "Don't worry. We'll find her."

"Let me know if there's anything *legal* I can do," Miguel said.

We all agreed to do what we could. Three of the men— not including Marty or Ollie—were directed to wash and dry plates, cups, and silverware. They left the kitchen cleaner than they'd found it.

"I think it's time for us to get back to the shelter," Marty said. "Good night, Zoe. Thanks for supper."

As the men left with Marty, there were hugs and thanks. They looked as rugged and down-and-out as could be, but all the men seemed to have hearts of gold. Sometimes I wondered about their pasts, and thought my instinct might be a bit swayed by the good things they'd done for me. I tried not to worry about it.

Ollie left soon after. "I'll give you two some time alone. A word of warning, Miguel: whatever you do, don't touch her hair."

I could feel the blazing hot spots on my face as Ollie chuckled and left the diner. He was beginning to be like the older brother that I never wanted. How could he *say* something like that? I'd confided the secret to my curls to him in good faith.

Not that it mattered once the gel was dry. And I didn't expect Miguel to run his fingers through my hair or anything tonight. It was just embarrassing.

"Would you like some pie?" I tried to distract Miguel from Ollie's remark. "I still have a piece or two of Uncle Saul's peach pie left."

"No. I'm full. The biscuits were delicious." Miguel smiled. "I guess I should go."

"Okay." What else could I say? I had been expecting to continue the conversation that had started before the others had arrived.

"There was one more thing I wanted to say." He came up close to me and took the dish towel out of my hands. "About my intuition with you, Zoe."

He put his hands on my arms and stared earnestly down into my eyes. I knew he was going to kiss me, despite what he'd said about not being ready. I tried not to look too expectant or do any puckering. I always hate when girls do that in the movies.

"Oh?" I opened my eyes wide and parted my lips a little. No lip licking, either. That was a dead giveaway.

"I think you're a *very* good soul. Wonderful, in fact. I've never known anyone quite like you."

That was it.

He smiled, wished me a good night, and left the diner.

I had to sit down on a stool at the counter for a minute to catch my breath, and let go of the expectations I was trying to hide.

Well, he thought I was wonderful. It was a start.

I locked the door to the diner and turned off the lights. I was too tired to think about making my sweet and savory fillings for tomorrow. That meant I had to get up even earlier and make them while I was baking biscuits. It would have to do.

I took a quick shower and hopped in bed with Crème Brûlée. He was snoring so loud that I had to wake him. He turned over and put his paws on my face for a moment before he licked my nose and fell back asleep.

Even though I was exhausted, my mind kept going over all the possibilities that could have been hidden in the green beads.

Chef A. That was obvious. Everyone knew Chef Art wanted the Jefferson recipe. Was Terry alluding to that fact? Or was that a warning to Don?

Green chili. We'd searched for a green chili canister, and a canister with green chili peppers. Neither one of them seemed to be what we were looking for.

There was always the possibility that someone had found what we'd missed. But if that was true, why not take it to Chef Art?

Food truck. That seemed obvious, too. I would've guessed Terry's food truck rather than mine. He was only in the Biscuit Bowl a short time harassing me. He could've hidden something while he was there, but it seemed unlikely to me.

Either way, again we struck out.

Watch your back. Maybe Terry knew this other person was involved. He wanted Don to watch out.

None of it made any sense—except the part about someone getting to the recipe before us. Both food trucks were such a mess, how could we say for sure that the recipe wasn't there?

Suddenly it struck me and I sat straight up in bed. Crème Brûlée hissed and turned over, ignoring me as he went back to sleep.

"We've been thinking about it the wrong way." I jumped up and rummaged around until I found Detective Latoure's phone number. I arranged for her to meet me at police headquarters in thirty minutes and called a taxi.

I threw on some jeans and a T-shirt, pushed my feet into tennis shoes, and plopped Crème Brûlée into his basket. He didn't appreciate that at all, but I didn't want him to wake up and find me gone. No telling what kind of trouble he'd get into. Besides, it was dark, and I didn't want him to be scared.

My curls were a mess. I scowled at them in the mirror. I didn't have the heart to wash and fix my hair, so I pulled on a bright blue cap to hide them. "It's your own fault if you don't like it," I told my sometimes pesky black curls. "Every once in a while, you could stay in place by yourselves."

I looked as good as I was going to look. I grabbed Crème Brûlée and my handbag before I shot out the door. I locked it behind me, even though it seemed to be a useless gesture. If someone wanted to get in, they'd just break a window. Leaving the door open might be the lesser of the two expenses.

Despite the argument with myself on the matter, my more practical side won out, and the door stayed locked.

Detective Latoure was waiting for me when I arrived at police headquarters. I paid my driver, who wasn't happy about having a cat in his car, and went to meet her, holding Crème Brûlée.

"You brought your cat with you?" she asked. "Did he eat the startling new clue you think you've discovered that made you call me at this ungodly hour?"

"He gets scared at the diner if he's alone too long." I shrugged and readjusted Crème Brûlée's weight in my arms. "We haven't been there that long. He still misses the apartment."

Patti put her hands over her ears. "Please! I don't want to know that you're living in that old diner."

"Oh, sorry. Well, anyway, Crème Brûlée has nothing to do with finding the recipe." I explained my new theory about the clues Terry had left behind for Don to find. "We have to look at the taco truck again. I think I understand what Terry was trying to tell Don."

"That's over at the impound lot." She looked at Crème Brûlée. "I suppose he has to come, too?"

Crème Brûlée hissed at her as though he knew Detective Latoure was trying to exclude him.

"He won't be a problem. He'll stay in his basket in the backseat. I promise."

Patti smiled and made the mistake of trying to stroke my cat. She pulled her hand back quickly and sucked on her bloody finger. "I think he hates me. But with that body, I don't think he could get out of the basket if he tried."

I didn't tell her that Crème Brûlée could indeed get out of the basket. I didn't want to stand out here or take him home. I wanted to take another look at the taco truck.

"Okay. Let's go." Patti shrugged and pulled out her keys. "My husband doesn't like it when I go out at this time of night without a partner."

I laughed as we walked to her car. "He must hate you being a detective."

"You could say that. I was going to be a lawyer when we met in college. He's never gotten over me changing my mind. He really didn't like it when I worked vice."

"What made you change your mind? I can't imagine my mother suddenly deciding to be a cop."

"A friend of mine in college was killed." She opened the back door of her car for me. "It was one of those random things. He was mugged and put up a fight. There's not much you can do against a shotgun. I knew I wouldn't want to defend his killer in court. I know everyone is entitled to good representation. I couldn't be that person."

"What about your husband?" It surprised me that she was willing to open up to me this way. Maybe she was still half-asleep.

"He works as a corporate lawyer." She grinned. "We're not exactly on the same wavelength, if you know what I mean. We tough it out like everyone else does."

"That must be hard."

"You have no idea." She got in and started the car as I put on my seat belt. "What about you? Are you crazy, or just a rebel?"

"I think maybe a little of both. I take after my Uncle Saul more than my parents."

"I knew Saul. He was a devil. When he was younger, people thought he was a genius in the kitchen. I never could figure out why he gave it all up. He could've been as famous as Chef Arrington."

"That's the crazy part, I guess. He suddenly decided it wasn't for him anymore. Now he lives in the swamp with an albino alligator."

"I've heard rumors that there was a woman." Patti glanced at me for confirmation as we stopped for a red light on Government Street.

"I guess I was too young for that. If there was a woman who brought him down, I've never heard anything about her. But you could be right."

We'd reached the impound lot. The officer let us through the gate. There were tall lights shining down on all the vehicles there, trying to prevent theft. They gave the whole area a weird orange glow. I saw Terry's taco truck right away.

I left Crème Brûlée sleeping in the back of the car. Detective Latoure and I walked to the taco truck. She opened the door with a key from her pocket.

"So, what's the new insight?" Patti hopped up into the back.

"It's this." I carefully pulled away the green chili calendar from the back door. "I was thinking maybe *watch your back* could have more than one meaning. What if it meant the back door? And we were all looking for something that *held* green chili. This calendar has different chili peppers on it every month. I got a free one, too. This month is green chilis."

As I spoke, I looked at the back of the calendar image. There was something taped to it. My heart skipped a beat as I excitedly pulled the tape from it.

The paper was very fragile. No telling what kind of damage had been done to the old recipe. It was still intact, signed by Thomas Jefferson. It was amazing to see it.

"You know, they had a lot of different ways of spelling the same words we use today," I told Patti. "I probably should be wearing gloves. I didn't think of it."

"You found it!" She smiled and held out a large plastic bag that she withdrew from her pocket. She put on latex gloves and carefully handled the recipe. "I didn't think we'd find it."

Now for the second part of my plan. "Since we found it, I'd like to use it to get Delia back."

I could see her immediately recoil from the idea. "Absolutely not! This has to be returned right away."

"If you return it right away, there won't be any reason to keep Delia alive," I reminded her.

"You don't even know for sure what happened to Miss Vann. She could've left town, for all you know, Zoe. I can't risk this recipe to let you play around at being a detective."

I'd thought about this objection before I'd called her that night. "What about if you keep this a secret for another day or two and we make a copy of it? I could try and exchange that for Delia. If nothing else, I could possibly draw out the killer with it. That would be even better for you, right? You'd have the recipe *and* the person who killed Terry and Don."

She thought about it for a moment. "You couldn't use the real recipe."

"Okay."

"But maybe I could keep this quiet for a few days. What are you thinking?"

TWENTY-NINE

We had to find a good forger to fool anyone with the document I planned to trade for Delia. Uncle Saul suggested Ben Weathers. Miguel and I went to visit him at his antique shop on Friday morning.

"Did Uncle Saul mention that his friend did time in prison for forgery?" Miguel asked as we drove to South Water Street.

Rain had come in from the gulf and was sweeping the streets of Mobile. Not a good day to be out in the food truck, and yet I felt a little let down that I might lose all the momentum I'd gained with Chef Art's help.

Delia needed rescuing, I reminded myself. My plan had to work. Miguel wasn't pleased with my plan when he'd heard it. "Did I mention how many things could go wrong with this plan? I can't believe Detective Latoure is going along with it."

The proof of Detective Latoure's willingness to try and

catch the killer—as well as taking the credit for finding the Jefferson recipe—was in my lap.

A historian from the Mobile History Museum had authenticated the recipe yesterday. He'd agreed to keep quiet about the find. He'd put the document into a protective envelope where it could be viewed without being touched. He'd also warned that the recipe needed to be returned as quickly as possible, as he ogled the slice of history.

"It's going to be fine, Miguel," I told him. "There are always things that could go wrong, but that doesn't mean they *have* to go wrong."

"You walking around telling everyone that you have the recipe and are going to sell it to Chef Art is a bad idea. Don threatened you, and he wasn't even sure you had it. How do you think the killer is going to react with the *certain* knowledge that you have it? He's killed at least two people already to get the payoff from Chef Art."

"I've thought of that. And that's why I'm staying at my father's apartment until this is over. He has security. After today, I'll only have a good copy of the recipe, so it can't be lost again. The worst that can happen is that the killer will figure out where to find me, and he'll kill me before I can sell the fake to Chef Art."

"Oh. If that's the worst that can happen—I think we should scrap this idea and come up with another one."

I put my hand on his arm as he drove. "Don't worry. I know this is going to work. Uncle Saul says we can trust Ben Weathers to keep his mouth shut about the forgery. Detective Latoure will have people at the benefit dinner. It's all going to be fine, and we'll have Delia back."

I wasn't as sure as I sounded, but what choice did we have? I figured the biggest risk was the killer trying to get the recipe *before* the dinner. I hoped staying at my father's apartment would take care of that. In addition to security at the apartment, Detective Latoure had two men stationed downstairs in the lobby. I was probably safer there with the fake recipe than I had been without it at the diner.

Miguel parked the car in the same spot Uncle Saul had parked when we'd visited Ben. "I hope you're right. It seems risky to me. As Detective Latoure pointed out, we don't even know for sure that the killer has Delia."

"I think we're pretty clear about that." I got out of the car. "Delia didn't just run off on her own. If it wasn't for my mother messing up the exchange, we'd have her back already."

Miguel came around the side of the car. "I can see there's nothing I can say that will change your mind."

"That's probably true. Shall we do this?"

Ben was thrilled to get a look at the Jefferson recipe. He spent ten minutes marveling at it, turning it around, and examining every part of it.

"I love holding history in my hands. You know, this seems like only a recipe, but Jefferson and his chef—who was Sally Hemmings's brother, by the way—changed how we think about food in this country. It would've been tragic for this to have ended up in a private collection." He looked up and grinned at me. "Unless of course it was mine."

I could appreciate his sentiments. It was fascinating. It struck me even more so because crème brûlée was involved. What were the chances?

"Now, let's see. I think I have exactly the right paper here to make this realistic." Ben put on his glasses and slid a piece of antique paper from a plastic pouch. "If someone who knows what they're doing looks at this too close, you're dead. I could tell you that it's a forgery with a few minutes to examine it. You need to do what you have to do and get out of there, Zoe. I wouldn't want Saul saying I got his niece in trouble."

Of course, Ben didn't know what we had in mind. I'd only told him the barest information. It was better that way.

Detective Latoure was hoping that Chef Art wasn't the killer and wasn't the person who'd kidnapped Delia. Neither one of us could be sure. She certainly didn't want to arrest the popular celebrity, especially not at his own, very high-profile, party.

I didn't want that to happen, either. It would make me doubt my instincts about Chef Art. When I'd called him, and told him I had found the recipe, he'd almost sounded disappointed.

I couldn't tell; maybe he was disappointed that he might have to kill me, or that he'd have to pay me the million dollars he'd promised Terry.

Whatever it was, I didn't let it get to me. I had to steel myself in case Chef Art was the culprit. If I was wrong about him, I was wrong.

Ben began copying the information from the Jefferson recipe to the forgery with excruciating patience. He offered several times to let us leave the recipe with him and pick it up later. I didn't have to nix that idea. Miguel said no very quickly.

That meant I had to wait on his customers that came in while he was working. There weren't many on the dismal day. One man came in for a chair Ben had procured for him. A woman came in to browse but left without a purchase.

"Hey!" Ben looked at me over the top of his glasses. "I'm doing this for free, Zoe. The least you could do is sell something for me."

"Sorry. I was trying. She wasn't interested."

"She sounded interested to me. I thought you'd be a good salesperson since you have that food truck and all. How's that going, by the way? You were all over the news with Chef Art. Is he your new mentor?"

"Not exactly. He kind of owed me a favor."

Ben grunted. "I guess that runs in the family, or I wouldn't be doing this, either."

"Great. Can we have a little less talk and a little more forging?" Miguel said.

"Keep your pants on," Ben said. "This has to be done just right. If I misspell one word, it could be a dead giveaway."

The rain came down even harder, making the antique shop seem smaller and darker. No other customers came in. Miguel spent most of his time on his cell phone with a client. I walked through Ben's shop looking at all the wonderful old pieces he had there.

"I'm done." Ben took off his glasses and blew on the ink he'd used from an old fountain pen. "Like I said, someone who knows his business is gonna spot that this wasn't written with a quill pen. That would be bad. If you're trying to sell this to a person who is only looking to turn it over and make some money, you should be okay."

I knew he was trying to get more information from me about what was going on. I hoped he could stay quiet about what he knew. It was a big secret to keep for someone like him.

"Thank you for your help." I picked up the forgery and looked at it.

"You're welcome. Tell your uncle I owe him one less favor. Someday, he's gonna owe *me* a favor or two."

"I'll tell him."

Ben squinted up at me as he looked at the real recipe again. "You know, I'd heard this was lost—that the sale to Chef Art didn't go through. You aren't involved in that, are you, Zoe?"

"Not at all." I smiled at him as I took the Jefferson recipe. "I wouldn't do anything like that, Ben. My mother would prosecute me in court herself."

Miguel and I left the shop, darting out into the heavy downpour. When we were inside the car, he said, "You're a very smooth liar, Zoe."

"I wasn't lying. I'm not involved in the sale to Chef Art. I'm only trying to get Delia back."

He laughed as he started the car. "Selective truth, then."

"Maybe. I guess we better get the real recipe back to police headquarters before Detective Latoure sends out a search party for us."

We went over the plan again as we drove across town in heavy traffic. It seemed no one wanted to be out walking or riding their bikes on a day like this. That led to more cars on the road.

I was surprised when we got to police headquarters that Suzette's Crepes was parked outside. The weather was so bad that I knew no one would stop to eat. Still, there was a strong part of me that wished I was out there, too.

Miguel and I ran upstairs. We returned the real Jefferson recipe to Detective Latoure. She took a look at the forgery and pronounced it ready for the benefit dinner.

"Are you ready, Zoe?" She stowed away the plastic envelope that held the million-dollar recipe.

"As soon as I pick up my dress from the cleaners, I will be. I'll be glad to get this over with."

"Just remember we need you here by four P.M. to fit you with the wire. Make sure you keep to yourself the rest of today. You don't need to put yourself in harm's way any more than necessary. Let us do our job."

"Of course." I smiled at her. "I completely understand."

She grimaced. "You're a terrible liar. Just be careful, huh? I don't want this whole thing blowing up in my face."

After Miguel telling me I was a great liar, I was surprised at Patti's words. "You don't have to worry. I'm not going to do anything to get myself killed before I go to Chef Art's benefit dinner."

She glanced at Miguel. "Imagine that being your only motivation."

"I guess everyone is different." Miguel shrugged and picked up the forged recipe. "We'll see you tonight."

"Are you going to keep that?" I nodded at the recipe in his hand as we left Detective Latoure's office and headed back downstairs. "That would mean you have to go to the dinner tonight."

He looked a little red-faced as he gave the fake recipe to me. "I'm sorry, Zoe. You know how I feel about it. You'll be in good hands with the police. There wouldn't be anything else I could do to make it any better."

Except for being there with me. "I suppose that's true."

We'd reached the front door. Miguel looked at his watch.

"I can take a taxi back to my father's apartment." It was a completely awkward moment. "There's no reason for you to run back and forth across town."

"I *do* have to be at the courthouse in thirty minutes. If you wouldn't mind?"

I smiled and took out my cell phone. "Don't worry about it. I'll see you tomorrow. Have a good day in court."

Miguel looked as though he wanted to say something else. Whatever it was didn't come out. "Be careful, Zoe. I'll talk to you later."

I told myself it was just as well. I didn't want to be all clinging and nagging him. Tommy Lee and I were over. That didn't mean I had to be insecure about not being with a man. I was a small-business owner now.

I called for a taxi, squared my shoulders, and went outside to wait under the overhang.

I thought I might as well get my dress while I was out. It would be wrapped in plastic anyway. I might as well get everything ready.

Lucky for me, Crème Brûlée was a little familiar with my father's apartment. He'd settled in there much better than he had at the diner. He liked familiar surroundings and cushiony things. We weren't that much different.

Frankie at the dry cleaner's had my dress ready to go. I hadn't worn it in a long time. I'd tried it on before I decided to wear it. The elegant black party dress had a little red embroidery at the neckline and waist. It was always perfect whenever I wore it.

I paid Frankie and stood around making small talk for a while. I realized I wasn't looking forward to hiding at my father's apartment.

I felt like the chances were better than average that the killer would wait until the benefit dinner. What could it hurt for me to do a little shopping?

I was pretty sure my black heels needed to be replaced before dinner. I still had some money. I started thinking about treating myself to lunch and shoes.

That ended up taking most of the afternoon. I sprang for a manicure, and a cute little black hat with a veil that had a touch of red that would be perfect with my dress. I got the shoes on sale so I felt justified spoiling myself a little.

"What in the world have you been doing with these hands?" Penny, the manicurist at my usual salon, asked when she saw them. "Have you been mixing concrete or something?"

"No. I started my own business. I own a small diner and a food truck now."

She looked as though I'd told her that I was about to jump off a bridge. "Why on earth did you do a thing like *that*?"

It was a question I was used to answering. I wished it wasn't—and I wished no one else would ask me in that tone of voice again. It might be time to look for another salon, even though I'd been coming to Penny's for years.

Of course, who knew when my next manicure would be? My toes curled in my shoes as they imagined what she'd think of my lack of pedicures.

All of that led to lunch at the small café, Lavender Blue. I loved the quaint, hole-in-the-wall atmosphere, and the food was fantastic. I ordered my usual roasted vegetable orzo and sat back with my lime water to wait.

Across the crowded room, I saw Tommy Lee with Betty from the bank. It still amazed me that the two of them had managed to find each other. It annoyed me a little, too, even though I knew I was better off without him in my new life.

I was depressed, despite telling myself all those wonderful things about being in business and doing what I really wanted to do. I'd never thought of myself as one of those women who had to have a man all the time. But maybe I was.

That was even more depressing. I ended up splurging for the Grand Chocolate Surprise. It was really good. Then I started feeling guilty. Maybe that was better than being depressed.

I spoke with Lavender, who owned the café. We'd talked before about food, and many other subjects relating to food. I'd admired her for the last few years since I'd started coming there. She was in her midforties, and was very successful. She was also not afraid to be herself. I could tell because her long, straight hair was dyed a soft shade of purple. She was famous for it.

"That's wonderful news, Zoe." She held my hands and smiled. "I can see looking at you how good it's been."

"It hasn't been without its problems," I confided. "I'm still not sure if I'm going to make it."

"Of course you will. If not this time, then the next. This place isn't my first attempt at owning my own restaurant." She gestured at the soft lighting and plants. "There have been failures. Each time, I got back up, saved my money, and tried again. You will, too."

Even though she'd managed to pinpoint my greatest fear, I felt much better when I left. Even the rain had stopped when I got outside. It made me feel like everything was going to be okay. People who didn't know me might not think I could do this, but I knew they were wrong.

I grabbed a taxi and headed back to my father's apartment, full of chocolate and positive energy. I paid the driver when I got there, and stepped out on the sidewalk. The doorman tipped his hat to me.

"Zoe!"

I glanced up, and there was Marty. I got the oddest little *zing* when I saw him. It wasn't a good thing. "How did you know where to find me?"

"Ollie told me. You have to come with me. We found Delia."

THIRTY

In all fairness, I *had* told Ollie where I was going to be staying in case of an emergency. This seemed to constitute that emergency. I didn't blame him for telling Marty where I was.

Still, all the hair stood up on the back of my neck. I wondered what was wrong.

I was surprised that Marty had come to get me. Why hadn't Ollie called me to let me know that something had happened? "Where is she? Is she okay?"

"She seems to be fine, Zoe. I brought my car so we could go right over and get her."

I looked at him with his old jeans and T-shirt barely covering his tummy. Beyond him, parked on the street, was an old Buick that had seen better days. I hadn't even realized that he had a car. It made sense then why Ollie hadn't called and why Marty had come to get me.

I shivered a little, despite the warm afternoon sun on my

head. Something still felt wrong, no matter how I tried to talk myself out of it.

"Did you call the police?" I noticed the doorman's ears perked up when I mentioned the police.

"You know how we are with the police." Marty shrugged. "We thought about getting you and figuring out what to do after."

"Okay." I glanced at my watch. I still had an hour before I had to be at police headquarters to be fitted for the wire they wanted me to wear. "Let me drop my stuff off upstairs. I'll only be a minute."

"I'll go with you." Marty glanced at the doorman. "He doesn't look too happy about me hanging around. I think he might ask me to leave before you get back."

It made sense. It all made sense.

Still, I had a growing fear in the pit of my stomach.

I smiled at the doorman, who knew me well. "We're going upstairs for a minute, Bodie."

Bodie nodded, his critical eyes on Marty. "Whatever you say, Miss Chase." He used to be a security guard. He seemed to observe the world with as much suspicion as if he'd been a police officer. But a guest was a guest.

Marty and I walked through the posh lobby. There were a large number of people hanging around, especially for midday on Friday. I thought they were probably police officers, undercover, assigned by Detective Latoure. I smiled at each of them in case my life might be in their hands.

"Nice place," Marty whispered. "Do you live here when you're not at the diner?"

"No. My dad lives here. I live at the diner. I couldn't afford this."

He shrugged, and we walked into the elevator together.

I pressed the button for the fourth floor. "Where is she?"

"She's been tied up in the basement area under the

shopping center the whole time. We were right on top of her and didn't realize."

"Maybe we should call the police and an ambulance. Traffic was bad out today. They could be there before us." I took out my cell phone. "I know you don't like the police, but I don't have any problem calling them. Delia could be dehydrated or something."

"No. She's fine. She said she's been fed regularly, and she's okay. We don't have to worry."

The elevator stopped on the fourth floor and we got out. "Still, I think I'd feel better if someone takes a look at her. There could be complications. And where is the man who kidnapped her? The police should be there in case he shows up."

"Let's get out of here," Marty suggested.

Did he seem a little more nervous than usual?

It could be this setting, I thought.

I opened the door to my father's apartment. Silence greeted me, which was good. I knew Crème Brûlée was happy if he wasn't howling.

I put everything down on the chair by the door, glad to get it out of my arms. "I'll call the police. I won't mention the shelter, or you. I'd feel better knowing everyone was safe from the killer. If he doesn't know we've found Delia, he could be on his way back."

I looked at Marty as I spoke. A change came over his face. He didn't look friendly and helpful as usual. To make matters worse, he took a large, ugly gun from his jacket pocket.

"No one is going to get hurt, Zoe, as long as you hand over that recipe."

"Marty?" My knees felt a little weak. So much for my good/bad radar. I think it was trying to kick in, but it was too late.

I quickly reminded myself that I had been really preoccupied since I'd met him. I probably needed to pay more attention to the people around me. Usually, I did that, but perhaps I'd been slack since I opened my business. I definitely didn't see this coming.

"Let's not make a big deal out of this. You give me the Jefferson recipe, and I'll leave you here for your rich daddy to find. I think that's a fair trade."

"But you've been at the shelter for years. Ollie told me so. You're the glue that holds them together."

"Yeah, well, it was too good a deal to pass up. Chef Art contacted me about keeping an eye on Delia, in case she and Terry were in on the theft of the recipe. I knew this was *my* time. I knew I could take that recipe from Terry, and sell it to Chef Art myself. Just like *you've* been planning."

I'd forgotten for a moment that he thought I was supposedly selling the *real* recipe to Chef Art at the dinner tonight. It was the story I'd told everyone.

It was a good thing he wasn't clued in on the *whole* plan.

At least it *seemed* like a good thing.

"And Delia really is under the shopping center, and she's okay?"

"She's fine. I had no reason to hurt her. I was even thinking she might like to leave with me once I have a million bucks in my pocket. Delia is fun."

"Oh." I didn't know what to say. My mind kind of blanked out.

What was I going to do?

"So, hand it over. I'll tie you up on one of those cushy chairs and get out of here. No reason to panic or get all bent out of shape. I promise I won't hurt you."

I wondered if he'd made that promise to Terry and Don. It was enough to jump-start my mind. I had to do something fast.

It didn't matter that he took the fake recipe from me. The chances were that he'd never know the difference.

But it also meant he'd get away. I couldn't let that happen. I had to delay for a few minutes. There was also the worry that he might not only tie me up and leave once he had the recipe.

"I don't have it with me."

The gun came closer to my face. "What do you mean?"

"Miguel kept it with him. He was afraid I'd lose it before we could sell it to Chef Art."

"I knew Miguel was too good to be true. All that talk about helping people—he's been your accomplice through the whole thing, hasn't he?"

I thought about Miguel. *Did I want to bring him into this?* It seemed like my only way out. "Yes. It was all his idea."

Marty looked unhappy about that. He rubbed his chin but kept the gun pointed squarely at me. "But you can get it, right?"

"Yes." My mind raced ahead to all the possibilities. "One phone call. He's supposed to bring it over later. I could ask him to bring it now."

"Okay. Do it."

I looked at my cell phone and regretfully erased 911. I put in Miguel's number and waited while the phone rang.

"Put it on speaker." Marty put the gun to my head. "Tell him to get it over here right away. That's it. If you say anything about me, you're dead. Got it?"

"I've got it."

Miguel picked up the phone. "Hi, Zoe. What's up?"

"Can you bring the Jefferson recipe over right away?"

"What?"

I glanced at Marty. "I need you to bring the *real* recipe to my dad's apartment right away."

"The *real* recipe?"

This wasn't going to be easy. "Yes. I only have the forgery. I need the *real* thing. Right away."

Before Miguel could answer, Marty took the phone from me and turned it off.

"That's enough. We'll wait for him to get here. Sit down

over there, Zoe. I'm going to have to tie you up to keep you from trying something stupid and heroic."

I sat in the side chair. Marty had come well prepared. He took some duct tape out of his pocket and used it like a rope to tie me to the chair. He was about to put duct tape on my mouth when I stopped him.

"How am I going to tell Miguel to come in when he gets here?"

"I'll take care of that. You sit back and let it happen, okay?"

It didn't seem like I had much choice. He put the duct tape across my mouth. I hoped Miguel somehow understood that I was in trouble. I wasn't sure if I'd be able to pick up on that from what I'd told him. I hoped he could.

Marty knelt on the carpet at my feet and began duct-taping my legs to the chair. I heard a sound from the bedroom door. Crème Brûlée was coming in to see what was going on.

"Shoo!" Marty tried to flick him away from the chair.

Crème Brûlée looked up at me and meowed loudly. He was probably hungry, and he didn't like to be ignored.

"I said get away, cat." Marty gave him a push with his hand.

That was a little too personal for Crème Brûlée. He yowled and sank his teeth into Marty's hand. Marty slung him back on the carpet. As I was about to feel sorry for my cat, Crème Brûlée came back like a warrior.

He jumped on Marty's back as Marty was trying to keep my legs still. For once I was glad my kitty was so fierce. Crème Brûlée bit the back of Marty's neck and dug his claws in. Marty jumped up and down, even rolled over trying to dislodge him. He couldn't budge Crème Brûlée.

I would've applauded my cat, if I'd been able to move my arms and hands.

Marty had dropped his gun on the floor as he'd tried to get Crème Brûlée off of him. He hadn't noticed it yet. I was afraid, when he did, that Marty might shoot him.

"Get off of me, you little monster!" Marty finally managed to get Crème Brûlée off of his back and held him by the scruff of his neck. He stalked to the front door as Crème Brûlée continued to scratch at him and hiss.

Marty opened the door, ostensibly to throw Crème Brûlée out into the hall. Miguel and two police officers were standing right outside.

Forgetting for a moment that he was holding a fully loaded cat, Marty appeared stunned by the three men at the door. Crème Brûlée took his opportunity to twist his big body over. He latched onto Marty's arm with his teeth and claws.

Marty let out a scream. "Get this thing off of me!"

The two police officers grabbed him. At that point, Crème Brûlée dropped gracefully to the carpet. He sauntered over to where I was tied up and sat down to complain that his food bowl was empty.

Miguel rushed over and quickly got the duct tape off of me. Not a pleasant experience.

I threw my arms around his neck and thanked him repeatedly. "I didn't know if you'd get the idea over the phone. Thanks for rescuing me."

"I don't think I should get the credit for that." He glanced at Crème Brûlée. "You really need an attack cat warning sign."

I reached down and lifted Crème Brûlée, hugging him, too. He bit my nose, licking it once after, but it was clear he was done playing around.

"He's hungry." I grinned at Miguel. "I'll be right back."

When I returned, there were more police officers, including Detective Latoure. Miguel was answering questions. Marty was gone.

"I'm glad this worked out okay," Detective Latoure said. "I think we have the murder weapon, and enough evidence to put Marty away for a long time."

"Thank goodness." I told her about Delia. She dispatched

a paramedic unit and a police car. "I hope he was telling the truth about where to find her."

"He probably thought he had nothing to lose by telling you," Patti said. "People like to brag about what they've done. Most of the time, they are their own worst enemies."

"Well, I was really glad to see Miguel. I was hoping he'd understand. I couldn't say much."

Miguel smiled. "Since I knew I didn't have the *real* recipe, and we were thinking someone could make a move on you before you could accomplish the fake sale to Chef Art, it wasn't too hard to figure out. I'm glad you're okay, Zoe."

Detective Latoure shook her head. "I hope you've learned something from this, Zoe. Leave this kind of thing to the professionals."

"Don't worry. It will never happen again."

THIRTY-ONE

Woodlands was the name of Chef Art's mansion. It was alive with music and lights, inside and out, as I arrived. It was as splendid a sight as I'd imagined it would be.

I felt a little like Cinderella going to the ball. I didn't plan to come home with a prince, but I was awestruck by all of it.

There were dozens of moss-covered live oaks lining the drive to the main house. Men and women from around the world, elegantly dressed, were assisted from their cars by red-jacketed footmen who invited them into the huge foyer complete with a glittering, forty-foot chandelier.

I knew all the details of the mansion. I'd read about it many times in magazines and seen it on television.

The mansion was a combination of Greek Revival and Italian styles, with huge white pillars in the front. It was said to be one of Mobile's finest antebellum mansions.

I saw the massive double parlors and grand circular staircase for myself as I waited in the receiving line. It had been built in 1855 and had become the center of social life in the city. The mansion survived the war with very little damage because it was used as a hospital.

The double doors to the mansion were wide open. The night was mild, and the party spilled over from the house to the grounds. Outside, there were buffet tables laden with every type of food imaginable, and surrounded by a Dixieland band.

Inside were even more tables with food and drink, complimented by a string quartet. There were flowers and candles in every nook and cranny. The aromas were equal to the wonderful sights.

I had to admit I was enjoying everything—except being alone.

I knew I'd get used to life without Tommy Lee. This had been a test of my resolve. I'd almost asked Ollie to come with me. I wasn't sure if he'd put on a tux or not. It didn't matter anyway. He wouldn't leave Delia's side at the hospital.

The doctors had pronounced her fine, a little dehydrated and exhausted from her ordeal, but Marty hadn't hurt her. I'd been so glad to see her.

"Good to see you," Chef Art greeted me in the long line at the door to the mansion. "I've heard about your ordeal trying to save the Jefferson recipe for me."

I wasn't sure what to say. Did he think I still had the real recipe?

"Don't worry." He laughed. "I managed to acquire the recipe from the museum. They were looking for donations. I gave them a hefty one. Now the original is safe with me. Thank you for your help, Zoe Chase. Please enjoy yourself tonight."

"I'm glad you got what you wanted," I said. "You know it hurt a lot of people, though, right?"

"You can't make a cake without breaking a few eggs."

With that bit of callous wisdom, I was sort of pushed aside to wander into all the rooms in the mansion. Each room had a different theme in color, flowers, and food. It was a remarkable event. I could see why people paid a lot of money to be there.

I sneaked my phone camera out a few times when no one was looking. These were ideas from master chefs around the world, some of them right there, talking about their dishes. I couldn't resist capturing the moment. Later I could peruse the pictures and guess what the ingredients were, and how they were made.

I mingled with senators, governors, and famous movie stars. It was fun, if a little lonely. Everyone but me seemed to have brought a date.

"Zoe?" My father looked surprised to see me there.

"Daddy?" I looked at him in his sharp new tux. "You look great. Did you come alone?"

He laughed a little. "No one comes alone to a thing like this, honey. Audrey is over there at the dessert table."

I didn't look. I knew Audrey was his woman of the month. I hadn't met her, and wasn't looking forward to it. After a while, they pretty much looked the same to me.

"Where's your date?" My father glanced around the crowded room. "Did you come with Tommy Lee?"

Before I could answer, an arm slid smoothly around my waist. "She's here with me, sir," Miguel said.

I couldn't believe my eyes. "I thought you said you wouldn't come to something like this." I admired his nicely tailored tux and white ruffled shirt. He looked like an old-time riverboat gambler.

"When the right invitation comes along, sometimes you have to go for it." He smiled down at me. "A new friend of mine told me that. She said you have to grab your dream when you can."

"Well, I owe that new friend a big thanks. She knows what she's talking about."

Suddenly a loud alarm rang. The red-coated footmen, who'd welcomed everyone into the mansion, began ushering everyone back outside.

"Is there a fire?" I asked, looking around.

At that moment, Chef Art stalked past us, a murderous expression on his face.

"I wish it was a fire, Miss Chase. It's something *far* worse. Someone has managed to steal my Jefferson recipe!"

Miguel took my hand, his sherry brown gaze warm on mine. "Shall we dance?"

I put my arm around him. "Yes, please."

RECIPES FROM THE BISCUIT BOWL

I felt like crème brûlée should be mentioned here, even though I technically didn't make it. It was so important to the story (not to mention the name of my cat!) that I'm including it anyway.

Crème Brûlée

Crème brûlée is also known as burnt cream. It has a rich custard base with a contrasting hard layer of caramel. It is usually served cold. The custard base can be flavored with orange, chocolate, coffee, or whatever you like. I like mine best plain, as in this recipe.

   6 egg yolks
   6 tbsp. white sugar or sweetener
   ½ tsp. vanilla extract

2½ cups heavy cream
2 tbsp. brown sugar or brown sugar substitute

Preheat oven to 300 degrees.

Beat egg yolks, 4 tbsp. of white sugar, and vanilla in a bowl until thick. Set aside. Stir cream in a pot over low heat until it comes to a boil. Immediately stir cream into the egg mixture. Beat until combined. Pour the mixture into the top of a double boiler and let it heat about 3 minutes. Remove immediately and pour into shallow baking dish. Bake for 30 minutes then remove and let cool. Refrigerate for at least an hour.

Combine brown sugar and remaining white sugar. Add this mixture to the top of the set custard. For an exciting finish, use a long lighter to "burn" the sugar. Hold the lighter about 4 inches from the top and move it slowly across the sugar for a few seconds. Great drama!

If you're not looking for drama, turn on the broiler and place the dish under it until the sugar melts. Keep track of it because it will burn if you aren't careful. Take it out. Allow the mixture to cool again in refrigerator until custard sets again.

Ollie's Spicy Gumbo

It took me a while watching Ollie make this so I could write it down. Here's what I have.

1 pound dry red kidney beans
¼ cup olive oil
1 large onion, chopped
1 large green pepper, chopped

2 tbsp. minced garlic
2 stalks celery
6 cups water
2 bay leaves
¼ cup chopped cayenne peppers
Fresh parsley (Ollie says you know how much parsley you
    like)
2 tsp. fresh thyme or 1 tsp. dried thyme
¼ tsp. dried sage or 1 tsp. fresh sage
½ tsp. paprika
½ tsp. oregano
1 pound andouille sausage (or spicy vegetarian sausage)
    cut into chunks
Salt and pepper to taste
Rice (optional)

Rinse and then cook kidney beans after soaking overnight.

Add oil to a large frying pan and sauté onion, green pepper, garlic, and celery.

Add cooked kidney beans to 6 cups of water. Stir sautéed vegetables into beans. Add bay leaves, cayenne, thyme, sage, parsley, paprika, and oregano. Allow to come to a boil then reduce heat to low and simmer for about 2 hours.

Stir sausage into the mixture and continue simmering for another 30 minutes.

Make rice (if you like) according to directions on package. Serve the gumbo over rice.

You can also serve in biscuit bowls, but use 3 cups of water in the gumbo instead of 6!

Cherry Filling

This filling is fast and really good in biscuit bowls—and in pie, of course!

    4 cups pitted cherries
    1 cup white sugar or sweetener equivalent
    ¼ cup cornstarch

Simmer cherries over low heat about 10 minutes. Be careful not to scorch! Mix sugar and cornstarch together and add to cherries. Return to low simmer and cook until thick, about 2 minutes. Allow to cool before using as filling.

How to Make Biscuit Bowls

I'm sharing my trade secret here for those of you who can't get to Mobile and get one from me!

    2 cups white flour
    ¼ tsp. baking soda
    1 tbsp. baking powder
    1 tsp. salt
    6 tbsp. butter or vegetable shortening
    1 cup buttermilk

Preheat oven to 450 degrees.

Combine the dry ingredients. Cut the butter into the flour mixture until it forms coarse balls. Add the buttermilk until the mixture is slightly wet. Turn the dough out on a floured board. Gently roll or pat dough until it is about ½ inch thick.

Fold the dough three more times then carefully press down to about 1 inch thick.

Here's where the normal biscuit recipe changes for biscuit bowls.

Spray vegetable shortening into a muffin tin. Use a cutter to cut circles of dough. Place these circles into the openings in the tin, pressing down the center gently. Bake for about 10 minutes until brown. The biscuit dough will rise around the circle, leaving a well in the middle for the filling.

The biscuits don't have to be deep-fried right away, but don't wait more than a few hours. The freshest biscuits will make the best biscuit bowls. If you can't use them right away, freeze them for later.

To deep-fry, simply drop the biscuits for 2 minutes into a deep fryer set on high. You want them to be crisp but not greasy. Be sure to use good-quality vegetable oil in your deep fryer.

Becca Robbins is happy to help research a farmers'
market and tourist trading post—until she has to
switch her focus to finding a killer...

AN ALL-NEW SPECIAL
FROM NATIONAL BESTSELLING AUTHOR

PAIGE SHELTON

Red Hot Deadly Peppers

A Farmers' Market Mini Mystery

Becca is in Arizona, spending some time at Chief Buffalo's trading post and its neighboring farmers' market to check out how the two operate together. She's paired with Nera, a Native American woman who sells the most delicious pecans—right next to a booth with the hottest peppers money can buy.

When Nera asks her to deliver some beads to Graham, a talented jewelry maker inside Chief Buffalo's, Becca is grateful to get a break from the heat. Little does she realize that the heat's about to get cranked up even more—because Graham has been murdered, and she's the one who finds his body. She soon discovers that Graham was Nera's cousin, and that her uncle was recently killed, too, after receiving a threatening note. Becca begins to think the murders may have something to do with the family's hot pepper business. Now she must find the killer, before she's the one in the hot seat...

Includes a bonus recipe!

paigeshelton.com
facebook.com/TheCrimeSceneBooks
penguin.com